Blood in Tavasci Marsh

Also by Lakota Grace

The Pegasus Quincy Mystery Series

Death in Ghost City
Blood in Tavasci Marsh
Fire in Broken Water
Peril in Silver Nightshade

BLOOD IN TAVASCI MARSH

by

LAKOTA GRACE

Version 1.0 – September, 2017

Published by Lakota Grace at CreateSpace

ISBN: 9781549804571

Discover other titles by Lakota Grace at www.LakotaGrace.com.

CHAPTER ONE

I wasn't looking for trouble my first day back after mandatory leave for use of deadly force. I hadn't expected to kill a man in the line of duty either, which is what got me the leave.

My name is Pegasus Quincy—Peg to my friends and enemies, of which I have a few in both camps. I'm a recent police academy graduate in this small mining-turned-tourist town. Once the third-largest city in Arizona during the copper boom, Mingus now boasted a population of four hundred good souls including two sheriff's deputies: Shepherd Malone and the rookie, me.

Although I didn't feel so rookie now after the shooting of that psychotic man. I worked through it the best I could, day by day.

Shepherd didn't make it any easier, having assumed the role of chief boss-and-advice-giver the minute he transferred in to replace me during the mandatory leave. He'd been sending me regular phone calls and text messages, most of which I'd ignored.

So that's why this morning when the young man parked his restored Trans-Am in front of our office and walked in, I knew I had a choice. I could either hide behind the do-nothing assignments that my new partner had relegated me to, or I could deal with this guy's problem.

I dealt.

"Have a seat," I told the Trans-Am driver as he entered the front door. On closer inspection, I'd put his age at mid-20s, a little younger than me. "How can I help you?"

He gave me a woeful smile and settled into a chair in front of my desk. "My name is Howard Nettle. I used to live in these parts until a few years ago." His light brown hair needed a cut and his pale blue eyes peered at me earnestly.

He rummaged in his pocket and pulled out a business card. Turning it so that the name faced me, he presented it. "I'm the manager and co-owner of Big Al's Used Cars in Phoenix. You've heard of us?"

Phoenix was about two hours' drive and a world removed from our small mountain town. "Can't say as I have."

"I'm the guy that rides that ostrich onto the car lot and says, 'Hey, have we got a deal for you.' You know, the TV commercial?"

I didn't watch television, but anybody who'd ride an ostrich deserved consideration. "Oh, *that* Howard Nettle. What brings you to Mingus?"

"My father is missing—at least I think he is."

I got out my notebook and started writing. "And your father is?"

"Calhoun Nettle, Cal for short. He lives over by Tavasci Marsh, outside of Clarkdale."

"And you think he's missing because?"

"I wrote a letter inviting him to go deer hunting with my stepson and me. But when Daddy didn't answer my letter, I drove up to check on him. I don't think he's at the house."

Howard had reverted to the old Southern habit of referring to his father as Daddy. I could still catch a bit of twang in his voice. But his assumption that something was wrong made me pause. "Why didn't you just call him?"

"It's complicated. The home phone blocks my calls. And when I drove out to the place, Momma ran me off with a shotgun."

He looked about ten years old, woebegone at being banished. But I'd heard this "ah shucks" line before. There was something more going on beneath the surface. "I'm not sure this is a police matter, Mr. Nettle, unless you feel there's been foul play."

"Call me Howard." Intertwining slender fingers, he leaned forward. "Look, here's the story. I moved down to Phoenix where I started work at the car dealership. One thing led to another, and I asked Pietra—she's Big Al's daughter—to marry me."

All kinds of family. I wondered if the ostrich was related. "Go on."

"I'd lost touch with my folks at that point, so I didn't see any reason to ask them to the ceremony—they're plain country folk, you understand—wouldn't fit in. And we lost touch after that. It's been almost four years since I've been back here to the Verde Valley. I was hoping this visit might be a way to bridge that silence."

He'd made a choice, putting his new family before his old one, and reaped the consequences. I didn't consider selling used cars as a high-status job, but maybe it was to him. I wasn't the one to judge. I was from hill country, and I didn't respect people like Howard who put status before family. But not talking to a son for four years seemed extreme, even for that slight. "And you want us to do what?"

"Well, I thought maybe you could phone my sister Janny and find out what's going on. You're a woman and all. Maybe she'd talk to you."

I rolled my eyes at the "woman" comment. "Why don't *you* call your sister?"

Howard Nettle looked unhappy. "Momma ordered Janny not to speak to me, and my sister won't cross that line." He dug in his wallet, fished out a dirty slip of paper and handed it to me.

The paper had been unfolded and refolded so many times it had turned soft and frayed along the creases. The faint lettering said "Janny" and gave an address and phone number in Cottonwood, a small town down the mountain from Mingus.

I tried to return the scrap of paper, but Howard pushed my hand away. "I've got to get back to Phoenix. Big Al wants me on the lot. Gotta sell those cars, you know?" He gave me a sorrowful look. "Please, will you help?"

His request raised all sorts of red flags—why was he coming to a police station for an intervention he should handle himself? And why was I even considering a proposal that might overstep my authority?

Yet his plea for understanding resonated. I had recent experience of working under someone like Howard's overbearing father-in-law. Maybe that's why I agreed to call Howard's sister even though it was outside the bounds of normal police activity. What could it hurt?

Howard bumped into my partner on his way out of the station. As the door slammed, Shepherd inclined his head toward his office. "Quincy, when you're free, in here." It wasn't a suggestion.

"What was that all about?" He gestured toward the door.

"Man says his father is missing. Wants us to investigate."

"Did he file a complaint?"

"It's complicated."

"Well if he didn't file the proper paperwork, we can't help him." His tone was dismissive.

Shepherd had been transferred to this outpost of the Anasazi County sheriff's office when I was on mandatory leave. Now instead of my being the sole cop here in Mingus, there were two of us. And Shepherd didn't let me forget who was senior. His gruff voice and ramrod-straight back matched his rule book view on life.

I sat in front of the desk that used to be *my* desk and moved a chunk of obsidian Shepherd had placed there. He shifted it back to its previous location.

"First day back on the job," he said, "and you think you can make all the decisions and break all the rules. Things like that get people shot. But I guess you know that." He leaned back in the chair and interlaced fingers over a gut that strained his shirt buttons. "We need to understand each other. I wasn't there and I don't know what happened when you shot that man. But I've been on the force thirty years and I've never had to use my firearm."

How do you answer that one? After the shooting, I'd broken down a few times—always when no one was around. Then I settled into a brittle who-gives-a-damn attitude, ignoring the sleepless nights. It would pass.

"I have a few months left until retirement and I want them to be peaceful ones." Shepherd gave me a wintry smile. "I took this assignment as a favor to the sheriff. He wasn't too happy with the way things were going up here, and frankly, neither am I."

In my defense, they weren't here when that man was killed. I was.

"You made an appointment to see the counselor yet?" he asked.

I brushed an errant hair back into the long braid I wore down my back. "Not yet." Counseling was mandatory before I could get my Glock back, but I didn't want to go down that road. I was fine.

"See that you do before the day is over."

I'm six feet tall with red hair. When I get upset, even a little irritated, heat starts to rise under my freckles like mercury in an old-fashioned thermometer. I turned my chair so Shepherd wouldn't notice the steam.

He wasn't finished. "Since you haven't been cleared to use firearms yet, I want you on foot patrol. You know how to write parking tickets?"

"I've done a few." Not, I'm sure, as many as he had.

"Why don't you write a few more," he ordered. "Don't forget to make that counselor's appointment." He flipped open a crossword puzzle book and picked up a pencil.

***

Late that afternoon I sat in my office and my mind returned to Howard Nettle. I reached in my back pocket for his sister's number and pulled out the counselor's card instead. I hoped she was gone and I could simply leave a message. That would satisfy Shepherd and put off the inevitable for a while longer. I needed my Glock back, but I wasn't in a hurry to spill my guts to some stranger.

Unfortunately, she answered on the first ring, with a voice low and cultured, a bit of British in the vowels. I pictured a dignified older lady with sterling gray hair, a stout figure, sensible shoes.

I introduced myself and asked for an appointment. She didn't seem impressed with my statement that I killed a man. She had an appointment the next day, in fact. I took it.

I'd handled worse in my life than some Brit lady-doctor. I'd just agree with whatever she suggested, mouth a few mea culpas, and get on with my life. A weapon on my hip would contribute greatly to a positive state of mind. I felt naked without it.

The call to Janny Nettle, Howard's sister, was easier because I slipped back into professional mode where I knew all the answers. She seemed hesitant to talk about her brother over the phone, but agreed to meet me after her shift ended that afternoon at the Dollar Store in Clarkdale.

10

The Verde Valley was populated with small towns. Mingus, on the mountain, had been the mining community. Clarkdale, at the base of the range, had housed the smelter for the copper. It in turn merged into Cottonwood, where farmers produced the beef and produce to feed both. The last still had a great farmers market in the summer.

In the good old days, I would have driven an official vehicle to meet Janny Nettle. But I'd totaled the town's sole squad car chasing the man I had killed. During my mandatory leave, Shepherd appropriated the replacement SUV.

I walked down the steep hill to my grandfather's house to borrow his pickup truck. He wasn't home, but the keys were right there under the floorboard. Half the town knew that. He didn't lock his house, either. This was Mingus, he said. We don't lock things up here. Maybe he was right. Maybe he wasn't.

***

The discount store edged one of the roundabouts punctuating the road from Clarkdale to Cottonwood. More than a dozen traffic circles had been built around the valley before the city fathers listened to the voice of moderation. The circles did prevent head-ons and T-bone accidents, for which I was grateful. But local drivers cursed the tourists who negotiated the roundabouts at a crawl, stopping at every traffic entrance.

I pulled into an open parking spot with a Ready Ice machine to the left, a soda machine and a video rental box to the right. Video streaming had sounded the death knell of the video stores in the valley, and we were left with this poor imitation of a movie rental opportunity. A poster on the store window advertised cheap cigarettes. It was next to one for a gallon of milk, both apparently life essentials in the eyes of the establishment.

Janny Nettle gave me a wave when I entered the Dollar Store, probably recognizing me because of the

11

uniform. She looked to be older than Howard, maybe in her early thirties with a feminine version of his snub nose. She smiled at one customer, complimented another's finds, and checked out a third with efficient ease. I wandered around until she finished with her customers.

I roamed the aisles looking for bargains. It shouldn't be called a "dollar" store, though. For every $1 sign, I saw lots of $2 and $3 placards.

When I turned the corner, a little girl about seven blocked the aisle while deciding on a purchase. Her brown hair hung down in tangles, and she carried one hand in the pocket of her overlong jumper. She finally settled for a glittering princess tiara and marched up to the front, prize in hand. I followed her.

Janny gave her a big hug. "Find something you liked, honey?" The little girl nodded and clutched her tiara to her chest after Janny checked it through. Then Janny turned to me and held out her hand. "Sorry. One of our clerks didn't show, and I had to work a second shift."

She gave her little girl a pat. "Aurora, meet Officer Quincy." Aurora retreated behind her mother's back and peeked out at me. Janny had a harried look on her face. "I hate to ask you this, Officer, but might you give us a ride home? My car's got a flat. I hitched a ride to work, but now I need to get Aurora home."

I had empathy. I was driving my grandfather's borrowed wheels, myself. "Not a problem."

"Thanks! Give me a minute to check out. Watch Aurora for me, will you?"

Whether it was small-town trust or the fact that I was wearing a uniform, the little girl accepted her mother's direction and followed me out of the store. She planted her tiny body next to my big frame on the curb. Then she awkwardly unwrapped the tiara and jammed it firmly on her head. The fingers that had been hidden in her pocket were deformed and a puckered scar ran down her right forearm.

She'd brought a notebook and pencil with her, and drew with her left hand, quick sketches of the people coming in and out of the store, capturing the action with line gestures.

Janny joined us a few minutes later and we climbed into the pickup for the short drive to her apartment. Janny fumbled in her purse and pulled out an inhaler. She breathed in deeply, then capped the inhaler and returned it to her purse. She leaned back against the bench seat and closed her eyes.

When we pulled into the apartment parking lot, I reached over and touched her shoulder. "We're here."

She yawned and opened her eyes. "Must have drifted off. My apartment's on the second floor." She gathered her things and lifted Aurora out of the truck.

The rundown apartment complex contained four units up and four down. A symphony of old Kenmores clunked away in a vacant laundry room in front of us, the door wide open. Trusting tenants. I lost more than one good bra to laundry room gremlins.

When we approached the steps, a skinny gray-haired woman wearing a pink CSI-Las Vegas sweatshirt waved from a bench. She had the sunken cheeks of a meth addict, a sad reality of small-town life. With a lack of the drug enforcement resources of a big city, we fought with drug addiction and meth labs on a too regular basis. The woman's smile lacked a few teeth, but her eyes were bright as she peered at us.

"Pay her no mind," Janny said. "That's just the resident snoop."

Every apartment complex had one. Those folks with too much time on their hands who used it to pry into lives more interesting than their own.

Once in the apartment, Janny brushed a jumble of unfolded clothes off the small couch so I could sit while she took the little girl into the other room to get her ready for bed. The apartment was maybe two hundred feet square, if that.

A half-person kitchen completed one end of the living room and the single bedroom opened directly off the living room with only a three-quarters wall for privacy. The apartment lacked a smoke detector although the bracket for one still hung on the wall. Smells of bleach and old grease made the air heavy and dense.

A moment later Janny returned from the other room. "I fed the baby with some snacks at the store. Not good for her, I know, but what can you do?" Her eyes held a tired look. "Can I offer you some refreshments, Ms. Quincy?"

While the water boiled for instant coffee, she opened the dormitory-sized refrigerator and pulled out a quart of milk and two shriveled apples. She reached into a drawer for a paring knife, cut the apples into precise slices and arranged them on a plate.

Janny's voice held that faint hint of an Appalachian twang that her brother's had, and hill country hospitality dictated that whatever you had, you offered to guests. I recognized it because I'd been raised in eastern Tennessee where anything less would be considered ill manners.

Janny filled two mugs with hot water and instant coffee and poured in a dollop of milk. Then she put the fingers of one hand through the two mug handles, lifted the plate with the other, and set everything down on a TV tray in front of the couch without spilling a drop.

I was impressed. I'd tried waitressing once, and flubbed up on everything. I'd only lasted a week before they fired me. "You had experience in the restaurant trade?" I asked.

"That's my weekend job, cocktail waitress at Rainbow's Folly."

14

"That means you're working seven days a week. When do you get time off?"

"Don't. Can't afford to. You saw my baby's hand. Got a doctor wants to take it on. He'll operate dirt cheap, for a bone doc anyway. That still means a ton of money, but we'll manage. Momma watches Aurora while I work. And I make good tips."

I took another sip of the coffee. "Having your car out of operation must make it tough. Bad flat?"

"It's one of the regulars down at the bar," she explained. "He's been after me to move in with him. Won't. So he lets the air out of my tire."

"You want me to go talk to him? Be glad to do that for you."

She shook her head. "I'll put air in it tomorrow before I go to work. Neighbor next door has a bicycle pump that I borrow." She seemed to accept the fact as an ongoing condition of existence. Then, "You said you talked to Brother Howard. How is he?"

"Says you won't speak to him."

"Haven't, for years."

"Why not?" I asked.

"He was there when the whiskey still exploded and Aurora was hurt. Instead of helping, Howard just ran. Maybe she wouldn't be crippled if he'd stayed." She took another apple slice, looked at it blankly as though her mind was in another time and place.

"Howard came to go hunting with your father, but says he didn't show."

Janny laughed harshly. "Liar. Howard is scared of guns. He'd never go hunting with Daddy, not in a thousand years. He's just sniffing around the money."

"Money?"

"Green gold, Momma calls it. Developers want to turn our land into a golf course development for all those retirees from Phoenix. They offered a million dollars, but

Daddy turned 'em down. Said the property was worth two. All that money for a piece of swampy land." She sighed.

"Seen your father recently?"

Janny stiffened and her voice chilled. "No, I haven't."

Interesting. Some tension there. I wondered what she wasn't saying. I opened my mouth to ask her when she stood up and gave an exaggerated yawn.

"Time I was getting to bed. Early day tomorrow. Say hi to Howard-the-coward for me." She escorted me out the door with the skill of a bouncer ejecting an unwanted customer.

I stood on the landing for a moment, hesitating, then walked down the stairs. Let the poor woman get her rest. She deserved it. She and that poor child.

As I reached the pickup, a shaft of light gleamed from the neighbor's half-opened door. I wasn't the only one taking notes.

I sat in the truck for a moment still feeling the hostility that crackled in the air when Janny Nettle said goodbye. Three things were clear: she was uncomfortable talking about her father, she felt the need to end the conversation right then, and she all but booted me out of her apartment in direct contradiction to her old-country ways.

On the other hand, if no one had broken the law, it wasn't my business. I'd done what I promised. The inquiry into the Nettle family had hit a dead end, and I intended to call Howard in the morning to tell him so.

That was before we discovered the dead body floating in Tavasci Marsh.

CHAPTER TWO

Shepherd took the call the next morning. He rapped on our adjourning window and beckoned me into his office. "That was Robert Miller, ranger at the Tuzigoot Indian Ruins. He spotted a floater in the swamp."

We hurried to the parking lot and jumped into the SUV. "Buckle up," Shepherd ordered, switching on the light bar and siren.

We bounced off the curb onto the road and barreled down the switchbacks toward the valley below us. The SUV sped through the roundabout at the Cement Plant entrance, rammed through Clarkdale, slid right on Broadway and then skidded left on the road to Tuzigoot Ruins.

Shepherd turned off the siren as we coasted to a stop in front of the ranger station. He checked his watch, smiling. That trip usually took twenty minutes, but he made it in ten.

"Watch and learn," he instructed as we marched up the front steps.

Ranger Miller waited for us at the top. "Glad you could make it so soon. Just a little nervous about this, I can tell you." Miller was a skinny guy with fine blond hair thinning on either side of a high forehead. Tortoise-shell rimmed glasses made his eyes look even larger.

Shepherd stepped in front of me to shake his hand. "Deputy Malone, here. This is my subordinate, Peg Quincy."

His subordinate! What was Shepherd pulling? I worked for the sheriff, not for him.

Miller accepted the statement without comment and led us into the Visitors Center. The central room was filled with artifacts taken from the Indian ruins. A group of tourists circled a docent lecturing about the Ancestral Pueblan peoples who had lived here hundreds of years ago.

Miller gave the tour group a nervous look. "Let's go into my office where we can talk undisturbed. I'd just as soon keep this whole business private. When I was in Yellowstone, the press got wind of a climbing accident there and we were swamped with looky-loos for weeks." He unhooked a half-door and we followed him behind the counter and down a hall.

The desk and chairs in his compact office were puke-green government issue, but the Hopi Kachina figure behind his desk was not. Protected by a glass case, the figure had outstretched feather-covered arms and stood more than two feet tall. An eagle dancer, with what looked to be authentic feathers.

Miller gestured to it as he sat down behind his desk. "Beautiful, isn't it. The tribe had to get special dispensation to collect the eagle feathers. And it's made by a woman. Usually, only the men carve the Kachinas out of those cottonwood roots. I've got her name around here someplace."

Shepherd didn't seem impressed. "Nice," he grunted.

Whether his lack of enthusiasm was for the carved statue itself or the gender of its creator, neither bode well for our relationship: I was a woman and I happened to like Native American art.

There were two mismatched chairs in front of the ranger's desk. Shepherd dropped into the most comfortable seat. I shuffled behind him to fold my tall frame into the small chair next to the wall.

"Where's the dead body?" he asked.

"Middle of the marsh," said Miller. "An ultra-lite pilot from the Cottonwood airport spotted it as he flew over."

Shepherd turned to me. "You getting all this down?"

I hastily retrieved my notebook and scribbled away. "You said a marsh?" I asked.

Shepherd cut me a sharp glance.

"Tavasci Marsh," Miller said, "was formed by an oxbow in the Verde River. It is filled with rushes and cattails, creating good habitat for migrating waterfowl. Birders from all over the world—"

Shepherd interrupted the ranger's practiced tourist lecture. "You investigate the body?"

I kept my head down. Note taker, that's me.

"Of course not! I watch CSI. I know the rules."

He smiled like it was a joke, but I got the feeling it wasn't for him. Some folks take their television seriously.

"I've got one of my interns blocking tourists from entry to the murder site," Miller said.

"Might not be a murder," Shepherd replied. "Could be an accident. Let's take a look."

We followed Miller out a side door onto a pathway that circled Tuzigoot Indian Ruins. The Ruins had been a pile of rocks on the oval hilltop until Work Progress Administration workers rebuilt the walls in the thirties, uncovering more than one hundred rooms in the dwelling. Some of the lower rooms even contained burial sites. Still fuming at Shepherd's arrogance, I mentally banished his presence to one of the deepest ones.

Then taking a deep breath of fall air to clear my mind of such nasty thoughts, I focused on enjoying the warm day. We'd had a spell of balmy weather, followed by a dusting of snow on Black Mountain. Now it was almost summer hot again. Nature was teasing us, but real winter would arrive soon enough.

"Turn left here." Miller led the way down steps from the ruins to Tavasci Marsh. The park intern squatted on the ground next to a shallow landing, staring into the brackish water. He jumped to his feet at our approach and pulled a moored rowboat half onto the shore.

Shepherd hesitated for a moment, looking at the boat. "Hard to get in and out of those things with my trick knee." He patted his leg. "I'll secure the perimeter. Peg, you go with Ranger Miller. Call and tell me what we got." He settled on a boulder to watch.

Interesting, his sudden delegation. The snarky side of me wondered if it was fear of the water or just plain laziness.

The marsh was shallow here, no more than a foot in depth, but Miller said it deepened to ten feet in places. No way that we could wade out there to investigate. He held the boat as I stepped in. I steadied for a moment and moved to the front bar. Miller climbed in after me and settled on the back bar while the intern pushed the boat off the shore. Dropping the oars into the oarlocks, Miller angled the boat with a practiced stroke and glided into the marsh.

"Can't use a motor here because the weeds tangle in propeller blades." He handed me a GPS. "I've programmed in the general location. You keep us on track."

We pushed through cattails now brown and crisp with autumn dryness. Their roots merged into the brown water below, sending up a miasma of rotting vegetation.

"How far to the body?"

"I'd say maybe five hundred feet give or take."

"That's not very far," I observed.

"Not on dry land, maybe. This marsh is about a hundred acres, end to end, but narrow at this point, and filled with reeds and tangles. How we doing on direction?"

I glanced at the GPS. "Edge a little to the left."

He maneuvered the rowboat with one paddle. Something plopped into the water next to the boat, and I started.

Miller chuckled at my alarm. "Bullfrog, probably. The early settlers introduced them to the marsh. Going to make a cash crop out of them. Didn't work out. You ever eat frog legs?"

"No, thanks." Not on your life would I touch those slimy things—enough to turn me vegetarian.

"Watch your head," he cautioned. "It's going to get tight here." The rushes closed in on the boat and sunlight disappeared for a moment. Then a dark shape appeared ahead of us in a clearing. The dead body.

I'd been dreading this moment. I'd seen dead people before, but never a floater. The instructors at the Police Academy tormented us with images of fragile flesh slipping off fingers like a glove. They described ravaged faces, lips and eyes eaten by crabs. My stomach clenched as we drew close.

The corpse floated face down in about six feet of water, the head hanging below the surface. The body looked to be male, wearing bib coveralls with crisscrossed back straps. One pant leg caught on a sharp branch protruding from a nearby beaver lodge, and the hands waved idly in the boat's wake.

I pulled my phone from my pocket, snapped some quick photos and sent them to Shepherd. I glanced back at Miller. He had one hand clasped over his mouth and his eyes were huge. I wasn't feeling too hot myself. "Back us off and take some deep breaths."

He did so with alacrity.

I thumbed Shepherd's number on the redial. "Get the photos? Want me to contact the sheriff's office?"

"No, I'll do that," he said quickly. "Send Miller back with the boat and you secure the scene."

My jaw tightened. Making brownie points with the sheriff over *my* discovery. And how the heck could I "secure the scene" when it was all water? I didn't have gills.

I could have protested, but I was too stubborn. Secure the scene? Fine, I could do that. The only dry land was the beaver lodge in front of me. It would serve.

At least I could arrange to sit where I didn't have to look at the corpse. Nobody could approach this watery scene without my hearing them. "Move the boat wide and circle to the other side of the beaver lodge," I said.

When we reached the opposite side, Miller grabbed a branch cemented into the rock-hard dried mud to steady the boat while I clambered up.

Oar splashes receded as he left, and the marsh noises resumed. A red-wing blackbird gave a liquid cry and two coots set up a chorus. I ducked as a Cooper's hawk swooped over the reeds. Finally, all was silent.

To get better traction, I took off my mud-stained shoes and socks, rolled up my pants. The marsh winds dried my sweaty toes and I climbed higher on the lodge. I sneaked a look over the top.

Yeah, the man was still there, one water-soaked arm bumping against the lodge. I ducked back down again. He wasn't going anywhere, and neither was I. Sticks poked my backside and I wedged my arm around a knot of wood trying to get comfortable.

My thoughts returned to the corpse floating on the other side of the rough hillock. Could the dead man be Howard Nettle's missing father? If so, how did he get here? With an effort, I shut out the image of that close and unwelcome companion floating on the other side of the beaver lodge. The water recovery team would be here soon.

Chapter Three

By the time the underwater recovery team appeared, the weather turned colder and all sensation had left my feet. The two men in the boat wore black wet suits, zipped open at the neck with the hoods folded back. I waved to them as they approached the beaver lodge

They tossed me a mooring rope. "Tie this around something, will you?" one of them asked. "You can be our tender."

They reached over to shake hands and introduce themselves. James Glen was the tall one. He had shaggy brown hair and a mustache to match. Rory Stevens was a runty little guy with curly black hair, younger than my own twenty-nine years.

"The underwater team members are all volunteers," James said. "We're sworn deputies, on regular duty in Prescott. Got the call and came over the mountain to join the fun."

Rory peered at me. "Who-eee. You're tall."

"And you're short," I said, irritated.

"Then we'd make a good couple. Ever date anybody my size?"

Was he hitting on me? Here, dressed in a wet suit and prepared to retrieve a dead body?

"Sorry," I said, "I'm going with somebody." Well, not exactly. Flint Tanner hadn't spoken to me since that new lady banker came to town. I encountered them one morning bending heads over café coffee. I resisted the urge, just barely, to plunge a stake through his heart. But Rory Stevens didn't need to know that.

"Maybe another time," I said.

He frowned and turned away.

I wanted to tell him it wasn't his size. Or maybe it was, but I could see he was embarrassed at my response. I'd had enough razzing over my own height. I knew how it felt. "Hey, I'll call you the next time I'm in Prescott," I said. "Maybe we can take in a movie."

He rewarded me with a grin. "It's a date. Let's take a look at the present you have for us." I held the boat steady while they suited up with metal air tanks and scuba gear, testing the air lines, wetting face plates. Then, they slid over the side of the boat to investigate.

I climbed up the mound to watch. Soon both surfaced, one on either side of the corpse. James shoved his mask to the top of his head and shouted to me. "In the boat, you'll find a rolled-up body bag."

I climbed over the sticks and branches of the beaver lodge, grabbed the bag, and crawled around the side of the mound to hand it to him.

"We always bag a body like this in the water, away from possible family members on shore," Rory explained. "Seeing a person turned into a bloated corpse traumatizes survivors. Doing it this way frustrates aggressive picture takers, too. It stops photos of a dead loved one showing up on the Internet."

I shuddered. I couldn't imagine anything more awful than to open Facebook and have such a photo waiting for me.

Opened, the water-recovery body bag looked like a sleeping bag with a top of opaque plastic, a mesh bottom to drain water out, and graspable handles on all four sides. Rory laid it on top of the water, parallel to the body and pulled the top portion of the bag away from the corpse.

Quickly and efficiently he and James pulled the bag under the corpse and gently cradled the dead man, careful to include all limbs and clothing within the bag, Then they zipped it closed, their actions quiet and respectful. When the body was secure, Rory held it while James ducked under the water to plant a marker buoy where the corpse had been.

"We'll be back as soon as we get him loaded in a Stokes rescue basket for the ride to the morgue," Rory said. The two men glided through the water toward the landing at Tuzigoot Ruins towing the bag between them.

"Don't go away," Rory called over his shoulder.

As if I had anywhere else to go. I retrieved my shoes and climbed carefully into their boat to wait. It felt good to stretch out my legs in a level position.

Half an hour later I was unnerved by two black heads popping up next to the boat like oversized otters. Rory removed his mask and shook his hair, tilting his head one direction and then the other to ease neck tension and clear his ears. He and James pulled stanchions from the boat and strung jackstay lines to start an underwater search in front of the beaver lodge.

I guess I've watched too many avalanche movies. I assumed they'd hold onto the lines and poke sticks along the bottom. Instead, they removed their flippers and walked in a back-and-forth pattern, feeling through the cloudy, murky water with their sensitive neoprene booties.

I watched them for a few moments, their locations marked by fine silt plumes roiling to the surface. When Rory next appeared, I called to him. "Mind if I borrow your boat and head to shore? It's getting cold out here."

"Go for it. This may take several hours. We'll swim in and retrieve it when we're done."

I placed the oars in the locks and rowed through the reeds back to the landing. When the nose of the boat hit the edge of the bank, I shipped the oars, slung my shoes around my neck, and waded toward shore. My right foot hit a sinkhole and I plunged into the water, halfway up my thigh. I swore and yanked my foot from the sucking ooze. Another uniform, ruined.

When I hauled the boat up on the beach, Shepherd's amusement greeted me. "Nice maneuver there." He rose from a comfortable folding chair and put down a coffee mug. "You take over the perimeter-zone access control. I've already strung the barrier tape at the top of the path."

He signed the crime scene logbook with a precise signature and handed it to me. Whistling, he strode up the hill, abandoning the marsh. I sat down in the chair, shuddering as the cold breeze hit my wet uniform.

The logbook had my name, with arrival time and purpose filled in, and below that his entry and those for Rory and James. The medical examiner's crew had arrived while I'd been sitting on the beaver lodge, signed in, gathered the dead body, and signed out. Darned efficient.

However, while I was delegated to the cold damp amidst the reeds and muck, Shepherd awarded himself a dry-land folding chair and coffee. Guess that's how management works.

My stomach growled. What time was it, anyway? No lunch, breakfast a distant memory. I wondered if Shepherd had left some coffee. I jiggled the mug, disturbing the half-inch of cold sludge in the bottom. In the excitement of the moment, I hadn't brought a jacket, either, and the night air crept closer like a wolf circling a kill.

Replacements should be here soon, assuming Shepherd remembered to send someone to relieve me. Wouldn't put it past him to "forget" for a while, though. That seemed to be how his mind operated.

Three long hours later, a uniformed officer came swinging down the path. Gratefully, I signed out and turned logbook control and responsibility over to him.

The Visitor Center was closed when I reached the top of the hill, all tourists departed. The wind had died down and an unearthly quiet surrounded the ghosts of old Pueblans, those souls interred within stone walls.

There was meager cell phone coverage. Just enough to call my grandfather, HT, for a ride home.

"Be right there," he said.

It took him twenty minutes to arrive, rather than Shepherd's speed-demon ten, but I didn't care. HT had the heater up full blast, and the warmth curled my toes. He must have sensed my need for quiet and made the drive to Mingus in silence. I felt corpse-like myself, after spending long hours with a dead body. I was tired and discouraged, and ready to quit for the day. But I was resentful, too, about the way I'd been treated.

When HT pulled into his drive and turned off the engine, I paused before opening the door. "I didn't have to sit out there in the swamp that long," I complained. "Shepherd was messing with me."

HT chuckled. "When I was little I used to help my granddaddy with his carpentry. He was always sending me to the shop for a left-handed monkey wrench or a wall stretcher."

The light bulb went on. "In other words, I was sent on a snipe hunt."

He squeezed my shoulder. "Come on inside, Peg. I'll make us some hot chocolate."

"Thanks, but I'm heading down the hill to my apartment. Things to work out."

"Suit yourself," he said.

The night turned dark and sleety as I walked down the street to my studio apartment. When I reached my front door, even the stray cat had deserted my porch stoop. The same bitter wind that echoed my mood swept down the mountain to disturb the reeds in Tavasci Marsh. I was alone, the way I had chosen to spend most of my life. At least I was alive, not taking up space on some morgue shelf.

And somewhere out there a killer lurked, waiting for us to find him.

CHAPTER FOUR

Inside my apartment, I stripped off the wet, ruined uniform and tossed it in the corner. I stood in the shower, letting the welcome heat soak into my bones.

When the window was steamed and the water frigid, I stepped out and pulled on my pink robe. Even though the man who had worn it once in a former relationship had left, the robe still held warm memories, pleasing on this cold night.

Food was next. Opening my refrigerator in my kitchenette, I took stock. Not much there. I hacked some mold off a lump of cheddar cheese and cut it into bite-sized pieces, added some crackers, and a forkful of bread-and-butter pickles. Then I popped the top on an Oak Creek Ale and dropped into my favorite red armchair to eat my supper.

This studio apartment had worked for me when I first arrived in Mingus, but now it felt cramped. Hard to entertain guests when the couch faced the bed, only four feet away. For some reason, an image of Rory Stevens, the scuba diver, entered my mind. I'd always been partial to black, curly hair. I pushed the thought into a compartment of my mind reserved for possible-but-not-likely opportunities.

I tried to read for a bit—an Ian Rankin mystery I'd picked up at the drugstore in Cottonwood—but my eyelids kept drooping. I scraped the remains of my dinner into the trash, dumped the empty bottle in the recycle bin, and crawled into bed.

***

In the early morning hours, an odd buzzing near my head woke me. I swatted at the night table trying to hit the alarm clock, but the noise continued. I struggled upright and saw my cell phone glowing on the night stand, Shepherd's name on the ID.

I grabbed it and punched the talk button. "Hello?" I mumbled.

Shepherd's deep voice grated in my ear. "I'll be by in fifteen minutes. We've got an ID on the dead man." He hung up.

The clock said two a.m., but that didn't seem to count in Shepherd's book. I scrambled out of bed and pulled on my last clean uniform. Splashed some cold water in my face and plaited my hair into a hurried braid. Still not awake, I pushed my feet into socks and shoes and pounded down the stairs, just as Shepherd pulled into the driveway.

I opened the door and scrambled in. "What's up?"

"That corpse you found at Tavasci Marsh? It's Calhoun Nettle. Some janitor found the driver's license when he sluiced the morgue channels. License must have dropped to the floor when they transferred him out of the body bag."

"They sure it's him?"

"The medical examiner on duty compared his face to the photo. It's Cal Nettle, all right. We need to make a death notification to the family."

A lot of strange things happened in the dead of night at the morgue. Someone would have their head handed to them for losing that piece of identification—glad it wasn't me.

The light of a rising moon illuminated the mountain ridges on the far side of the valley as we drove down the hill. The black coffee that Shepherd had picked up helped, but I shook my head, trying to clear the late-night cobwebs.

Shepherd seemed to know where he was going, taking the curves at a fierce clip. Didn't the man know any speed except too-fast?

"You know the Nettles?" I asked.

"Last time I was out there, about four years ago," he said. "Explosion at Cal Nettle's moonshine still. The eldest boy, Lucas, was killed. A little kid burned pretty bad, too, as I recall."

That would be Janny's daughter, Aurora. But Janny hadn't mentioned this older brother, Lucas. Secrets in the family. And now I was carrying a few, too.

I should have told Shepherd about my conversation with Janny. I could call Shepherd a son-of-a-bitch, which he surely was, but there'd been opportunities to fill him in, and I hadn't. A cardinal sin in any organization, particularly ours. Even now I kept quiet, not willing to be drawn into controversy over my interview with Howard Nettle and the unofficial conversations with Janny. What I did on my own time was my business.

"Quiet over there," Shepherd noted. You okay with this death notification?"

"I'm fine." I straightened on the seat and put my mind to business. "How many kids total?"

"Four. Lucas, the eldest, dead now. Three after that." He counted them off. "Next came Janny, then Ethan—he'd be over twenty-seven now, and the youngest, Howard."

Lucas had been Cal's favorite, Shepherd told me. When he died, Howard became the scapegoat for the family tragedy. Shunned, he left the valley. That jibed with Howard's tale to me. On the other hand, if the father needed someone to blame for the tragedy, Howard might have been the most convenient. And then Janny had followed suit, blaming Howard for Aurora's injury. It didn't make logical sense, but then family dynamics rarely did.

Shepherd took another slug of coffee and negotiated the next roundabout with one hand as we sped through the deserted streets of Clarkdale. Several miles out of town we circled around the far end of Tavasci Marsh and then turned right at a hand-lettered sign nailed to a sycamore snag: "Keep the hell out. This means you."

"Getting close," Shepherd observed. He put the coffee mug in the holder and negotiated the narrow dirt road with two hands. Potholes formed dark craters in the headlights and the vehicle swerved one direction and then the other, as the SUV negotiated the curves. We detoured around a fallen cottonwood tree and approached a house concealed among the shadows.

When Shepherd came to a stop, the SUV headlights illuminated a ramshackle house with hand-hewn timbers supporting an unpainted porch. A chain-link fence, four feet high, surrounded the house, a half-open gate marking the front. The wire sagged and bowed in spots as if rammed by a heavy vehicle.

I reached for the door handle and Shepherd touched my arm, cautioning me to wait. Two black shapes hurdled around the side of the yard, baying like air-horns on an eighteen-wheeler. One dog circled the SUV, nose to the ground. The other stretched paws up my window, nails scraping against the glass and jowls slathering. He made a short series of cries, deep "oowoofs."

"How's it feel to be treed like a varmint?" Shepherd chuckled. "Redbone coonhounds. Nothing in the world like them. Boy should be coming out soon."

A light went on in the front window and the door opened. Shepherd's "boy" turned out to be a young man, tall and lanky, with a down-turned shotgun in one hand. Shepherd lowered his window four inches, aimed the spotlight on the man, and shouted, "Police. Put down your gun and leash your dogs."

The man shaded his eyes with one hand and peered into the light. Then he leaned the gun against the wall of the house and walked down the front steps. He gave a shrill whistle and slapped the side of his leg. "You, dogs. To me."

The dogs abandoned the patrol car and rushed him. They nosed his crotch, long tails wagging. He grabbed their collars and chained them close to the porch. Only then did Shepherd open his door. I did the same and followed him into the yard.

"Ethan? Deputy Malone." Shepherd reached out his hand to the man. "I was here a few years ago about your brother. Sad affair, that." The men shook hands. Shepherd turned to me. "This is my subordinate, Deputy Peg Quincy."

"Peg?" Ethan examined me. "Janny told me about your meeting with Howard. Come up on the porch."

Shepherd gave me a quick sidelong glance.

I shrugged. The telling could wait. I joined the two men on the porch landing.

"All right if we step inside the house, son?" Shepherd asked.

Ethan nodded and pushed open the door, motioning us in.

"Is your mother here?" Shepherd's deep voice was quiet, yet firm. "We need to speak to both of you."

Ethan's jaw set as if anticipating our news. "You want to speak to Janny and Aurora, too? They're bunking with me in the trailer."

"Might be best."

Ethan stepped into a back hall and called softly to his mother. I heard her murmured response, and then he reappeared. "I'll fetch the others."

He let the screen door bang on his way out and I jumped at the sound. I wasn't looking forward to what would happen next.

Shepherd exhaled heavily and settled into a worn chair. "I'll talk," he ordered. "You watch the family's reaction."

Fine with me. I pulled two wooden chairs from the adjoining dining area and sat down facing the couch. A late-dinner smell of fried onions and stale fish hung in the air, closing around me.

I rose and paced the room. On the mantel was a sepia picture of a bearded man in a black felt hat. I examined it closer. Cal Nettle? He wore a long-sleeved denim shirt and canvas pants with suspenders. He had a sharp, no-nonsense mouth and piercing eyes that looked straight out of the photograph. The image did not resemble the bloated corpse we had pulled from Tavasci Marsh.

The front door opened with a blast of cold air, and Ethan re-entered with the other two. Janny had slipped on a gray sweatshirt and jeans, but Aurora was still dressed for sleep in a ruffled flannel nightgown. She hugged a stuffed yellow bunny with a ragged ear and giggled a little. Her mother shushed her.

Janny pulled Aurora down on the couch and clutched a pillow to her own chest. It was fringed with green, a picture of a young Elvis embroidered on the front. Ethan settled into one of the straight-backed chairs. I licked my dry lips and tried to ignore the lump in my throat while we waited in silence.

Finally, the last member of the family, Ruby Mae Nettle, appeared. She wore a faded chenille bathrobe pulled tight about her. Long silver hair flowed like a waterfall down her back and green eyes blinked at the bright light. She hesitated for a moment in the doorway and then entered the room. The two men half rose to acknowledge her.

"Sit here, Momma," Janny said scooting over to make room. She squeezed her mother's hand as she sat. All eyes centered on Shepherd. A wall clock ticked down the seconds.

"Mrs. Nettle, I have terrible news for you." Shepherd's statement was formal leaving no room for mistake or error. Your husband, Calhoun Nettle, is dead."

Ruby Mae was still for a moment, absorbing the words. Then she snapped her head rapidly back and forth, the gray mane hiding her face. She screamed, shriek after shriek filling the room and spilling into the hall, the noise assaulting my ears. I thought it would never end.

Abruptly she stopped and glared at us. "Get out of my house. You don't belong here. Cal is coming home soon and I have to get supper ready for him. He allus likes a hot meal. He don't want you here." Her voice rose hysterically and she started to scream again.

Janny scooped up Aurora and handed her to me. "Here, you take the baby. I'll settle Momma down." The little girl felt warm and awkward in my arms, and I hid my own tears of upset in her soft hair.

Janny stood in front of her mother and reached for her hand. "Come on, Momma, let's go in the other room for a little while."

As they rose, Ethan joined them, and for a moment, all three clung together. Then the two women moved from the room, Janny holding her mother upright with one arm tightly around her shoulders.

Ethan sat down on the now vacant couch, hiding his face in his hands for a moment. Then he rubbed his cheeks and looked at Shepherd. "I love my momma. Hard to see her in that state." His voice cracked and he swallowed awkwardly. "Guess I'm the man of the family now. You best tell me what happened."

Shepherd was matter-of-fact. "Cal's body was found floating in Tavasci Marsh. The estimate is that he'd been there for some time."

"How'd he die?"

"We're not sure. We'll get back to you on that. Or Peg will. She's our Family Liaison Officer."

A F.L.O.! When did that bird fly the nest? I could just hear him. You'd be good at it since "you're a woman." Next he'd be asking me to serve tea with my little pinky crooked! I tuned back into the conversation as Shepherd changed to interrogation mode.

"Sorry to intrude at this time, Ethan, but I need to ask you a few questions."

The man nodded.

"When did you last see your father?"

"Monday, so that would make it five days or so."

"When on Monday?" Shepherd asked.

"Probably about ten in the morning. He was going over to Darbie's house."

"Darbie?"

"Darbie Granger. She lives over in Cottonwood, got a little trailer over there."

"And Darbie is?" Shepherd prompted.

"My daddy's other wife."

Aurora had fallen asleep, with her legs hanging off my lap and one thumb in her mouth. I shifted her weight to one arm and retrieved my notebook to scribble down this new person's name.

"Oh, they weren't hitched or anything," Ethan explained. "Momma would never give him a divorce. Said she and Daddy were married 'til death do us part.' But something had to give. Darbie is eight months pregnant, and she swore she wasn't going to bear an illegitimate child."

"And Miss Granger's address?"

He gave it to us, and I wrote that down, too.

"What was your daddy's mood when he left here?"

"Upbeat. He'd been talking to the real estate folks about selling this place."

That would be the one million dollar deal. I knew about it and Shepherd didn't. I had a small moment of triumph until I remembered I'd concealed that bit of information from him, too.

Janny came out of the bedroom and I transferred the sleeping Aurora into her arms. My forearm stung as it prickled back to life. Janny moved to the door and Ethan rushed to open it for her. Janny said she'd put the little girl to bed and come back to talk to us. Her steps echoed on the porch stairs, then faded.

"What were your relations with your father?" Shepherd asked.

Ethan thought for a moment. "They weren't good. I'll be honest with you about that, sir. After Lucas died, things got worse. The old man hit the bottle heavy. He beat the dogs, and I wouldn't be a party to that. No cause to be mean to God's creatures."

"Did you fight?"

"Some. Nothing serious. You know, pushing back and forth."

"Did you kill your father, Ethan?"

The crucial question. Shepherd didn't need to Mirandize since Ethan wasn't in custody, but would a possible confession stand up in court if he wasn't? I wasn't sure.

"No, sir, I didn't." To my ears, Ethan's statement was definitive and convincing.

"Anything else you can tell us that might be helpful?"

"He was my daddy. You find the son-of-a-bitch that killed him or I'll do it myself." He clenched his fists so tight that the knuckles whitened.

"No need to threaten, son. We'll do our job." Shepherd turned to me. "Peg, anything?"

I looked up from my note writing, caught unaware. Shook my head. My time to be included in the interrogation and I couldn't come up with one simple question.

"Okay, Ethan. You stay close now. We may have some more things to ask you. Peg, give him your business card so he can call."

I dug in my pocket and encountered nothing. My cards had melted into a sodden lump in the marsh and I hadn't been in the office to get new ones.

Shepherd tightened his lips and dug out one of his own. He crossed off his name, scribbled mine in, and handed it to Ethan. "Any concerns, you call Peg. That's what she's there for."

I hadn't felt this inept since fourth grade when I missed "intelligent" in the weekly spelling bee. Should have thought ahead, had cards ready, had questions to ask. My ears reddened and humiliation stung my cheeks. I accompanied Ethan to the trailer to bring in Janny. At least I remembered that much, to prevent suspects from talking to each other.

Shepherd put Janny through the same line of questioning. The only new information for me was that Janny had moved back to the home place. It seemed that her too-ardent suitor had flattened her tires once too often.

Shepherd scribbled my name on another of his cards and handed it to Janny. He left one for her mother, too. "Peg will be by in the morning, Janny. You just let your mother sleep for now." Then, "Your daddy was a fine man."

The snoozing dogs didn't even glance up as we walked by. Out in the squad car, I expected Shepherd to tear into me for not telling him what I knew about the Nettles, but he didn't. We drove in silence to Mingus.

He pulled up to my apartment and turned off the engine. "Peg…"

I froze.

"You did good tonight. Hard, facing a family like that. Tears are okay, just don't let 'em interfere with business." He paused. "Some things to settle between us, but they can wait."

I didn't know how to respond to that, so I stepped out into the dark night without speaking.

He rolled down his window as I passed by. "Get some rest. I'll see you at the station later this morning." He backed out and drove down the street. His brake lights winked at the corner as he turned on to Main and then he was gone.

Later, when I dropped into bed exhausted, I picked up the alarm clock and peered at its face. If I were lucky, I'd get two hours of sleep before the work day started all over again.

CHAPTER FIVE

The next morning, Shepherd was in his office sipping tea when I arrived. He looked terrible. I hoped the bags under my eyes didn't match his. But his uniform was starched and pressed and mine wasn't.

"Today," he announced, "I want you and Ben to clean that extra room behind your office. Get all the dust and trash out. When you're done with that, run some laps in uniform up and down Main Street. Time you shaped up."

"What?" I asked, not believing my ears.

"You heard me." He wasn't kidding.

Maybe it was my lack of sleep or maybe the tone of his voice, but I'd reached my limit. If I only held a pair of deuces to his royal flush, I'd still call in this poker game. I put my hands on my hips and glared. "I don't notice you running the streets much. How's *your* shape?"

The tea mug stopped half way to his lips. He set it down slowly.

The resentments I'd been stockpiling exploded into the tense air. "Another thing, why introduce me as your subordinate? I'm a deputy, just like you. And my being a Family Liaison Officer? Who gave you authority to change my title? The last time I looked, you weren't even a Field Sergeant, much less a Captain."

"You done?" His jaw set.

I shoved my own jaw out a half inch. "Are you?"

He lobbed a final one over the net. "Your uniform's wrinkled. You modern women above ironing?"

I didn't need this. "Look, I'm a deputy doing my job. Maybe you should do yours, instead of—"

He pushed an envelope my direction. "This came for you from Dr. Westcott, the counselor. Add anger management to your session topics." He smiled tightly. "I'll have your official appointment as Family Liaison Officer by day's end. Count on it."

I crushed the envelope in my fist, turned on my heel and left his office. To prove my even temper, I refrained from giving him the finger of doom. Ben, our office assistant, mimed a high five as I swept by. I slammed my office door and dropped into my chair, still adrenalin-charged. Then I ripped the envelope open. I crashed to earth. Inside was a billing statement from the counseling office, $50.00 for a "no show" charge. In the commotion of finding Cal Nettle's body, I'd missed my appointment with Dr. Westcott.

I intended to reschedule right away, but then Ben knocked at my door and handed me a pink message slip. Janny Nettle wanted me to phone. She was up early, probably hadn't gotten much more sleep than us. Counseling could wait. I dialed her cell number.

"Hi, Peg. Thanks for calling back. And thanks for coming out last night. It meant a lot to Momma."

"Hard for you Janny, to lose your father that way. Again my sympathies. What can I do for you this morning?"

"Three things, actually. First, I called Howard. He's coming home soon as he can get time off work. Then, Momma wants you to visit later today, too." Her organized voice ticked off the requests, almost as though it was a way to stave off grief.

I wondered if I could be that dispassionate if something happened to HT or my mother, even as lost as she was in her dementia. It would be an agony for me, but perhaps Janny felt different about her father.

"Then, I talked to Darbie," she continued. "Can you go see her?"

Darbie Granger, Cal's other wife. "Is she aware of your father's death?"

"I called her early this morning after you left," Janny said. "Darbie used to be my best friend. She still is, but living with Momma curtails my social life some. Darbie's at home now if you want to call her." She gave me Darbie's phone number and hung up.

I called Darbie and got directions to her trailer. She sounded young and upset. "I'll be here all day," she said. "Don't have much else to do with the baby coming."

Funny how these things work out. I'd planned to avoid Shepherd after our argument, but I needed wheels. I walked the short steps to his office and knocked on the door. At his grunt, I opened it and walked in. "Going out to interview Darbie Granger. Need to use the SUV."

He didn't say a word, just tossed me the keys.

"I'll brief you when I return."

He gave me a level stare and returned to his cup of tea, unresolved business cleaving the air between us like a butcher knife.

My breath fogged the air as I walked out to the SUV. Cold this morning, with a chance of snow flurries by week's end. Winter weather here would be nothing like the ice storms in Tennessee, but slick mountain roads could be challenging, no matter where they were.

Halloween was coming, and the shop windows already displayed holiday decorations as I drove down Main Street. Hopefully, storms would hold off until after the Spook Night Festival, that last-of-season income boost for the store owners.

I swung the SUV around the curves and bends leading out of Mingus and down the hill to Cottonwood. I stopped at the mini mart there and got a Diet Coke, lots of ice. Then I crunched the ice, piece by piece on the way out to Darbie's as I replayed the argument with Shepherd. No one could be that inflexible, surely. On the other hand, he'd had thirty years of practice.

By the time the cup of ice was empty, my calm had returned. Darbie's trailer was on a dirt road on the edge of town. The cottonwoods had lost their leaves early this year, but plate-sized sycamore leaves still clung to the white branches looming over my vehicle.

The trailer was an old Airstream, all silver aluminum and curved sides. The front jack was propped on cinder blocks and the wheels were uncovered. Not a permanent home, then. By the side of the door sat two white plastic chairs and a small table. An old border collie rose from a worn rug by the trailer door as I pulled to a stop. He approached my car and gave a half-hearted woof.

A young woman made awkward by pregnancy leaned on a wobbly side railing as she descended the two fold-down steps at the trailer's front door. "Hush you. Lay back down."

The dog looked at its owner and returned to the rug with a deep sigh.

Darbie Granger extended a soft hand. "Hello, Officer Quincy. Glad to make your acquaintance."

She was in her late twenties, medium height and thin except for her pregnancy. Her brown hair hung in casual ringlets to her shoulders. But it was her eyes that drew my attention: The same vivid green as Ruby Mae's. Cal had noticed that, too, I'd bet. Drawn to what he was missing at home?

Darbie's smile lit up a face that might be plain without it. "Come visit with me. It'll be good to talk to somebody besides my dog." Her voice sounded lonesome.

She gestured to the chairs. "We used to sit out here, Cal and me, and watch the sun set through the trees."

A rough pottery jug with purple coneflowers and white fleabane decorated the table, and a wind chime in the branches of a mesquite tree mingled with the sound of the river beyond.

"Nice place," I commented.

"Thanks. Cal promised me a real house when the baby came, but now..." She sniffled. "Janny called me. I haven't slept a wink since. Can I get you something? Still have some apricot bars left. Maybe sweet tea or...?"

I pictured her climbing down those uncertain stairs from the trailer, holding full glasses of tea. Didn't want her stumbling and hurting herself. "Thanks, I'm fine." I fished out paper and pen from my pocket. "Mind if I take notes?"

"If it helps bring Cal's killer to justice."

"Can't guarantee that, but we'll try. Cal was on his way to see you last week?"

"But he never got here. On my word, I swear he didn't."

"And you didn't call to see where he was?" I asked.

"Cal didn't like me to call. Ruby Mae watched him close, that jealous bitch."

"But you worried when he didn't show up?"

"I was frantic! I texted Janny, but she didn't know where he was, either."

"This would have been what day?"

She stopped to remember. "Monday, I think. That's trash day for us here. Yes, Monday, I'm sure."

That matched what Ethan Nettle had told us. It seemed reasonable on the surface. Or Darbie could be lying about Cal not visiting her that day. Especially if he showed up to tell her that he'd changed his mind and decided to stay in the marriage with Ruby Mae. A jealous woman, even a pregnant one, could murder out of rage and frustration.

"Tell me about your relationship with Cal," I said.

She got a faraway look in her eyes. "He was my hero. He had a reputation for temper, but he never showed that side to me, not once. A musician, did you know that? His guitar over there." She pointed to an instrument leaned up against the trailer.

Darbie settled into the telling of her story: How her folks had kicked her out when she sucker-punched her dad after an argument and how Janny found her the bartending job at Rainbow's Folly. "I rented this trailer with my first paycheck—But you asked about Cal..."

I nodded. "How long did you know him?"

"Since Lucas's death, about four years now. Cal stopped in at the bar where I worked. He'd talk and I'd listen. But then one night he got falling-down drunk. I grabbed his keys and drove him here after work. I figured he could sleep it off before going home. Nothing improper, you understand—I've got a pullout couch." She looked up earnestly.

"And then?" I asked.

The words tumbled out of her as if she needed to justify the relationship. "Well, one thing led to another. Cal had a way about him, hard to refuse. He was lonely and I felt sorry for him. I never intended it to come to this, that's for sure." She smoothed her dress over her belly. "He asked me to get an abortion, but I refused. I told him he had to make it right. And he was going to."

She raised her left hand to display a silver band cast in a Celtic knot with a small red stone in the center. "See this promise ring? We said our vows to each other, and that's all that counts. I was the love of his life."

I'd heard that tale before. But the knight didn't always ride up on his white horse to save the day. Sometimes he bolted the other direction.

"How did you and Cal get along?" I asked.

Her green eyes narrowed. "You asking if I hurt him?"

"Did you?"

"How could you even think such a thing! We had our little spats like any couple, but nothing serious. He took care of me, and I loved him, as hard as I could. I'd never turn against Cal like his family did."

"His family?"

"Ruby Mae, I mean."

"They argued?"

"She's a horrible woman. Cal detested her, that's why he chose me." She crossed her arms tightly. "Ruby Mae's spite rules her miserable life. She's capable of anything."

"Such as?"

Darbie took a deep breath. "One time Ruby Mae caught Cal making a cradle for little Cal, Jr. She smashed it with a sledgehammer, right down to kindling and then burned it. I was heartbroken. She had no cause to do that."

Seemed reasonable to me. Ruby Mae struck me as the type of mother who put her own children before all others. She'd seen the new baby as a rival to her own. "Anything else?"

Darbie sniffed. "Cal refused to ruin our time together talking about that vile person."

"Where did you and Cal go when you dated?"

She looked down. "We really didn't go anywhere. Ruby Mae wouldn't allow that. She'd find out—this is a small town—and I didn't want to get Cal in trouble. I just fixed him dinner here. That man did love my lemon meringue pie. We'd sit and talk. One thing led to another." She blushed.

Convenient for Cal Nettle, lonely for Darbie Granger. But this trailer was a long way from the wetlands where we'd found his body. "You ever visit Tavasci Marsh?" I asked.

She shook her head. "Nasty swampy place. Gave me the creeps. Full of mosquitoes."

Gave her the creeps *when?* How'd she know that if she hadn't been there? I hadn't noticed any flying insects when I'd been sitting on that beaver lodge. Maybe they'd already flown south before winter settled in. Smart bugs.

46

"You working?" I asked.

"Not for the last month or so," she said. "Terrible backaches. Cal was so sweet. He'd rub my feet and put a cold cloth on my forehead. He promised once the home place sold we'd leave this ugly old town, move someplace nice like Lake Tahoe. That Ruby Mae, always messing things up."

"Like what?"

"Never mind, I didn't mean anything. I can't be losing my temper like that." She stroked her belly. "It's bad for Cal, Jr."

"What about Cal's grown children?" I asked, persisting. There was an undercurrent, just below the surface, of untold secrets and half lies.

"Howard hasn't been around for a while, least I haven't seen him. I had a crush on Howard once, did you know? And then I ended up with his father. Funny how things sort out. And then Cal and Janny had their falling out."

I raised an eyebrow. "They argued?"

"A lot of blame flying back and forth when poor Lucas was killed and Janny's little baby girl was crippled. I don't blame Janny one little bit if she got mad at her daddy. She never talks about it, and I don't bring it up. But girlfriends stand behind each other."

And tell untruths and invent alibis where none exist? I filed the thought away. "What about the younger son, Ethan?"

"Cal was so wonderful, I don't understand why Ethan would pick a fight with him. But yes, they argued," she admitted.

"Anybody else?" I asked. "What about someone outside the family that might wish Cal ill?"

She thought a moment. "Cal ran moonshine whiskey for a while. Of course, that was before we met—I'd never have anything to do with that. But he associated with some rough people then. Talk to Otis Stroud, that's Ruby Mae's brother. He lives out there, takes care of the machinery on the place. As close to a man-friend as Cal had."

I gave her a card and offered my arm when she rose. She laughed. "Don't be silly. I'm not helpless."

Not helpless. I'd remember that statement.

Darbie slowly mounted the front steps, and the old dog lumbered after her into the trailer.

Driving back, I pondered on how life twisted us in strange directions. A year ago, Darbie didn't expect to be where she was. For that matter, neither did Cal Nettle, now lying on that cold slab at the morgue. Howard Nettle might want to keep an eye out. It appeared Darbie Granger liked unavailable men.

Someone hated Cal Nettle fiercely enough to kill him or loved him enough to do it. Ruby Mae Nettle and Darbie Granger were both contenders for the honor. I couldn't wait to hear Ruby Mae's take on the Darbie affair.

I stopped in Clarkdale to call Shepherd. "Finished talking to Darbie Granger. Going out to the Nettle place to see Ruby Mae. Want to ride along?"

CHAPTER SIX

Shepherd's tone was brusque. "Busy here. You handle the interview with Ruby Mae. But get back to the office in time to fill me in before day's end. Abner may want me to brief the press."

Busy doing what? Finishing another crossword puzzle? It didn't take long for Shepherd to settle into my space. Who did he think he was, presuming a first-name, best-buddy relationship with the sheriff, Abner Jones, planning his "expert" press conference?

It was near noon, so I stopped at Su Casa, the best Mexican restaurant in Clarkdale to have some chili rellenos and a glass of sun-brewed ice tea before heading out to the Nettles' home place. The manager said hi. We were on a first name basis after the shooting case a few months ago. When I finished, I called Ruby Mae and let her know I was on my way.

The SUV bounced and squeaked through the eroded clay ruts on the road to the Nettle place. The afternoon sun paled behind high cirrus clouds. I opened my window and caught the screech of a scrub jay, and then closed it when the dust cloud enveloped me. I'd have to hit a car wash on the way back if Shepherd wanted to make his press debut with a shiny vehicle on display.

I pulled the car in a circle at the house, gave the horn a short tap. The canine welcoming committee didn't show, so I cautiously entered the yard. The door to the house opened and Ruby Mae came out on the porch. "You're fine. Ethan shut the dogs up in the back kennel. Careful of that porch railing, meaning to fix that."

I walked up the steps and shook her hand. "Sorry to bother you, Mrs. Nettle, but a few questions still."

"Call me Ruby Mae, everybody else does, girl. Come in and set a spell." She touched my shoulder.

Ruby Mae appeared more in control of her emotions this afternoon. Her frame was big-boned but flat, front and back. Today, she dressed in a green-and-white checkered shirt tucked into worn blue jeans. She blinked against the sun as we shook hands, her eyes that startling green.

Why had Cal strayed? I'd heard the death of a child will do that to parents sometimes. They start blaming each other for the loss they're feeling inside. For Calhoun Nettle, death had put an end to painful grief that drink and a new woman failed to do. In fact, I imagined he wasn't feeling anything right now.

That meant, though, that Ruby Mae now had two losses to contend with, both son and husband.

"Pleased to make your acquaintance, again," she said in her soft, hill-country twang. "I know your granddaddy."

That told me two things: First, HT would grill me about this meeting, and second, if Ruby Mae Nettle and I counted cousins back a ways, we were probably kin. She might open up more to me than to others, but she'd also expect me to keep family secrets, and I couldn't do that. I wasn't her friend. I was the Family Liaison Officer thanks to Shepherd. I straddled a very splintery fence.

"Let's sit in the kitchen. Coffee's done perking." She pulled an old metal-banded glass percolator from the range and poured coffee into two mugs, one labeled "property of Smokey's Motel" and the other from a Tip's Market. My mother used to do that, too. Always came home from a trip with a suitcase full of hotel towels. It's stealing, mama, I

50

told her. She didn't see it that way. Maybe Ruby Mae didn't either.

"Cream, sugar?" she asked.

I shook my head.

We sat at a small wooden table in a corner of the country kitchen. Ruby Mae had already set the table in anticipation of my visit. Puff-plastic placemats held two decorative plates, one chipped at the edge. She brought another plate to the table and settled comfortably. "Here's beaten biscuits, left over from breakfast. And some of my strawberry jam, not as good as last season, a little runny," she apologized. "Eat, and then we'll talk business."

I knew about country-style beaten biscuits, that buttery-flour combination beaten with a wooden spoon into an ambrosia of delight. The jam was even better, capturing the essence of a warm summer day. When we had eaten, I touched my finger to one last crumb and lifted it to my lips.

Ruby Mae freshened our coffee and leaned her elbows on the table, hospitality satisfied. "Now, what can I tell you?"

"First, I'm sorry for your husband's passing. That must have been a terrible shock to you."

"Those first minutes last night took me terrible. Janny, my angel, bless her for being there. I thought some on it this morning. I shoulda known you wouldn't be bringing good news before the cock crowed. Maybe I just didn't want to hear you say it."

"Ruby Mae, I need to ask you some questions."

"Ask away." Those green eyes drilled into mine, and I encountered the whip-steel mind behind them. Ruby Mae was nobody's pushover. Cal met his match here, and yet he had left for Darbie Granger.

"How was your relationship with your husband?"

"We married at nineteen, been together ever since. But folks grow apart, that's natural."

"Grow apart?" I asked.

"We didn't sleep together if that's what you're suggestin'. Shook the house with his snoring. I told him one day, 'you want me to fix you breakfast, I need my rest.' So he moved his stuff to the trailer, bachelored with Ethan." She sighed. "Ate all his meals here, though. Sometimes I think he liked the cooking better'n me. Three times a day, year after year, I fixed his food just the way he liked it."

Both pride and regret echoed in her voice.

"Did you ever disagree, fight over things?"

"In all those years, selling this homestead was our only battle. I wanted to move to town, get a little place so I could watch Aurora until Janny got off work, afternoons. But Cal wouldn't hear of it. I told him, you keep stalling, those developers will build that golf course somewhere else. You'll still be here at ninety, tripping over roots and patching this leaky roof. Me, I wanted to move to that Del Webb development." She looked at me. "You know they got a swimming pool big as a pond? And bingo, some nights."

"But Cal wanted to stay here?" I prompted.

"Stubborn as a one-eyed mule. He said they'd have to drag him out of here, feet first. Well, now he's got his wish. But maybe I'll get the last laugh."

"How so?"

"Them real estate folks already telephoned to pay their respects. Janny must have told them he was gone. They asked if I still wanted to sell."

"And do you?"

"I might. That money could fix little Aurora's hand, get a proper stone marker for Lucas's grave. Maybe help Janny go back to school." Her tone was thoughtful. She gestured toward my mug. "More coffee?"

I put my hand over the cup and shook my head. "Ruby Mae, Ethan said last night that he fought with his father."

"Oh, that. Just a little tussling between two bull elk. Nobody got hurt, much."

"Cal had a temper?"

"When he was drinking, something fierce. He'd pick a fight with Ethan, and they'd holler and yell like the Lord pulled the final curtain. Good thing we don't have neighbors close, what would they think."

"Fight over what?" I asked.

"Them coonhounds that Ethan is breeding, mostly. When Cal got to drinking, he might have misused them dogs some, I don't know. But those two men of mine always made up. Their feuding didn't last through the cool light of dawn."

"What about your other son, Howard?"

She tensed. "What *about* Howard?"

Apparently, there were limits to confiding in almost-kin.

"Ruby Mae, Janny told me a little but I need more to understand what happened. Howard hasn't been here since the whiskey still exploded?"

She eased back in her chair and her eyes moistened. "Happened about four years ago, seems like yesterday. Cal was running moonshine, pushed too hard to make one last run. He'd heard Cyrus Marsh was about to shut him down."

Cyrus Marsh used to be the only law in Mingus. I'd replaced him when he died of a heart attack, none too soon for some of our townspeople, it seemed. Cyrus was of the old school, made his own set of laws. "What went wrong?" I asked.

Her eyes blurred with tears. "The pressure must have gone too high on the distiller, blew that thing to smithereens. Tipped a propane tank into the bonfire, and the whole place lit up. Maybe it was God's will. Lucas burned something terrible. He lasted a day in the hospital, nothing they could do. I never left his side the whole time. They drug me off his body when he passed." She rubbed knuckles of one hand with the other hand, soothing herself.

"And Aurora?"

53

"That poor baby girl. She never shoulda been out there."

"The explosion, whose fault?"

Her mouth straightened in a tight line. "Never you mind. Has nothing to do with this." She crossed her arms and sat silent.

"Remembering painful times can be hard, Ruby Mae," I said. "When did you see Cal last?"

She relaxed, ready to return to the present. "That would be Monday, about five days ago now. He'd said he was going to town to take care of some business."

"What business?" I asked.

"That slut." She spit out the words. "What sort of a name is that, anyhow? Darbie, Barbie, whatever. Like one of them funny-looking dolls."

"What was Miss Granger's relationship with Cal?"

"She had no right to come between a husband and his lawful wife. That Jezebel, I'll kill her!" Her fist banged on the table and the plate of biscuits crashed to the worn linoleum floor.

Ruby Mae jerked to her feet and pulled a corn broom and black dustpan from a closet. She swept the plate shards and ruined biscuits into the dustpan with abrupt motions and dumped them into the trash muttering to herself.

Then she slammed into her chair and huffed a shivery breath. "Cal loved me, swore on our family Bible he was going to break it off with her. That's why he went to town. I promised him that would be the end of it, that I'd stay on, not make trouble if he did. That woman claims anything else, she's a liar. She's not going to get one red cent from the land sale after I'd worked and scrimped and saved. Not one red cent.

"That's all I intend to say on the subject." She rose to her feet, the conversation ended. "Bid your granddaddy good day for me," she said. "He's always been a good friend of ours."

Meaning right now I wasn't. I shook her hand, walked out the door and down the stairs. No fun interrogating family, even kin twice removed.

I checked my watch. It was getting late. I weighed my options: was it better to arrive late or show up with the SUV in this condition? Clarkdale had a quick car wash, and I ran the SUV through to sluice off the dust. Even so, it was dark when I pulled into the parking lot for the sheriff's station.

Ben had gone home and Shepherd was perched impatiently on the edge of his office chair. "About time. Where you been?"

"Cleaning up the SUV. Want to debrief now?"

"Can't. Late. Got responsibilities." He grabbed his coat. "Need a ride?" he asked as an afterthought.

"I'll walk home. Some things to wrap up here." And then, I deliberately blocked his exit and held out my hand. "Sorry. My temper got riled this morning. No sleep makes me crotchety."

"Get used to it. That's police work," he said bluntly. But then he offered his own hand, and we shook. "We'll work on it. But understand: I'm still the SIO on this case."

Senior Investigative Officer. Fair enough. It didn't change things much between us, but at least we had a neutral zone defined. He left the office, and I breathed easier.

Ben had left a message on my desk from Dr. Westcott. The counselor again. Maybe my shortness of temper would start to ease the further I got from the killing of that man. To be honest, it still haunted me at night, all that blood.

I set the message aside to season and completed the notes on the meeting with Ruby Mae. Shepherd wouldn't know I was doing them after the fact if I didn't tell him. It was seven o'clock when I again remembered the counselor.

I picked up the telephone to leave a message. Surely she'd be gone by now.

"Denise Westcott here."

Caught. "This is Peg Quincy. Sorry I missed my appointment. It's been busy up here."

"Yes, I heard. But keeping appointments or at least calling to cancel is important in your recovery."

Recovery from what? I was fine, no problem with me. I broke into her lecture. "When can I come see you?"

"What times do you have free tomorrow?"

"Just got in, don't know my schedule yet." That sounded lame, even to me.

"Ring when you find out. I'll work you in," she said in that cultured British voice and hung up.

I did resolve to call her, first thing. But the next morning matters took an unexpected turn.

CHAPTER SEVEN

I walked to the station, breathing fog clouds into the air. Sun dogs formed in the sky, meaning our weather would be changing soon. The comforting aroma of fresh coffee, Ben's Blue Mountain special blend, greeted me as I opened the station door.

"Made you a pot," Shepherd announced from his office. "Grab a cup and let's talk."

The coffee a peace offering? Shepherd's mood was hard to predict, switching from judgmental supervisor to best buddy in an instant. Not sure which I preferred, but with a night of sleep, I was in a better mood, too. I poured a cup and buried my nose in the fragrant steam. Then I walked into Shepherd's office and sat down.

Whatever had been bothering him last night seemed to have passed. "Where's Ben?" I asked.

"Entrance exams down at Yavapai College."

Our office assistant, Ben Yazzie, already had one degree, but they had a new enology program that intrigued him. He said the knowledge of grapes would help his Navajo Shaman training. I didn't follow his line of reasoning, but was glad to see him moving ahead. He deserved better than clerking for a small-town sheriff's office.

"What'd you find out yesterday?" Shepherd asked.

I described my visits to Ruby Mae and the very pregnant Darbie Granger. "Darbie seems to think Cal was leaving his wife for her, but Ruby Mae said just the opposite."

"Not surprising. Women believe what they want to hear."

And men, too, I wanted to add. Two minutes into a conversation with Shepherd and I was already biting my tongue. "Darbie lives in a trailer on a dead end road with only an old border collie for company. Deserted out there."

"Convenient for Cal, that way."

I couldn't argue with that.

"What's Darbie's relationship with the other Nettles?" he asked.

I considered a moment. "She's good friends with Janny, attracted to Howard, blood enemies with Ruby Mae."

"Not surprising. Ruby Mae is a strong-willed character. Did Darbie talk about Lucas? I heard some tale about them being involved before the boy was killed."

Lucas, too? Ms. Darbie got around. I shook my head.

"Any chance Darbie could have killed Cal?"

"A distant possible," I said. "She mentioned conflicts with her own dad, and Cal was old enough to be a father figure to her. A rejection there would be unsettling."

I took another sip of coffee. Moved the rock on Shepherd's desk. He left it there. Definitely in truce-making mode. "But Cal would be too heavy for Darbie to lift, dead weight. If he died at her place, she'd need help to move the body to Tavasci Marsh."

"That's a fact. Did you ask her if she killed him?"

"Uh, no." I hated to admit that blatant oversight.

"She probably wouldn't have told you anyway. It takes a skilled interrogator to gain a confession."

Which I obviously wasn't, in his opinion.

"Okay, we'll keep her on the list," he said. "What about Ruby Mae?"

"She makes good biscuits."

He smiled. "That she does. I ate a few when I investigated Lucas's death. Cop bait, she calls them. Wouldn't be surprised if she's used that maneuver once or twice with the ATF guys. A sharp one, our Ruby Mae."

Alcohol, Tobacco, Firearms. Ah, the moonshine still. "You think part of her reaction when we made the death notification could have been a performance for our benefit?" I asked. "She'd calmed down when I talked to her. If we're going with family connections, I think she's a better bet for the murder than Darbie."

"Why?" His gaze sharpened.

I ticked off the reasons. "She wanted to move to help her kids, and Cal stood in the way. Not to mention that affair with Darbie. Pretty hard to ignore when the woman's so pregnant."

"Ruby Mae's a tough lady. She's weathered worse than a husband with a wandering eye."

"But if he were actually going to divorce her this time?" I asked.

"Good point."

"Or maybe the reason goes back further than Darbie. Losing a son is a terrible tragedy. If she found out Cal was to blame for that...."

Shepherd nodded. "Tough on the whole family. But four years later?"

I shared the details about my meeting with Howard that first day. "If he's back in the picture, maybe he said something?"

"A long shot, but we'll keep Ruby Mae on the list, too." He took a sip of his green tea.

Never could understand how folks drink that stuff. Donkey piss.

Shepherd looked at me as if reading my mind. "They ever get that whiskey still up and running again? That was Otis Stroud's baby. He was responsible for keeping that old machinery operating. Man's a wizard with anything mechanical. You meet him when you were out there visiting with Ruby Mae?"

"He wasn't around. What's so special about Otis?"

"Otis Stroud..." Shepherd began. He leaned back in his chair. "Came out from Tennessee about the same time Cal married his sister, Ruby Mae. Heard rumors that Otis *had* to leave, killed a man back there in a bar fight. He ran the whiskey operation for Cal. Has possible connections to the Phoenix bad guys, but never charged. No respect for the ladies, either. Always keep him in front of you, Peg. Call for backup if there's any sign of trouble with that one."

Fair warning. But I'd held no patience with male physical intimidation since my growth spurt started in high school. The Krav Maga, that Israeli combat defensive training I'd taken in the Police Academy, helped, too. I'd be cautious when I met Otis Stroud, but I wasn't backing down, either. My motto was: be a cop first, a lady second.

"Write up your meeting with Howard and your visits with those two women before you leave tonight. I didn't see a summary report on my desk this morning like I asked for." Truce over. *Supervisor* Malone had returned.

He was the one left early last night, and I didn't recall any request for a report. I choked back that need to prove myself right. I could've written one up before I left, and I didn't.

"Best I go talk to Otis, get his statement," Shepherd said. "I want to be certain that whiskey still isn't operational again. Man's work, but you can tag along if you want to." He peered over his reading glasses at me.

Was there a hint of humor in his voice, or was he pushing my buttons with that "man's work" comment? Either way, I wouldn't give him the satisfaction. "Works for me. When?"

"Now. No notice this time, we'll deal with the dogs when we get there."

As he drove down the winding road to Clarkdale and beyond that to the Nettles' homestead, I kept my seat belt fastened tight. That man did like to slice the sharp edges off the corners.

I hadn't called the counselor, Dr. Westcott, but I'd remembered her at least. That should count for something. No problem, I'd touch base with her later. I didn't know what my schedule was yet. That was the truth.

When we arrived at the Nettle place, all the vehicles were gone, the place silent. Shepherd pulled our SUV into the drive and turned off the engine. Then he opened the window and helloed the house.

Ethan appeared from the barn, wiping his hands on his blue jeans. He tossed too-long bangs out of his eyes and walked up to the SUV. The man could do with a haircut. I tucked an errant strand of my own hair behind one ear.

"Big dogs are penned. Momma went to pick up Aurora, and Otis is at the feed store. Come see the pups."

We got out of the car and followed Ethan to the near barn. In one corner he had built a six-foot square whelping box. When we approached, a redbone coonhound bitch rose from the pen and stepped carefully over the sill of the adjustable door.

"Folks, meet Red Sheba and her family," Ethan said with pride.

The pups appeared about six weeks old, all round bellies and stubby legs. They tumbled over each other and squeaked in eagerness to follow their mother.

Even Shepherd was impressed. "Nice. You sexed them yet?"

"Three boys and four girls. They've almost outgrown this box. I'll be constructing a play area for them soon. Training them on 'coon tails," he said.

"You aren't shooting raccoons?" I asked.

"No, ma'am. My cousins in Tennessee collect tails off roadkill and ship them to me on dry ice."

I sat down on a corner seat of the box and touched the velvet-soft, sunset-red fur of one exploring pup. It immediately suckled my finger. Always hungry at this age. "What are those bars around the pen's inside?" I asked.

"I built the box special with pig rails. Gives the pups someplace to hide, protect them when they're little. Sheba's a good mother, but breeds this large can kill pups by laying on them."

"Good man," Shepherd said.

Ethan's face shone in the praise. He had a man's body, but a youngster's need for approval. "I'm trying to do the best I can. My brother Lucas created this breeding program before he died. I aim to continue what he started." His voice sounded wistful. "Come to the porch and I'll fix you some lemonade. Momma should be back soon."

As we moved from the barn, Sheba re-entered the box, plopping down with a whump and the pups swarmed her side. When we got to the house, Ethan disappeared through the door and soon returned juggling three Mason jars filled with lemonade, iced and sweet-tart.

We perched on the steps, Ethan on the highest, Shepherd one down, and me on the lowest board. I leaned against the porch railing but straightened as it sagged behind me. A Bendire's thrasher in the high branches of an old sycamore trilled an intricate warble, and we basked in the mid-morning sun waiting for the rest of the Nettle family to return.

A gangly adolescent coonhound loped around the corner. When Shepherd reached out his hand, the dog shied away.

"Sorry," Ethan said. "Reckless is spooked by strange men. Gets on fine with the ladies, though. Aurora's his favorite."

As if on cue, the young dog approached me and lay down with his chin across one of my shoes. "What happened?" I asked.

Ethan's face darkened. "Daddy about ruined him and that's a fact."

"Tell us about it, son," Shepherd said, his voice gentle.

Ethan rubbed a hand over his narrow chin. "Daddy insisted on hunting late one night. He'd do that when he got to drinking and remembering Lucas. Tripped over a log, blamed the pup. That started it. Then Reckless rolled in the remains of a dead squirrel, stunk something fierce. He's a young dog. They just do that." Ethan's voice was defensive. "And next, the pup treed a possum instead of a coon."

Ethan clenched his fists and the dog jerked upright off my shoe. He climbed up the steps and wedged against the man. Ethan smoothed the dog's ear and leaned against his side, his eyes moist. "Daddy took off his belt and started beating Reckless, like he did me when I was little. Know you're 'sposed to honor your parents, but I couldn't stand it, I plain couldn't."

"You fought?" Shepherd asked.

"I grabbed that belt out of his hand and threw it away. Punched him hard. Called for Reckless but he'd disappeared. Came to my senses, then. Not right taking advantage of a man's been drinking. I left Daddy to sleep it off and went to the trailer. Reckless didn't show until the next morning, and he's been like this ever since." He patted the dog's side.

"And your father?" I asked.

Ethan looked up in surprise, as if he'd forgotten I was there. "The next morning he swore it never happened. To his mind maybe it didn't. I let it be."

"But you didn't forget."

"How could I, with Reckless here?"

Two vehicles swung into the drive, a blue sedan and behind it, a man driving an old Ford pickup truck with sun-faded red paint. That had to be Otis Stroud, Ruby Mae's brother.

Reckless gave a joyous bay and leaped off the porch. He pounced on the side of the sedan, just as the hounds had done on the SUV our first evening here. Aurora opened the door and climbed out. She leaned down so the dog could lick her face, and then skipped toward us, her crippled hand braced against the dog's fur.

"Let's go help your mother," Shepherd said to Ethan. "And I want a word with your Uncle Otis." The two walked toward the vehicles. Aurora approached me, touched my hair shyly in passing, and clattered up the steps into the house, Reckless at her heels.

Shepherd greeted Ruby Mae at her car and said something in her ear. Then he walked to the pickup and pulled a feed sack out of the bed. He lifted it to one shoulder with some difficulty. I could have done better. It was only a fifty-pounder. Otis hoisted another sack and disappeared around the corner of the barn. The man appeared to have a sinew-hard strength, with arms darkly tanned. I'd be able to judge him better at close range, though, and I intended to.

Ethan opened the car's back door and pulled out two sacks of groceries. He handed one to his mother and followed her toward the house.

I stood and dusted off my pants. "Hello, Ruby Mae. Good to see you again. Can I help?"

"I got it. You say hi to your granddaddy for me?"

I reddened. "Soon," I said.

"Do that, now. You best catch up with your side-kick." She jerked her head toward the barn and then climbed the porch steps, treading carefully, holding the groceries. Ethan followed close behind her.

***

The far end of the barn had been partitioned off from the whelping area. Light from the second-story loft door dimly illuminated a collection of vintage farm implements: a wooden plow with an iron point, a hand threshing machine, a corn sheller. One wall held a huge hay fork. Next to it were collars and traces for long-vanished work animals. Nothing used in decades, all preserved by past generations for a future need that never came.

In one corner of the barn sat another pickup, a 1929 Ford, lovingly restored, its brass gleaming in a blade of sunlight thrown by a high window. Cal's truck? If so, who would inherit it? I'd seen grown men come to blows over a father's signet ring. This truck was much more valuable, especially to men who prized fine machinery.

I pictured Otis and Ethan in a toe-to-toe struggle. Ethan had the youth, but I read Otis as an experienced street fighter. If Ruby Mae intervened, maybe it wouldn't come to that. But when the patriarch of a family died, it was hard to predict the new matrix.

The two men looked up as I neared. Otis was about forty, with a big head and small eyes. A worn circle of fabric in one shirt pocket outlined a can of chewing tobacco. He had a rank odor like a wild animal caged too long.

Otis surveyed me like a Saturday-night John deciding how much to offer. "Who're you?" he asked. His voice had that raspy hardness of a lifetime smoker now denied his habit.

It was a challenge I accepted. Getting in his face, I stuck out my hand. "Deputy Peg Quincy, from Mingus."

He spat to the side, reached in his pocket for the can, stuck another plug in his cheek, and slowly slid the can back into its resting place. "Heard about you." His eyes were dead, like pools filled with rotting leaves.

I'll bet you have. Take my hand, you bastard.

When he did, I matched him grip for grip. He was strong, I'll give him that. But I'd been arm-wrestling champ at the Police Academy and I held my own. Finally, Otis dropped his hand, his fingers twitching. Shepherd stood behind him, watching the exchange. A smile drifted across his face and disappeared.

"Now then, Otis," he said, "time we mosey down to that old whiskey still. Want to make sure no bears destroyed your equipment."

With lightning reflexes, Otis grabbed at a fly buzzing around his head. He opened his palm to view the mangled insect. It was still alive, although its wings were crushed. Carefully he set it on the Ford's hood and watched it struggle up the curved surface.

"Kill the damn thing, Otis," Shepherd said.

"Nah. It'll die soon enough." He turned on his heel and spat again at the ground, barely missing my shoe.

We walked abreast down a dirt road behind the barn. In the noonday sun, the animals and birds turned silent as we hiked about a quarter-mile through a small meadow and over a hill. Tuzigoot Ruins filled the horizon as the Tavasci Marsh spread before us. The road ended at water's edge and a single-file path entered the swamp.

"What about it, *Ms.* Quincy. You up to a hike?" Otis flashed tobacco-stained teeth, inviting me to follow directly after him.

Shepherd quickly stepped in front of me. "I'll take the middle, Otis. Peg, you bring up the rear."

Part of me prickled at Shepherd's intervention, and part of me was relieved I didn't have to smell Otis's animal stench in front of me. He had a sure-footed familiarity on the path, but both Shepherd and I sometimes misstepped as we tried to predict which hillock was solid and which slid off toward the murky water.

We'd been hiking for about ten minutes, the overgrowth getting thicker and wet areas increasing as we angled diagonally into the marsh. The rough path remained weed free as though someone trod it regularly, but to either side, pools of dank water appeared and then vanished from view behind tall reeds and marsh grasses.

Sweat blurred my vision and I wiped my eyes. "How much farther?"

"Why? You tired?" Otis sneered.

I grunted, not willing to engage. We'd be out of here soon enough. The man was a sore loser, that was all. I pumped my fist in memory of arm-wrestling victory.

Otis picked up the pace, striding long. Shepherd and I hurried after him; my eyes on the path to keep my footing sure, Shepherd stiff with an arthritic hip. Then Otis jerked to an angled halt and his elbow jutted out. Shepherd bumped into his motionless figure and sidestepped, splashing into the water to regain his balance.

There was a sound like a recoiled spring snapping, and Shepherd cried out in pain. He doubled over, clutching his calf with both hands. Blood seeped through his fingers, turning the water black. Two rusty metal bands with jagged teeth sliced into his leg: A bear trap, set at water's edge to protect the whiskey still.

Shepherd screamed and slumped forward into the water.

CHAPTER EIGHT

I plunged into water above my knees, frantic to reach Shepherd before it was too late. I turned him so that his face was out of the water and he could breathe.

Blood gushed from the wound like an artesian spring. I tried to pull the jaws of the trap apart, but the spring was too heavy for me to pry open by myself.

Could I trust Otis? Probably not—he'd *set* the trap— but my partner's life was at stake. I had no other options, had to act now. "Help me?" I asked.

Otis looked at me and shrugged a half-hearted agreement.

I maneuvered Shepherd's body to the edge of the path so that his head was on dry ground. Then I splashed back toward the jaws tightening about his leg. "Get on the other side," I told Otis.

He waded in and together we reached under the water and forced the teeth of the trap apart far enough to reset the springs. The trap jaws chunked into a cocked position with a muffled thud, more felt than heard.

I painstakingly worked Shepherd's calf free of the rusty teeth, my fingers turning red with his blood. He moaned and blood surged from his crushed and mangled leg. I tried to be as gentle as I could, not wanting to spring the trap again as I struggled with the unyielding metal.

Finally, with a sucking sound, the jaws relinquished their grip, and Shepherd's leg slipped free.

Otis hefted Shepherd in a body hug, taking most of the weight. I grabbed his legs, the blood dripping down my arms. We staggered out of the water and laid Shepherd lengthwise along the narrow path. Otis stood breathing heavy at the exertion.

My mind calculated the next step to save Shepherd's life. "Give me your belt," I ordered.

Otis whipped it off and handed it to me. I placed it above Shepherd's knee, cinched it tight, and the bleeding slowed. But my partner's face paled as he slipped into shock. I wiped my hands, smeared with his blood, onto my uniform. He was stabilized but wouldn't last long in this condition.

With shaky fingers, I keyed my radio. "Officer down. Assistance needed. Send an ambulance." I gave our location.

Then I put my hand over the mike. "Is that whiskey-still still operational?" I asked.

Otis bent his head.

I returned to dispatch. "And send some ATF men out here. Got an illegal still."

Otis and Shepherd were both Verde Valley residents—they had a shared history. Maybe Otis felt a small guilt at hurting Shepherd. Or maybe he was like some bullies I'd known—call their bluff and they collapsed. Fine with me, either way. I was past caring, but I needed outside help for Shepherd.

I fished out my cell phone and glanced at Otis. "Ethan have a mobile?"

He mumbled the number and I dialed.

"Been an accident, Ethan. Shepherd stepped into a bear trap. We freed him, but it's bad. You got an ATV?"

"Old, but it works."

"Get it revved up and ready. Wait for the ambulance crew. Load them on that ATV, bring them and their gear out here to the still."

What else? My mind raced in overdrive, adrenalin-charged. "Next vehicle is going to be a cop car," I told Ethan. "Have Ruby Mae lead them out here, double-time. Tell them to watch the edges of the path. Don't know what other traps might be set."

My mind spun through all the contingencies: What about Aurora? Aurora had been traumatized the last time there'd been an accident in the marsh. Didn't want to leave the little kid by herself if Ruby Mae came to us. And the dogs at the home place—would they get vicious with strangers?

"Call Janny at work," I told Ethan. "Have her come home to take care of Aurora. And pen up the loose dogs. Don't want any of them getting shot."

That should cover it. I turned back to Otis.

"Now what?" he snarled. The immediate life-threat over, his hostile attitude had re-emerged.

"T-shirt," I ordered. Otis silently unbuttoned his shirt. He pulled off the undershirt and tossed it to me. Then he put his outer shirt back on and re-buttoned it while I fashioned a rough bandage around the jagged wounds on Shepherd's leg.

The T-shirt was sweat-stained, but that was the least of Shepherd's worries. What infection he didn't catch from that rusty trap, he might from the foul waters around us. The man was in for a long recuperation.

I loosened the tourniquet for a moment and retightened it. Shepherd's color was returning, but he was still unconscious.

The bear trap was next. I jammed a stout branch in its jaws to re-spring the trap. It snatched the branch with an explosive crack. The splinters of wood tumbled end over end into the swamp. That could have been Shepherd's leg bone.

I stepped around Shepherd's motionless body and grabbed his gun out of its holster. I pointed it at Otis. "Turn around." When he did, I cuffed him. I kicked his boot heel with my toe. "Up the path," I grunted. I wanted him out of the way when the med techs arrived to work on Shepherd.

I followed and a few paces later jerked him to a halt. "Here. Sit down and wait."

Otis awkwardly lowered to the ground and sat quietly, staring out into the marsh. Part of me wished he'd try to escape. I knew *exactly* where I'd shoot to disable him. That bear trap hadn't been meant for Shepherd—it had been meant for me.

Fifteen minutes later Ethan's ATV roared up, two wheels on the path and the other two tearing up the bank side and throwing up a geyser of muddy water. One med tech sat next to Ethan holding the rescue cradle skyward like a surfboard. The other tech perched behind, clutching the emergency medical kit.

The ATV slid to a stop in front of Shepherd, and the techs jumped off while Ethan reversed the vehicle to face the other direction. One tech checked Shepherd's vitals and gave me a thumbs-up. Efficient hands stripped away the bloody T-shirt, swabbed the wound with disinfectant and re-bandaged it.

Shepherd was loaded in, and the rescue cradle was securely fastened crossways on the back of the ATV. One tech leaned backward to hold the cradle in place and the other jogged behind the ATV steadying it, as Ethan gunned the vehicle back towards solid ground. The whole procedure took less than five minutes. Those guys were good.

Now a second group of people ran towards us: Janny followed by men in ATF jackets and a sheriff's deputy. What was Janny doing here? I'd asked Ethan to send Ruby

Mae as a guide. But the reinforcements were a welcome relief. Otis hadn't tried anything yet. I'd been lucky.

Janny gave me a strange, almost guilty look when she neared. She looked past me, and then I knew.

For in those short moments that my attention had focused on Shepherd, Otis had slipped into the water as smooth as a water moccasin, not even a ripple to show his passing. He had vanished into the marsh, handcuffs and all.

At least the whiskey still remained, I reassured myself, reason enough for the Alcohol, Tobacco and Firearms team to make the trip. But I was to learn even that target was elusive. My phone call to Ethan, while saving precious minutes for Shepherd, also warned the Nettle clan of a possible raid on the whiskey still.

With Janny assuming the role of guide, we ran into a series of too convenient delays. A recently fallen tree blocked the way and we had to push the branches to one side. Then the path split and Janny chose the wrong way to a dead end. We backtracked to the junction, losing several more minutes.

When we finally reached the site of the whiskey still, crushed grass showed fresh earth stains—evidence of equipment recently moved. The remainder of the little meadow was empty. Nothing left but tipped barrels and empty gunny sacks scattered on the ground. The main apparatus had vanished as silently as Otis had.

One ATF officer brushed at his wet pant leg. "Damn Nettle clan. Thought we had them this time." He glared at me. "You brought us all the way out here for this? Check your intel better next time." He snapped a few I-been-there pictures with his cell phone and left without another word.

"Lost Otis, did you? Piss-poor work." The second ATF officer scraped his shoe against a barrel stave, cleaving off a hunk of red mud, and followed his partner. Janny seemed to be the only one in a cheerful humor. Still avoiding my eyes she ran to catch up with the two men, flirting a little with them as they moved down the path.

The sheriff's deputy touched my shoulder. "They were loading Shepherd into the ambulance when we arrived. You saved his life, kid." Then he departed, too, leaving me alone in the disturbed, grassy space.

My return hike back to the Nettles' homestead seemed to take forever, and Shepherd's cautionary words echoed in my brain. "Don't ever turn your back on Otis." I *had* turned my back, and as a result, I'd lost him. Basic procedural error.

A merciless judge perched on my shoulder and pronounced my shortcomings: You should have cuffed that S.O.B.'s feet. Why didn't you *watch* him? Might as well have announced your raid on the whiskey still with a bullhorn, telling Ethan who was coming. What did you think he'd do? Offer them lemonade?

I didn't deserve to be wearing this uniform. I'd made one dumb rookie mistake after another, and as a result, the Nettles were free and Shepherd was in a hospital emergency room.

My eyes blurred and I tripped over a root, sprawling flat on the path. My knee hit a rock, tearing the skin and shredding what was left of my pant leg. My own blood seeped through the cloth, mingling with the bloodstains of my partner. Both palms were scraped raw, but I deserved the pain. The retention of Otis had been my responsibility and I blew it.

When I reached the SUV, the ATF men were gone and the house was vacant with no sight of the Nettle family. They were probably sawing the cuffs off Otis or reassembling the whiskey still in yet another location. Having a good laugh at my expense while they did it.

I climbed into the SUV and slammed the door. I beat my hands against the steering wheel and added my forehead for good measure. Then I swore, working through all my favorite phrases and throwing in a few repeats when I reached the end of the list. By the time I punched the key into the ignition and jammed the SUV into gear, the windshield was steamed with my hot words. Accelerating out of the yard in an angry skid of mud, I raced for the hospital. Would Shepherd be alive when I got there?

CHAPTER NINE

When I arrived at the hospital, I parked in the police slot near the emergency entrance. The nurse on duty had tired brown eyes that viewed my ruined uniform without expression.

"Yes?"

I presented my credentials. "I'm looking for a Shepherd Malone?"

She looked at the computer list in front of her. "Shepherd? We have an *Irving* Malone."

"That's the one. Can I see him?"

"He's in X-ray."

"What's his condition?"

"You family?"

"I'm his partner."

She shook her head. Apparently, partners were low on the nurse hierarchy. "Have a seat. I'll call you when he's back."

I flipped through an *Entertainment Weekly* so old even the tear out stubs were missing. I paced for a while and returned to the nurses' station. "How long do you think it'll be?"

"Can't say. Look, the cafeteria is just down that hall. Go get something to eat and I'll call you."

I left my cell number and walked down the hall to the cafeteria. It was past the dinner hour and the display area gleamed with polished stainless steel racks and empty serving trays, but not much hot food. I settled on a Diet Coke, a stale muffin, and a yogurt cup. Added a piece of cherry pie to cheer up my taste buds and carried the tray to a table near the window.

In a patio outside the dining room, a single white-crowned sparrow hunted for bugs. Fall-bare mesquite trees ringed the cement patio, their branches forming a ragged silhouette against the darkening sky.

I mouthed the tasteless muffin, took a forkful of the too-sweet pie, and pushed the tray away. Food didn't appeal to my roiling stomach. I wanted to know how Shepherd was doing. It was my fault he was here. The clock on the far wall stuttered at two seconds past the hour marker, then hiccupped and started again.

The sparrow pecked against the glass. Sorry, bird. I wouldn't even feed this stuff to you. I dumped the remains in the trash, took a last slug of the soda and tossed it, too. Surely Shepherd would be back from x-ray by now.

The nurse looked up as I approached her desk. "I was about to call you. You can come back to see him now." She clicked the lock open and I walked down the hall into the emergency triage room.

Most of the U-drapes were open, revealing empty hospital beds. At the far end of the room, a familiar voice droned behind an enclosing curtain. I pulled back the hanging sheet and saw Shepherd lying flat on the bed.

A nurse brushed past me, raised the head of the stretcher, and adjusted the head pillow. "Now do we feel better? I'll be right outside. Push this button if we need anything."

"Goddam medical 'we'," Shepherd grumbled. "I'd like to tell 'us' where to go."

Hadn't lost his bad temper, anyway. That was a hopeful sign. "How you doing?" I asked.

"They're talking surgery to repair the leg. Want to pump me full of dope, and I can't take pain pills. Call Dr.

Cravets. He knows my background. He'll tell them what to use." He gritted his teeth, as though what he wanted was a big shot of anything, right now.

"Will do. Is there family I can call?"

His face twisted with pain. "No, nobody." Changed the subject: "Heard you lost Otis. And the whiskey still was gone when you got there. Any *good* news on the case?"

I reddened and kept my mouth shut.

"Put out a Be-On-the-Lookout for that bastard. We need to put him out of commission." He paled behind the bravado, sweat drops gleaming on his forehead.

I promised I would and asked him if there was anything he needed.

"House keys in the tray beneath the stretcher. Take those, feed Fluffy and give her meds."

"Fluffy?" Never figured Shepherd to be a Fluffy type.

His wallet and keys were in the tray. I opened the wallet to check the home address on his license and put the wallet back with his cell phone. Kept the keys, and his service revolver for good measure. Never could tell when it might come in handy.

"I'll call Dr. Cravets and feed the critter for you," I said. "Don't worry about a thing. I'll be back in the morning."

"*Early* in the morning," Shepherd emphasized.

Two orderlies appeared at the foot of the bed to move him to permanent quarters. I didn't envy the night nurse, keeping track of an injured Shepherd with no pain medication. They wheeled the gurney down the hall.

Dr. Cravets was unavailable when I called and his answering service was noncommittal. I emphasized the importance of the situation. I didn't want my message stuck in a queue without action. "It's an emergency. They're doing surgery on Shepherd—make that Irving—Malone. They need orders to give no narcotics."

The operator assured me the doctor would call the hospital, and I moved on to the second promise I'd made

Shepherd—feeding Fluffy. Pet pig, iguana, hedgehog? Shepherd was a crossword puzzle addict, so the critter might be anything.

***

It was dark when I started my drive to Shepherd's place, but everything was close in Cottonwood, this small town situated between Black Mountain and the Verde River. From the Medical Center, I went down 89A toward the center of town and then right on a side street into the foothills, following the directions Shepherd had given me.

My stomach was waking up now that I'd left the antiseptic smells of the hospital, but Fluffy came first. Like a good partner, I was there, setting my own needs aside in the quest of Shepherd's pet-whatever. I'd grab a burger later.

Shepherd lived in a small guest house situated behind a two-story rambler. I walked down a flagstone path, beyond a small fenced garden. Two hummingbird feeders hung near the front windows. The solid front door had two deadbolts and the main key lock. Even in the relatively burglary-free Verde Valley, I understood Shepherd's need for caution. Being a cop changes your outlook that way.

The deadbolts opened smoothly, as did the well-oiled front door lock. When I groped for a light switch and clicked it, something swiped at my hand, hissing. I jumped inside the door, slammed it behind me, and stared at four reddening welts on the back of my hand. I lurched into a small kitchen and held my hand under the faucet. The numbing cold water stemmed the bleeding, but I jumped back when Fluffy stalked into view.

She was a tiny, black-and-white cat with a feathery tail that switched ominously as I reached down to pet her. The ears went back and I jerked my hand away just in time to avoid another attack. Son of a bitch! I was supposed to medicate *this*? I anticipated my coffee served on a gold tray when Shepherd returned to work.

I'd never had an inside pet, and in fact, only got within six feet of the feral cat who nibbled at the food I put out on my balcony. But I'd seen my uncle work with the animals on the farm back in Tennessee. He even had this special bridle used for worming horses, designed so they couldn't spit the stuff back out again.

Didn't see any bridle here. Too bad. It would make my life a lot easier. But it shouldn't be too hard. This beast couldn't be five pounds soaking wet—assuming you could get a cat like this near water.

In the refrigerator door, I found a half-full can of cat food and a vial of pink liquid. The label read "Hill-Top Veterinary. Give one full syringe twice a day." I unwrapped the cat food, dumped it on a plate, and syringed pink stuff on top.

I set it down and stepped away. Fluffy seemed hungry, but she sniffed once, and then pawed at the plate, trying to bury it. Come on cat, it didn't smell that bad.

Fluffy disappeared around the corner. When I pursued her into Shepherd's bedroom, she vanished under the bed. Pulling up the spread, I peered under. My knee, injured in the fall at the marsh, banged the wood floor and I winced.

"Here, kitty, kitty." Why do we say that to a cat? Fluffy didn't buy it, either. Two luminous eyes glared at me from a far corner, and she hissed. Would even this tiny ball of fluff defy me today?

I left the bedroom, closing the door behind me to confine her to the space. Grabbing a broom from a closet, I stalked back. My seat-of-the-pants plan was to force her from under the bed. Beyond that, I had no clue. It would come to me.

On my knees, I poked the broom at Fluffy and she retreated further into the corner. Another poke. She rushed past me, balked at the closed bedroom door, then raced around the perimeter of the room, and zipped into the bathroom. I slammed the bathroom door before she could escape.

Time for more pink stuff. I retraced my steps to the kitchen, retrieved the medicine from the refrigerator, and jammed it in my back pocket. Once back in the bedroom, I slammed the door behind me and stomped over to the closed bathroom door.

I went down on hands and knees and opened the bathroom door slowly, thinking to grab Fluffy as she tried to escape. She had other plans. A black and white paw zipped through, claws extended. Her head followed and I jerked back reflexively. She leaped on top of my back, all claws extended, riding me like a Brahma bull. I crashed against the bed and she released her hold and dropped to the floor.

I grabbed her, ducked into the bathroom, and slammed the door behind us. All four feet were scrabbling as the cat writhed in a boneless fury, trying to latch onto me. One back claw caught my palm and ripped a jagged wound. Swearing, I dropped the maniacal fur ball and she scooted behind the shower curtain. More blood ran down the sink as I rinsed the wound. Were cat scratches fatal? Shepherd owned me unlimited coffee service *and* a whole week's exclusive use of the SUV.

The medicine cabinet yielded a box of band aids and I tore two open with my teeth and applied them single-handedly to the bleeding wound on my palm. Time to finish this. I grabbed the bottle of pink liquid from my back pocket, reloaded the syringe, and set it on the counter. If I had to stake out this bathroom all night, if I had to grow a third hand, this beast would not win.

I yanked a bath towel from the bar and slowly drew back the shower curtain. Fluffy crouched in a corner, her eyes wide. I dropped the bath towel over her and bundled her tight like a burrito. In the towel's darkness, her fight disappeared and she went quiet. I wrapped the towel tighter and started feeling for body parts. Tail, no. Foot, definitely no. When I located her head, I slowly unwrapped it. Fluffy glared at me and strained to free one paw. Not yet, cat. I tightened my grip and wedged the bundle under my elbow.

Fluffy's ears flattened and a low growl rumbled from deep within the towel. Reaching over for the syringe, I held on tight, pulled back the neck scruff, and pried open her jaw with my other hand. Just a little wider, cat.

Fluffy sputtered and shook her head furiously when the medicine entered her throat. Instantly cat, bathroom, and I were splattered with pink liquid. Done! I dropped Fluffy on the floor and opened the door. She wriggled free from the towel and streaked under the bed.

I sat there on the toilet seat, catching my breath. How much pink medicine got inside? Didn't matter. Quest complete. Peg Quincy, victor. I swiped at the pink stains on my arms and rehung the towel. Shepherd could figure out the rose abstract on the walls for himself.

Then I returned to the kitchen where a zone of quiet reigned. I reached into a cabinet for a glass, ran a drink of water, and headed into the living room. Time to find out what this new partner of mine was all about. In a way, he'd given me permission. Offered me the keys to his house, didn't he?

I plopped into an oversized brown leather chair and surveyed the room. Some amateurish oils, mostly desert scenes, on the wall. No TV, but he had an old-fashioned phonograph. I set down the water glass and walked over for a look-see. Straight ahead jazz: Dave Brubeck and Miles Davis. And some fifties stuff in dusty albums: Elvis, the Brothers Four, Buddy Holly. Before my time. Hadn't he heard of Coldplay?

A small bookshelf held Westerns and casual reads: Louie L'Amour and Tony Hillerman, some Michael

Connelly and *A Game of Thrones*. He had the entire series of books by Martin. Of course he would, being Shepherd. I'd gotten bogged down in the first volume. Always meant to go back and finish it, but didn't see the need now that television had macerated it. A copy of the Alcoholics Anonymous big book. Interesting. That would fit his "no meds" request.

And some photographs. One, a small girl holding the black-and-white cat. A daughter? Shepherd hadn't said anything about family. Another photo showed a younger Shepherd in police uniform, posing with a trophy cup and a German shepherd. I picked it up. The engraving on the picture's frame said, "Grand Champion K-9 team, Irving Malone and the Kaiser of Destruction." Handlers sometimes brought their dogs home when they got too old to work, but no canine presence here in Shepherd's house, just Fluffy. She'd run off any dog that dared apply for the job of night watchman, anyway.

With a small meow, she rubbed against my leg as hunger triumphed over revenge. I returned to the kitchen, poured out the rest of my water in the sink and dumped the untouched pink-stained cat food into the trash. Time to find more food for the cat. In a cupboard, one shelf contained a bag of brown rice and another of dry pinto beans. Shepherd, a vegetarian? Fluffy's food was stacked in neat rows in the next cabinet I opened.

Grabbing a can opener from a drawer, I opened one can, plopped some in a dish and placed it on the floor. Then I rinsed out the cat's water dish and poured her some fresh. Not her fault I'd had a lousy day. She ate daintily, the magnificent tail straight in the air, waving back and forth like a plumed fan.

Better not push the armistice. Tomorrow faced another dawn we'd have to break together since she needed the medication twice a day. Cat box looked passable—I'd clean it tomorrow.

I went out the front door, making sure all three locks were secure. Before I headed back to the sheriff's office in Mingus, I dialed the hospital. The nurses' station gave me an update on Shepherd—no major changes, doing as well as expected, check back in the morning.

I negotiated the series of roundabouts on Highway 89A until the last one at Cement Plant Road. There, I circled three-quarters around and headed up the hill to Mingus.

It was after midnight and the roads were still when I rounded the last hairpin into town. Once the day-tripping tourists left, most of the town retired for the night. There were only a few pedestrians straggling home from the bars when I pulled into my parking space and climbed the stairs to my studio apartment.

There, I made coffee, poured some into a mug and walked onto the balcony. My breath formed vapor puffs in the cold moonlight. Within minutes the bitter wind penetrated my shirt, and I returned to the warmth of the apartment. I scribbled notes on the Nettle family to satisfy Shepherd the next morning, put some more iodine on the Fluffy scratches, and headed to bed.

My plan to sleep late the next morning was jinxed when the phone summoned me hours before daybreak.

CHAPTER TEN

I groaned and opened my cell phone to see a text message from Shepherd. "Feed Fluffy. Bring me some clothes." He must be feeling better. Or tired of hospital chow already.

"On it," I texted him back. The way I felt this morning, I didn't know if I could handle a phone that was brighter than I was.

After a quick shower, I stripped the Band-Aids off the Fluffy wounds and put on new ones. I pulled on jeans and a T-shirt and then stopped by the station to change into a fresh uniform compliments of the cleaners. Even if it was Saturday, I intended to look official driving the SUV. Cop weeks never seem to end, especially working with a partner like Shepherd.

On the drive down the hill to Shepherd's house, I reviewed what I needed, to deal with the cat. My heavy gloves were in the SUV storage compartment, but maybe a bribe would be a good idea, too. The on-duty clerk at the Dollar Store recommended a toy mouse and some cat treats. Chlorophyll flavored, she said, guaranteed irresistible. One way or another, the cat and I would come to an understanding.

When I reached Shepherd's guest house, I gathered my equipment and managed to open all three locks without dropping anything. Fluffy greeted me when I opened the door, tail waving gently in the breeze, all past indiscretions forgiven. Short memory, that cat. Or maybe she was just a day person, not a night owl. Could a cat be an owl? No matter.

I unwrapped the toy mouse and tossed it to her. She sniffed it once and ignored it. Perhaps I'd have better luck with cat treats? I lobbed one her direction and Fluffy tried to bury it. Not that I blamed her. They smelled like dead silage to me, too.

That left the main event. No reason to bother with the "Here, Kitty" routine. I might as well be making a peace sign to a street rioter. I yanked open the refrigerator with one hand, snatched the meds and slammed the door shut with my hip. Hands gloved up and holding a heavy towel at the ready, I waited until Fluffy's back was turned and grabbed her.

I hoisted the Fluffy-in-towel bundle onto the kitchen counter. Holding the bundle secure with my elbow, I jerked one glove off with my teeth, filled the syringe and stuffed the meds down her throat. Total time, beginning to end, ninety seconds. I pumped my fist in the air. Yes! If I ever washed out as a cop I could apply to be a Vet Tech.

Fluffy shook her head once and jumped off the counter. She rubbed a layer of fur on my clean uniform pant leg, stroking back and forth. Breakfast time. I dumped new cat food in her dish, changed the water next to it, and rehung the towel I'd used to subdue her. Cleaned the cat box.

Shepherd had asked for clothes. I went into the bedroom, opened dresser drawers and pulled out socks, underwear, and a T-shirt. What about pants? With that leg, he couldn't wear straight blue jeans. I settled on a pair of pajama bottoms, added some slippers and a straight razor from the bathroom.

I stuffed them all in a sports bag I found in the bedroom and grabbed a jacket from the hall closet for the cold day ahead. When I entered the living room, Fluffy was batting at the mouse. She saw me watching and stalked off, twitching her plume tail. So much for bonding-with-cat. I tried.

Half an hour later I entered the medical center and found Shepherd's new room. When I arrived at his door to present the completed paperwork, his bed was cranked up full. Somebody had found him some reading glasses and he was working crossword puzzles, in pen. Definitely feeling better. I handed him the Nettle incident report and the clothes.

He dumped the bag of clothes on the floor and grabbed for the file like someone had given him a special puzzle book. "Ah, the Nettles." He scanned through the pages before setting them aside for later. Then he inspected me over the glasses. "Nice Band-Aids. Cat fur on those pants, though. Packing tape always works for me."

I looked at him.

He continued. "Didn't thank you properly yesterday. Otis Stroud may be among the missing, but I've still got the leg."

"No surgery?"

"Skated by that one. I'll look like Frankenstein when I take all this off, though. Forty-eight stitches." He patted his leg, swathed in bandages from ankle to knee, a badge of honor. I had to admit—my cat scratches didn't compare to that magnificence.

"Due to be released this afternoon," he said. "Can't drive for a while, though."

That would break the heart of our department's entry for NASCAR.

"Pick me up here about two this afternoon," he ordered.

"Sure. Take you home then?"

"No, to the office. Haven't missed a day of work in thirty years, not starting now."

Less than twenty-four hours after a life-threatening emergency, and he was going back to work. Well, it was his life, not mine.

"You put out that BOLO for Otis?"

"Not yet. Plan to when I go in to work."

"Do that, then call the medical examiner's office—Somebody should be there—That place never closes—If they haven't done the autopsy on Cal Nettle yet, put their asses in gear—Your scuba buddies found anything more out there?—Call them—Howard Nettle back in town yet?—Check on his whereabouts—And contact Ruby Mae, see what funeral arrangements she's making—we'll want to attend." He paused for breath.

The man was a tap-dancing bunny rabbit.

"You make a note of all that?" he asked.

I tapped my head. "Up here."

"See you this afternoon. Two o'clock, then, don't forget. Thanks for feeding Fluffy." He picked up his puzzle book, the meeting over. I disappeared before he thought of something else for me to do.

I left the hospital and headed for Mingus. Half-way up the hill, my phone beeped with a text from Shepherd. I pulled to the side of the road and glanced at it. "Call your counselor?"

I'd ignore that message. Didn't need the added stress of a counseling session while I juggled my job and Shepherd's, too. None of his business, anyway. It would have to wait. The counselor would probably understand. What excuse hadn't I used yet with her?

Before I could pull back on the road, another text arrived: "Get me a cane." I shook my head, turned off my phone and drove the rest of the way to Mingus in uninterrupted silence. I was done playing answering machine for Shepherd's job-withdrawal anxieties.

***

The aroma of fresh coffee hit me when I walked in the door. Ben was working, making up hours for his out-of-

office personal time. He probably needed the money. He was back living with his uncle, Armor Brancussi, and the guy put the arm on Ben for spare cash whenever he could. Not easy for Ben, but he seemed to manage.

He gave me a high-five as I went back to my office, mug in hand. He'd even made a paper sign for my desk, "Acting Deputy-in-Charge, Mingus Sheriff's Department."

Shoes propped on the edge of the desk, I sipped the brew pensively, Zen-like. Life was good without Shepherd here to pickle up the works.

When I'd accumulated enough calming thoughts to write a self-help book, I fished in my pocket, and slowly withdrew my cell phone. I examined its gray perfection, turned it on, and set it quietly on my desk. It vibrated off the desktop and into the trashcan. I dropped my feet to the floor and fished it out. The caller ID said "Janny Nettle."

"Hi, Janny. Hold a minute." I put my hand over the phone and hollered to Ben. "Borrow HT's truck and drive to Walgreen's, buy a cane for Shepherd. Use this." I flipped him the office charge card. He gave me a mock salute and disappeared out the door. I crossed the first item off the Shepherd to-do list. When Ben got back, I'd assign him another. No need to waste a good assistant.

"Yes?" I said to Janny.

"Want to apologize for taking the long way around to the still yesterday," she said. "Momma said I had to do it. Is Shepherd okay?"

"Not good. He could have lost a leg with that maneuver, Janny. Where's your Uncle Otis?"

She skated right past that one. "Momma's planning the funeral. When will they release Daddy's body?"

"Soon, I think. I'll check for you." Part of my FLO responsibilities. Efficient Family Liaison Officer, that's me.

"We're lining up the pallbearers. Howard's coming up today from Phoenix."

I made another check on my mental Shepherd to-do list. Now we knew when Howard Nettle was arriving. My partner would be pleased.

Janny enumerated the pallbearers. "Ethan, and then Armor Brancussi and your granddad HT, that makes four, and... Shepherd. Would you talk to him for us? I know he's mad about that little accident yesterday, but Momma wants him to serve. He and Daddy go way back."

Didn't realize Cal Nettle was such a founding father of the valley. But maybe so. It takes all kinds. "I'll give it a try. Can't guarantee, though. With Howard, that's five. Who's your sixth?"

"Momma wants Uncle Otis to do it. He gives his word he'll turn himself in after the funeral." She talked fast, getting it all out in one breath before I could interrupt.

Doubtful Shepherd would agree to that one, but he wasn't here. So, no need to put out a Be-On-the-Lookout for Otis just yet. I didn't know where he was now, but I knew where he'd be in the near future. That counted. I crossed him half off the list.

Janny didn't sound sad, more like she was planning a family reunion, which in a way it would be with Howard coming home. All the family together, even Cal, for the first time in years. I wondered if second almost-wife Darbie Granger would show. She wouldn't be that stupid, surely.

Funerals weren't my thing, but I said I'd attend, as much for Janny as for the late departed, and rang off. I made a note to talk to Shepherd about the arrangements.

On a roll, I phoned the medical examiners' office next. Shepherd had pegged that one right. Someone actually answered the phone. I groaned when I heard the voice. It was Sidney Morrison—Solemn Sidney, we called him. He could put a raven to sleep with the minute details of death he found so fascinating.

"Just finished the autopsy. Surprised you weren't here to watch, Peg. Always fun to do a floater. First, you have to..."

My stomach heaved just thinking about it. "Never mind, I'll take your word for it. Did he drown?"

"No shoulder-girdle bruises, so nobody held him down. Some sand, silt, and weeds in pharynx and trachea, but not much in stomach or alveoli. I haven't done a diatom test on the bone marrow, but I imagine it would give us the same result."

Just my luck. Solemn must be having a slow weekend and figured he'd got a live one on the hook when I called him. But I played along. "...So Cal Nettle was dead before he entered the water?"

"Seems like it," he said.

"Cause of death, then?" Come on, guy, spit it out. What killed him?

"Massive blow to the back of the head. Caved that skull right in. We've dug out some wood fragments for lab testing. Somebody did *not* want that man alive."

I knew a few folks who could fit that description. "What about the tox screen?"

"Waiting on it. Some interesting stomach contents, though. Milk and apricots within a couple of hours of death."

Darbie's apricot bars. She had denied seeing Cal that day, even though Ethan assured me that she had. I kept reminding myself that witnesses—and suspects—lie. Even the nice ones.

Solemn read down his report. "On to the organs. Some indication of heart problems. Probably wouldn't have lived past sixty, that old ticker would have given out. Man had cirrhosis of the liver, too. Surprised he was still walking around. A heavy drinker?"

I thought of Cal Nettle's distillery. And Ethan's tale of the drunken man's hunt with the young coonhound. "Could be."

"And here's something for you..." He'd kept the best until last. There was a chirp of triumph in his voice. "Man was riddled with cancer. He didn't have but weeks, maybe a month to live. Folks get impatient, sometimes. All they had to do was wait."

It was a chilling thought. What would I do, if I had only months to live? Not something I wanted to dwell on. Every day, the old heart just keeps pumping away, and we ignore it. Until one day it doesn't.

But what it boiled down to was that Cal was near death, and somebody killed him anyway. Somebody that knew about the cancer, or somebody that didn't? Cal didn't die of his disease like he would have in the normal order of things. Somebody hurried the process along, and I had to find out who.

I gave Solemn the name of the funeral home the family had chosen. He said he'd fax the complete report, and I hung up. More paper for my partner—knowing Solemn there'd be some heavy reading. That ought to make Shepherd ecstatic.

Next, I left a voice message for Rory Stevens, the scuba diver. Asked him in my politest voice whether they had found anything further. It was a formal call, nothing personal, just business. But that small voice in the back of my head was asking why I called Rory and not his partner. Never mind.

Zing. That did it for most of Shepherd's list, and it was only eleven o'clock. Efficiency in action.

I called Ruby Mae and told her I had more questions. She invited me over for lunch, and I accepted. Plenty of time before I had to pick up Shepherd, and I'd scout out more information about the Nettle family along with the biscuits. The least I could do for almost-kin.

CHAPTER ELEVEN

When I drove into the Nettle homestead, the dog Ethan called Reckless was waiting for me, his tail swinging in a wide arc. I peered at the house hoping for rescue, but no one emerged. Gritting my teeth, I opened the door and swung my legs out.

Before I could straighten, Reckless leaped and planted two muddy paws on my uniformed chest. Nice red valley mud. I brushed at it, but only succeeded in transferring terra cotta smears to my pants. Forget the vet technician option—my new career choice should be in dry-cleaning.

"Shoo! Go away now." Ruby Mae appeared on the porch, and Reckless dropped to his haunches. She walked down the steps and took my hand. "Need to apologize. My brother Otis doesn't always think things through. Wasn't no reason to cause harm to anyone." She dropped my hand, social obligations satisfied. "Lunch ready soon. Go fetch Ethan from the barn."

I detoured by the front of the barn to check on the puppies. The seven red-gold youngsters had been moved to a makeshift puppy pen and tumbled over each other in their eagerness to reach me. Momma Red Sheba was nowhere in sight. They must be getting old enough for her to leave them. I leaned over the fence and cupped a soft head in my hand, ran my fingers along another's back, touched a third's floppy ears. My puppy-love satisfied, I straightened and walked to the end of the barn.

Ethan was sharpening a mattock, that combination of adze and axe, the blade held in a metal vise smoothed by many years of hard use. The old '29 Ford pickup was missing. Otis staking a claim already? Wherever he was hiding out, it probably wasn't here.

"Hi, Ethan. Your mother says lunch is ready."

"Be right with you." He twirled the lever to unlock the vise, hung the mattock on the wall, and wiped his hands on a rag. Each action was precise, unhurried.

I surveyed the possible weapons on the wall. Axe handles, scythes, even a sledge or two. Wouldn't take much to kill his father and then hang the instrument back in plain view. I'd know more when I got the configuration of a likely weapon from the crime lab. Had Cal been drunk or sober when he died? Either way, somebody wanted him dead enough to bash his head in.

Ethan and I walked back to the house with Reckless nudging my hand every second step. Then Ethan sat in the living room while Ruby Mae set the table and I freshened up. A piece of stained glass set in the bathroom window reflected yellow and red patterns on the worn linoleum floor, the light bouncing off the mud on my uniform.

I moistened a rag and rubbed at the worst of the stains. The cracked mirror above the sink mocked my dirt-stained face and I wiped some red mud off my cheek, too. Reckless sure knew how to spread the love around.

Ruby Mae served us lunch at the same kitchen table as before. Ham, fresh bread for sandwiches, homemade pickles, peach preserves, and an apple dumpling cake for dessert. That woman could cook.

We talked about matters in Mingus and the valley until the last of lunch was done and the table cleared. Then Ethan went back to the barn while Ruby Mae and I moved to the living room to discuss arrangements for Cal's funeral.

"We want the service at the First Wildwood Church in Clarkdale. Ever been there, girl?"

"No ma'am."

"Call me Ruby Mae, everybody does. Janny told you about the pallbearers..."

"About Otis," I interjected. "Any chance he could check in early? Shepherd and I would like to talk to him."

Her lips pursed in a frown. Guess not.

"The Right Reverend Billy Gerald's going to do the service. You met him?"

"Don't believe so."

"He's single, not much older than you are. Good catch, too. A young girl like you, time you were married, had some babies."

Me, date a man of the cloth? I wasn't an atheist, exactly, but hadn't been to church in years. I could see him already—scrawny chicken-neck, short-sleeved white shirt, black-string tie. Thanks, but no thanks. Puppies were all the babies I needed.

Ruby Mae moved ahead with the planning of Cal's day. "After the service, we're coming here for the burial in our home cemetery. Tell HT to bring that old backhoe of his, help dig the grave. Probably need to start that soon, before the weather sets in. What else?"

Ruby Mae seemed to be going over a mental list. I knew the feeling, having just finished one myself.

She continued. "Casseroles for the lunch after. Most of the neighbor ladies will bring one. What's your specialty?"

My specialty, if I even had one, was ambrosia salad from the grocery deli, with those cherry pieces and pineapple bits—loved that stuff. But some noodle thing with mushroom soup and crushed potato chips on top? Beyond my skill level. Possibly Isabel, HT's housekeeper, might help me.

"Ruby Mae, I need to talk to you about Cal's physical condition when he died."

She switched from event planner to grieving widow just like that, drawing a somber mask over her face. Funny how quickly that change occurred, like two separate people in there. I told her the news about the cancer, and she nodded.

"Doctor announced it to us, Cal and me. I didn't ever share it with the children, never seemed to be the right time. But we'd been waiting. He picked out his suit, been hanging in the closet there for months. Even chose what music he wanted at the ceremony. Easter music he said, never mind that it's fall. That's what he wanted, and that's what he'll have."

Ruby Mae's jaw set with the strength that molded her character. "We shared that cancer news way before that Darbie-bitch got her claws into him, that's for certain sure. Bet he didn't tell her about *that*." Her eyes glinted with homicide and it wasn't for her departed husband.

She leaned back in her chair and folded her arms. "So tell me," she said. "How'd he die?" I had the odd feeling she already knew the answer.

"Blow to the back of the head. How'd he get into the marsh?"

She gave me a knowing look. "Suppose somebody put him there. Maybe figured he'd be lost and never found again."

"Any idea who that *someone* might be?"

"Don't have the slightest," she said, giving me a narrow smile.

That lady had an iron one, have to give her that. I'd overstayed my welcome here, and it was time to pick up Shepherd. I rose and gave her my hand. "Please let me know if you need anything, Ruby Mae."

"I will, dear. Pay my respects to your grandfather."

I promised I would.

I peered out the door to see if Reckless was waiting in ambush. He must have followed Ethan to the barn, though, and I made it to the SUV unscathed. It was almost two-thirty. Shepherd would be prowling the hospital corridors, unleashing mayhem on the poor nurses. I hadn't meant to stay so long. Blame it on the puppies.

***

I screeched into the hospital loading zone, yanked on the emergency brake, and strode to Shepherd's room. He had dressed in the clothes I'd left and was arguing with the attendant when I entered.

"No chair. I'll walk."

"Sir, you have to ride in the wheelchair. Hospital policy."

"Damn the policy. I'm a taxpayer, same as you. I'm walking out of this place under my own steam."

I didn't have time for this. "Shepherd, get in the chair. Now! Time to go."

He harrumphed once for effect and climbed in. The orderly put down the footrests and set Shepherd's injured foot on one. Shepherd jammed the other in place. The man put the bag of clothes in Shepherd's lap and tucked in the cane Ben had delivered next to Shepherd's leg. Then he released the safety brake and steered the chair into the hall.

The orderly and I made small talk as we walked—what the outcome of the local election might be, whether the school bond would pass. Shepherd sat there without a word, hunched down as though fearful of being recognized. In the wheelchair, out of uniform, he seemed older and smaller in stature. We checked out at the reception desk and then moved through the automatic doors into the outside air.

"A bit cold, sir. Do you want your jacket?" the orderly asked.

"Don't need a coat, just get me in the damn car." He waited impatiently with the orderly while I retrieved the

SUV and drove back to them. I dumped the clothes and cane in the rear and then held the passenger door steady while Shepherd lifted from the wheelchair and grabbed the door handle, grimacing. He hopped on one foot to the front seat, hitched himself up and positioned his bad leg with both hands.

I closed the door and turned to the orderly. "Thanks for your help. Sorry he's been so cranky."

"No problem. He's probably in pain with that leg. He your dad?"

The remark hit me. I didn't have a father. He'd left us while I was still a child, escaping from my mother's drunken rages. But if I needed parenting, Shepherd wouldn't be the one I'd choose, that's for certain.

"No, he's not. Thanks for everything." There was an awkward moment, while I muddled about whether or not to tip him. Finally, I shook his hand instead.

I walked around to the driver's side and climbed in. "Got your seatbelt fastened?"

"Don't you be starting on me, too," Shepherd clicked the belt into the lock, stiffened his back and ordered, "Take me to the office."

Sure, why not. The guy was in pajamas and slippers, in distress with no pain meds, and he wanted to go to the office, not home. Without a word, I reached under my seat, retrieved his service revolver and handed it to him.

"On it," I said, and shifted the SUV into gear.

***

When we arrived in Mingus, I double-parked in front of the station and shut off the engine. Shepherd jolted awake. By the time I opened my door and walked around to help, he had already hopped across the sidewalk and stood waiting for me to open the station door. "Took your time," he said, fingers braced against the building. His

Code of the West bravado satisfied, he limped through the door, leaning heavily on the cane.

Inside the station, Shepherd refused assistance. He moved awkwardly to his office and collapsed into his chair. I shrugged and went to park the SUV. It was his high-necked pride, not mine. When I returned, Shepherd already had acquired a cup of green tea and was reading a law enforcement journal.

I went into my office, crumbled Ben's paper sign, and tossed it in the trash. No coffee perking in the kitchen, either. Sighing, I grabbed a bottle of water and knocked on Shepherd's door jam.

"Enter. That mud on your uniform?"

I brushed at it. Durned dog. Shepherd's eyebrows creased together with pain as I brought him up to date on the Nettle case. "Medical Examiner says it was blunt force trauma."

Shepherd pointed to a stack of papers on the desk. "Got the faxed report here. You talk to those scuba guys?"

"Call's in to them." I briefed him on the visit to Ruby Mae's.

"What about Howard? He back yet?"

"Due in tomorrow. Funeral's set for day after. Ruby Mae wants you to be pallbearer."

"Might be a challenge with this leg, but I'll manage. The whole valley will show up for this one, maybe even the killer."

"Who do *you* think did it?" I asked.

"Could be anyone. One of the kids. That pregnant lady. Ruby Mae. Her brother, Otis. Hell, even one of the shady folks who bought his hooch. We'll keep nosing around. Spook that wildlife from the brush, sooner or later." He looked at me. "You call that counselor yet?"

My own leg twitched. "Soon."

"Good. Need your gun available. Give me a half hour and I'll be ready to go home."

He would stay just long enough to make his appearance, keep his record intact. Maybe the guy was smarter than I gave him credit for.

He hollered after me. "Call Isabel. See if she can make me up some salve for this leg. Make it heal quicker."

Isabel was said to be a *curandera*, a medicine woman. She could identify more herbs growing in this valley than I knew existed. If anyone could help Shepherd, it would be her. I called HT's house and got her on the phone. "Shepherd says he wants something for his leg."

She thought for a moment. "He needs something for pain. He won't take that, but a salve to speed the healing, that I can give him. Stop by for it in a half-hour. I'll have it ready. Shepherd is a good man."

If he was such a good man, why did I get nothing but complaints and judgments coming my way? He was retiring in six months, though. I'd outlast him, easy.

Isabel put HT on the phone and we made arrangements for the grave digging. I got the impression his backhoe had been used more than once for that purpose. HT said he'd stop by the Nettles' place in the morning and start on the project.

I called the counselor next. She was gone, but her assistant was there. Didn't anybody in this valley take the weekend off? I made an appointment for ten on Monday. That should keep Shepherd happy.

Finally, I called and left another message for Rory Stevens. The guy was undoubtedly out playing in a pond someplace. He'd grow webbed feet if he wasn't careful.

In thirty minutes, precisely, Shepherd packed up his papers, ready to depart. I knew he was itching to drive the SUV, but I didn't trust his mind-over-matter attitude. I kept the keys and drove: first to HT's house to get the salve from Isabel and then down to Cottonwood to Shepherd's house.

We were almost there when I broached a subject that had been bugging me. "When I was feeding Fluffy I saw some photos."

"Yeah?"

"The little girl—your daughter?"

"Was. Her mother and I split years ago. Haven't kept in touch."

"Fluffy her cat?" I asked.

"A wild stray, came to the back door. Sheryl was the only one who could handle her. When she and her mother left, Fluffy stuck around." He adjusted the bandaged leg, trying to get comfortable.

"And the photograph with the German shepherd—that where you got your nickname?"

He nodded. "Kaiser. Loved that dog. My wife said I loved him better'n her. Might have been right. When he died, my heart went out of K-9 training. Never be another one like old Kaiser."

More information than I'd gotten about him since we'd met. I pushed a little. "Saw the Blue Book for AA on your shelf. You a recovering alkie?"

"What is this, the third degree?" His deep voice lowered an octave. "Stick to business."

Fair enough, learned what I needed to, anyway. When I pulled into the cottage driveway, Shepherd grabbed his cane and limped to the front door. I followed behind, carrying the duffel. He snapped his fingers for the house keys and I handed them over. He opened the locks and bent down to greet Fluffy. Then he turned to me and held out his hand.

"Appreciate everything you've done," he said gruffly. "You've got potential, Peg, but don't be so stiff-necked. Pick me up Monday morning about five-thirty. Want an early start."

Shepherd gave with one hand and took away with the other. Why should I care what he thought, anyway? Except I did.

I drove up the hill to Mingus ready to leave the job behind me. All I wanted was to go home and spend the rest of the evening with a hot bath and a cold beer.

But as I walked in the door, a call from Rory Stevens changed all that.

CHAPTER TWELVE

"Saw your messages," Rory said. "We might have found the murder weapon at Tavasci Marsh. You interested?"

"What you got?"

"A photograph. Like to show you in person. You free for dinner tonight?"

"Where?"

"At Grapes, there in Mingus," he said.

It was a lame excuse for a date, but I was hungry. "Okay, meet you in an hour."

Grapes was a tapas eatery specializing in fancy wines. The building had been a pony express and stage coach stop at the turn of the century. Now the historic structure housed this restaurant, serving excellent food in a quiet atmosphere.

I locked the office and walked down the street to my studio apartment. I changed out of my uniform into clean jeans and added a shimmery green top that set off my red hair, tassel-y earrings made of feathers and rhinestones, and a pair of high-heeled cowboy boots. Darned if I was going to wear flats, just to accommodate some short guy. Never had, wasn't starting now.

I walked up the hill to Grapes and reached the door just as Rory whooshed up in a yellow BMW Z4, top down.

"Nice wheels," I said as he jumped out.

"Thanks! I had a rich uncle who left it to me." He patted a fender. "I call her Tweetie-Bird."

Convertible driving had to be frigid coming over the mountains from Prescott to Mingus this time of year. Maybe he put down the top to make an entrance as he reached the edge of town—what I would have done.

Rory held the restaurant door open for me and we walked in. With the early hour, the dinner crowds hadn't arrived, and the hostess put us in a corner booth. We did the cop shuffle over who would sit with their back to the wall. Rory lost. I slid in and did a quick check of both the restaurant and the front door, looking for potential bad guys. Found none.

"How've you been?" Rory asked.

I had forgotten how alert his eyes could be. "Busy." I told him about the set-to with Otis Stroud in the swamp.

"That bastard. Are you okay?"

"I'm fine, and Shepherd's on the mend. We've got a BOLO out on the guy." Well, we did, sort of. Shepherd had requested it, and I would have done it, except I knew Otis would be at the funeral. That counted. Half of me felt protected by Rory's concern and the other half felt I didn't need any rescuing. Both halves were right.

"Shepherd's got a reputation in the department for being a cranky cuss. How you getting on?"

"Poorly, at times," I admitted. "What's he got against women?"

Rory took a breath. "Peg, he might not have anything against women, just against *you*."

I tensed. "Meaning what, exactly?"

He spread his hands in a peacemaker gesture. "Look, like it or not you're a rookie. If you hesitate at the wrong moment, his life could be in danger. Has nothing to do with whether you're male or female."

I was spared from a knee-jerk feminist rejoinder by the waitress's arrival.

Grapes specialized in wine flights, a row of tiny glasses used to sample a selection of wines, the theory being that you'd fall in love with one and buy a nice expensive bottle. Rory suggested we try a flight, and we picked a pinot noir from California, Chianti from Italy, and just for fun, something called Cycles Gladiator Merlot.

All expensive wines, and that usual niggle started in the back of my head. Just who is paying for this, and what do they expect as payback? I shook the buzz out of my brain when the waitress brought three small tasters for each of us.

Rory tried the merlot first. "Ah, I taste ruby red with violet hues, and is that a cedar aroma?"

"And you've been reading the menu." I laughed and sipped some myself. Not bad.

"Rory, what about you? No hang-ups like Shepherd has?"

"None I'd share in mixed company. I do like them tall, though."

Not a pickup line I appreciated. Was he going to be like some of the other guys I dated? "How does it feel to be *short?*" I asked bluntly. At six foot, I'd never had that problem.

He could have blown it off and made some funny joke, but instead, his reply was serious. "It sucks to be short. They called me leprechaun or ankle biter when I was a kid. Stuffed me in a dryer once. 'You're so short you're the last one to know when it rains.' I've heard them all."

Honesty on a first date. This was refreshing. "How'd you cope?"

"Humor, sometimes. There's always a comeback line. I was less than five feet tall until I got into high school. Then I had a major growth spurt. Made it all the way up to my present five foot eight."

Four inches difference between us, then. If the genders were reversed, that wouldn't make a whole heck of a lot of difference. I pondered that thought for a moment.

His eyes dared me to make a joke about it. I didn't, because my experiences were a mirror image of his. "Look," I said. "I haven't crossed my legs under a desk since fourth grade. What I heard was, 'How's the air up there?' It sucks to be tall."

We smiled at each other in mutual understanding. Then we tried the other two wine samplers, and had the waitress bring us a bottle of the Chianti. She whisked away the tiny glasses and poured us each a nice goblet full. Rory ordered the chicken saltimbocca—chicken breasts with prosciutto and mozzarella—what's not to like there? I selected the seared ahi tuna with ginger and wasabi. Wasabi, a close cousin to my favorite horseradish.

"How did you get into scuba diving?" I asked.

Rory took a sip of his wine. "Started out in gymnastics. That paid for college. But always loved swimming. Wanted to get into the SEALs. You know that old slogan: Join the Navy, see the world? I did, all underwater. What about you?"

"Track scholarships paid my way through school, psychology major. Ended up in Africa for a time in the Peace Corps. Came back to take care of my mom, then out here to re-connect with my granddad, HT. Haven't been too successful with that, as yet." Rory was easy to talk to. I liked that.

The waitress arrived with our food, got them mixed up, and we crossed plates after she left, my wrist touching Rory's. A zing of connection. The grilled tuna was superb, and so was the chicken. Rory reached a forkful, melting with cheese and basil, across the table for me to taste. Amazing! I shared the tuna with him, and his nose wrinkled at the piquant spices. But he was game to try it.

We did the usual get-to-know-you dance. I asked about his family—two older brothers, both taller than Rory. He asked about mine. Only child, I replied.

"What's one thing about you most people don't know?" he challenged.

I thought about the ballet I'd taken as a child until I broke my ankle. Ballet and being a cop probably don't go together. Too sissy, some might judge. Or the way I cried for days when my puppy got run over? Discarded that one, too. Cops hated the sensitive label. Decided on: "Got a tattoo in a private place." I held up my hand, laughing. "No, you don't need to know more than that. What about you?"

"I know Pashto."

"The Afghan language? How's that?"

"It was my backup plan. If I didn't make the SEALs, I was going into foreign language school. I figured knowing Pashto would give me an edge. Always important to have a Plan B. What's yours?"

"What would I do if I wash out being a cop? Be a private investigator, maybe. I seem to have a talent for finding things. But I'm happy where I'm at right now. Learning this deputy job is huge."

"I hear you."

And I got the feeling he really did.

The waitress cleared our plates and asked about dessert. Rory raised an eyebrow at me and I shook my head. "Just coffee then," he said.

When the waitress returned with two steaming mugs, Rory reached for a folder he had placed beside him on the seat. "Here's the main event. We found it tangled in the reeds at Tavasci Marsh."

I grabbed it and pulled out the photo. It was a picture of a flat stick, about the size of a baseball bat. "I've seen one of these before," I said.

"What? Here?"

"No, at my great aunt's house in Tennessee. She had one hanging on her wall. It's called a battling stick."

"What?"

"A battling stick. It was used to beat the clothes on the rocks when you washed them at the creek. I'll bet it's made out of red oak, too. The best ones were. My aunt kept hers as a reminder of how far women have come." I looked at the photo once more and put it back in the envelope. "Okay if I keep this?" He waved a palm in assent. "You think it's the murder weapon?"

"Could be. Forensics is testing it even as we speak."

Something more to share with Shepherd. "Time to leave," I said. "Early morning for me." It wasn't, really, but babysitting Shepherd all day had worn me down to a nubbin.

Rory nodded and signaled for the check. When it arrived, the waitress set it in the neutral ground between us. I grabbed, but he beat me to it.

"This time the gentleman will pay for everything," he said.

So I let him. Next time I'd get it. Shoot, maybe I'd even learn some Pashto in the process. If there *was* a next time.

"Offer you a ride home?" he asked as we left the restaurant.

I looked at the mini-sports car parked at the curb. No way could my long legs fit into that.

My hesitation didn't faze him. "Plan B," he announced, taking my arm.

He chose the street side of the sidewalk like a well-mannered gentleman and walked me back to the apartment.

When we arrived at my front door, he said, "Let me show you how we handle this." He stepped up on the landing and put his arms around me. "Consider Javier Bardem. He's my height." And then he kissed me slowly, thoroughly.

I enjoyed every minute of it.

***

That night I dreamt of romantic motorcycle rides down hilly roads in Greece, just me and Rory.

But when I awoke in the pre-dawn hours, my ghosts rose with me. Unbidden images of blood dripping down a wall, and a dying man sprawled on the floor coursed through my brain. I'd relived that scene countless times, examining it from all angles. I *had* to kill the man to free his hostage, no choice. That didn't make what I lived with each day any easier to bear.

I turned over in bed, trying to return to my romantic motorcycle dream, but sleep was elusive. Finally, I threw on a robe and walked out onto the balcony in my bare feet. The air was cold and still. I shook my head in an attempt to banish the night terrors.

I didn't have PTSD like the guys coming back from the war zones. Kept my temper under control, usually. Didn't drink to excess or numb out on weed. Would talking to someone help? Perhaps. Today, without fail, I'd call that counselor.

Wisps of fog curled around the corners of abandoned buildings on the street below. Sure you will, they whispered.

CHAPTER THIRTEEN

A front moved in the morning of Cal Nettle's funeral and gusty winds pushed dry cottonwood leaves into windrows in front of my apartment. My mood was unsettled and jangly as I picked out a long, dark-gray skirt and jacket with a plain white blouse.

The skirt was a buying mistake, a mid-calf pencil skirt that I regretted the moment I walked out of the store. An unexpected use for it here. I French-braided my red hair, added a touch of lipstick, and shoved my feet into flats, since I wasn't making a height statement.

HT and Isabel picked me up at ten for the services. Isabel had baked a casserole, so my nonexistent "specialty dish" wouldn't be missed. I sat with the crock warming my ankles on the way to the church. Our office clerk, Ben Yazzie, had elected to stay at the station and I wished I were there with him. Never did like attending funerals.

The First Wildwood Church sat on a hill overlooking Cottonwood, framed by a row of green-black cypress trees. The white church had a tall bell tower and as we entered the parking lot, it tolled the years of Cal Nettle's life, fifty-eight solemn tones, one after the other. Sometimes in the early days of the town, the bell peeled more than eighty strokes to measure the life of a pioneer. Janny's father would never see that age. I hoped I might.

HT, Isabel, and I walked up the front steps, the three of us a family. I hadn't had that for a long while, with my father's desertion and my mother's drinking.

The church was small, one long pew on either side of an aisle, about ten rows deep. Maybe room for a hundred or so, if you counted little kids squeezed in between parents. Not many of them at this type of service, though.

HT and Isabel went ahead, while I sat in back to observe the folks coming in. I squirmed to get comfortable on the hard, varnished-pine bench. Above me was an old-fashioned tin roof. White-washed windows let in pale light. A cross of twisted wood hung over the altar, and the chancel held seating for a small choir. It was a no-nonsense church, foregoing the fripperies of stained glass and statuary.

A plain wooden burying box rested under a spotlight in front. Did Otis make the casket? Families from the hill country of Appalachia sometimes followed this practice, a mark of respect for the deceased. The too-sweet aroma of lilies drifted by. The Nettles had requested donations to the local food bank, but some people sent flowers anyway. HT had done both.

As the people filed in, music played softly. Ethan Nettle sat facing the visitors, a guitar cradled in his arms. He strummed some hymns, but mostly it was music of his own making. His eyes closed as he played for his father.

Everyone stood as the rest of the family entered. Janny and Howard supported Ruby Mae who walked stolidly between them, her face set. Aurora followed with a strange woman by her side. That must be Howard Nettle's wife, Pietra. She had long black hair draping to her waist and a red, outsized hat that flopped and tilted as she turned her head. Strange choice for a funeral.

Behind them, Otis walked alone in an outmoded suit too short in the sleeves. He glanced at me and then stared straight ahead as he marched to the front pew, joining the family.

That brought up one small detail I'd neglected to tell Shepherd yesterday, that he'd be sharing pallbearer duties with Otis. My partner jolted upright when he spotted the fugitive, and then swiveled around to catch my gaze. I made a hands-up motion and hunched back in my seat. Shepherd had been blindsided, and I'd hear about it.

When the family procession reached the front, ushers removed the ropes that reserved the section, and the mourners filed into the front pew. Aurora squeezed beside her mother and Janny gave her a pat. Ethan put down his guitar and joined them. The congregation fell silent, waiting for the service to begin.

Darbie Granger slipped quietly into the back pew next to me. She wore a flowered summer dress in an empire style that emphasized her pregnancy. Her hair hung in soft ringlets, with pink and blue ribbons intertwined. She pulled off big sunglasses and gave me a sad smile.

The news of her arrival rushed to the front of the church like a football wave. Ruby Mae jumped to her feet, turned one-eighty, and glared at the intruder. She started to say something, but Janny tugged at her arm and Ruby Mae allowed herself to be pulled back down. She put her head on Howard's shoulder momentarily, and Janny touched her hair.

After Darbie, the preacher's entrance was an anticlimax. He entered from the side and strode to the pulpit. Reverend Billy was tall, with a striking pompadour of blond hair. He ran a hand over it as he climbed to the speaking area, smoothing the strands. He looked to be early thirties—Ruby Mae had been right there.

"All rise for the first hymn," he announced. " 'Fair are the mountains, fairer still the woodlands.' "

I grabbed a hymnal and searched for the right page. Couldn't find it and just mouthed the words, hoping nobody would notice. Churches created that kind of awkwardness for me.

Reverend Billy gave a short prayer and then everyone sat. I assumed some member of the family would give a eulogy, but instead, that task fell to the Reverend. He proclaimed Calhoun Nettle to be a sterling member of the community, a wonderful father, and a faithful husband.

I thought of the beatings that Ethan described and the mistress sitting beside me. My gut wrenched. Describing Cal Nettle in such terms was false, and I couldn't see how it made anybody feel better.

We sang two more hymns, a quavering tenor soloed a third, and the service ended. Reverend Billy called for the pallbearers, and they marched to the front in solemn cadence.

Sons Ethan and Howard paired in front, then friends Armor Brancussi and HT supported the middle of the casket. Otis and Shepherd brought up the rear, one on either side. There was some shuffling for balance, and then on an unspoken signal, the men lifted the casket by its handles.

The walk was a little lopsided. Armor had a bad hip from an old motorcycle accident and Shepherd's injured leg was still healing, but they managed. Otis and Shepherd didn't make eye contact the entire way to the entrance of the church, engaged in a silent truce for the ritual.

While I stood in line to greet the Reverend, I examined him at closer range. No string tie. In fact, it looked like an expensive Armani four-in-hand. When I reached the head of the receiving line, the preacher grabbed my hand and covered it with his other, trapping it. He held it a second too long, deep brown eyes staring down into my own. That made him over six feet tall, maybe six-two.

"Glad you could attend, Miss...Are you a member of the family?" he asked.

In hill country parlance, that statement meant, identify yourself. What's your connection here?

I debated telling him I was a third-cousin once removed, which I actually might be, and settled for: "Deputy Peg Quincy, from the sheriff's department. Nice words about the deceased." Half of the statement was true, anyway.

"Glad to meet you, Ms. Deputy Peg Quincy from the sheriff's department." He mimicked my tone. "Come visit my church anytime. No lawbreakers here, just honest sinners." He winked at me, released my hand, and moved on to the next in line.

Once in the churchyard, I stood there for a moment in the sunshine with the other sinners. Ruby Mae and the family gathered under a big cottonwood tree. No sign of Otis. Somehow I was not surprised.

Darbie Granger, her chin in the air, made her way toward Ruby Mae. Folks parted to let her through and followed after like kids in a schoolyard anticipating a fight. Howard and Ethan closed ranks around their mother when Darbie reached Ruby Mae's side.

"I'm very sorry for your loss," Darbie said, her voice barely a whisper.

Ruby Mae stood silent a moment and then reached out her hand the barest amount.

Darbie grasped her fingers.

"Likewise, I'm sure," Ruby Mae said, in an evenly modulated, Emily Post voice. Then she dropped her hand and turned away.

I thought that would be an end to it, but didn't reckon with Howard's wife. Pietra shoved her way to the front and shook a finger in Darbie's face. "Shameful! Cursed, carrying that bastard child."

Howard grabbed her arm. "Now's not the time. Tend to Momma." He pushed Pietra in the direction of the family group.

The tightness of his grip raised angry welts on Pietra's arm. She glared at him and reluctantly complied with his directive.

Howard grasped Darbie's fingers. "I apologize. My wife is unwell. See you to your car?"

Darbie daintily took his arm just above the elbow, tottering on heels too high for the uneven ground. The two moved in the direction of the parking lot. In the distance, Janny leaned down to soothe Aurora. I wondered how she'd explain to the child the unresolved family issues bubbling to the surface along with the day's grief.

Shepherd caught up with me as I opened the door of HT's pickup. "Ride with me," he ordered.

I followed him to the sheriff's department SUV and buckled up for the dusty drive to the Nettle homestead. "Where's Otis?" I asked, introducing the topic before he could.

Shepherd pulled into the funeral procession. "Slipped away, soon as the casket was loaded. You knew he'd be here?"

"Uh, Janny said he'd turn himself in, after the funeral."

"You *believed* her?" His tone held scorn. "Thanks for checking with me first."

"Check with you about what?" I retorted. "Family's decision to have him here, not ours."

"What happened to the Be-On-The-Lookout I asked you to initiate for the county?"

I said nothing.

"Would it be too much trouble for you to operate as a *team* for the remainder of the afternoon?"

My resentment flared like lightning in a too-dry forest. "Would it be too much trouble for you to *treat* us like a team?"

That was it. He jerked to the side of the road. A cloud of dust billowed around the SUV as the rest of the procession passed us.

Shepherd slowed his breathing with effort. He reached for the mike and patched through to our dispatcher, Melda. "Put out a Be-On-the-Lookout for Otis Stroud." He gave the man's description in a matter-of-fact tone and clicked off the mike.

He sat for a moment and then turned to face me. "You're a rookie—I need to respect that—but fighting with each other lets the bad guys win. That what you want?"

My color rose and I bent my head.

He continued in a softer voice, "I need to know you've got my back, Peg. Can we work toward that?"

How long this uneasy truce would hold was uncertain, but for the present, it was better than the constant sniping—I agreed with him there. I reached out a hand and we shook on it.

Shepherd gave a short nod and pulled in behind the last car of the funeral procession. We ate dust all the way to the Nettle homestead.

The small family graveyard crowned a hill behind the house. People sat on rickety funeral chairs in groups of twos and threes, the artificial turf beneath their feet garish against the red earth. The casket, supported by a mechanical lever, rested over the open hole in anticipation of the final lowering. HT's backhoe stood to one side ready to refill the grave.

The wind blew, picking up the red dirt and flinging it into eyes already burning from too much emotion. Women held onto hats with one hand and skirts with the other. In the distance one of the coonhounds set up a chop and a mournful bay, others followed until the whole pack cried, one tone piling onto the next. Then silence fell.

Reverend Billy began with the Seasons passage from Ecclesiastes, "A time to be born, and a time to die...a time to weep and a time to laugh...a time to mourn." He recited the words with honest feeling, and my eyes filled with tears as I remembered my grandmother's funeral, and also my mother, now lost to me in the fog of her dementia.

Reverend Billy invited each family member to say something. Janny and Ruby Mae declined, but Howard Nettle rose and stood by his father's raised coffin. He placed a hand against its side and brushed back his windblown hair. "My daddy and I argued, that's a fact, but in the end, I loved him, and he loved me. I'll miss him." He sat down, and Janny gave his hand a squeeze.

"Anyone else?" asked the Reverend.

Ethan shook his head. He leaned forward in his chair, hands in front of his face.

Reverend Billy intoned the final benediction, raising his voice so his words could be heard over the bracing wind: "We commit this body of Calhoun Nettle to the ground, ashes to ashes, dust to dust..."

The cables whined and slowly the casket disappeared from view. Reverend Billy handed a shovel to Howard who pitched dirt onto the casket. Howard passed the shovel to Ethan who repeated the action, the clods hitting the wooden box with a hollow echo. Janny reached down and trickled a handful of earth into the cavity, and Aurora, her little face solemn, dropped a yellow rose that she'd clutched during the service.

I stood to one side watching the mourners pass by. Some used the shovel, some bent to toss a small handful of dirt as Janny had done. Then they filed down the hill toward the homestead. Reverend Billy said something to Ruby Mae, nodded to me, and joined the others.

Ruby Mae stood there, head bowed, saying goodbye to her husband. Her head lifted when she saw me. "Give me a hand down this hill? I'm feeling a might wobbly today."

We walked down the long hill in silence, Ruby Mae's thoughts her own.

Darby Granger hadn't been at the graveside, and I doubted that she would attend the funeral reception. Still, Pietra would be at the ritual potluck and her presence meant trouble. The rest of the Nettle clan would attend as well, their nerves worn thin by the funeral service for Cal Nettle—that wonderful father, faithful husband.

CHAPTER FOURTEEN

While we were at the gravesite, Reverend Billy's church ladies set up a meal on plank-and-sawhorse tables. As Ruby Mae approached this next step in the community's grieving process, she dropped her hand from my arm.

"Can't take no more." Shaking her head, she walked up onto the porch and into the house.

Although I understood her reticence, the feast beckoned me. The serving dishes made a quilt mosaic on the table as the meal stretched in lavish abundance—ham, mashed sweet potatoes, homemade coleslaw. The enticing smells of Isabel's green-chili chicken enchiladas wafted my direction. In the dessert section, a red velvet cake and a pecan pie made my mouth water. In her mother's absence, Janny stepped into the role of hostess, welcoming people to the buffet. Eagerly they followed her suggestion; the folks must have been as hungry as me.

Before I could join the serving line, Shepherd pulled me aside. He leaned on his cane, sharp eyes assessing the crowd. "I want you to keep an eye out. No telling what might happen here."

"On it. Mind if I eat while I do that?" My voice was sharper than I intended.

He smiled, seemingly aware he'd pierced my armor.

My jaw clenched at his unspoken rebuke. I'd do as he asked, *after* I finished the first course.

I entered the line ahead of Janny and Aurora. Janny's manner had been subdued throughout the service. Burying her father must have been difficult. But now that the interment was complete, she seemed ready to engage in lighter conversation. "What did you think of Reverend Billy?" she asked as we moved forward in the line.

"Not what I expected," I admitted. "Married?"

"Was. His wife died of a brain aneurysm. She was right there hitting a golf ball on the back nine and just keeled over. Left those poor children. Reverend Billy's been having a time with them."

Not exactly what I needed, a built-in family with problems. Enough challenges in my life already. "I noticed the Reverend gave the eulogy. I expected a member of the family to do that."

"Well, Brother Howard had been gone for years. Wasn't proper for him to do it. And Momma couldn't bring herself to get up there in front of all those people."

"Understood. But not you or Ethan?"

She poked my shoulder. "Looks like the line is moving. Keep up or there'll be nothing left. Aurora, baby, go wash up and I'll make a plate for you." Aurora let go of her mother's hand, skipped up the porch steps, and disappeared inside the house.

We finally reached the head of the line and picked up plates and silverware. Steam wilted my eyebrows when I took the top off a slow cooker. I fished out a couple of meatballs, then I forked some homemade pickles from a big jar, and a piece of southern fried chicken from the next platter. I glanced around to see if Shepherd was looking and added a homemade biscuit, too.

Since they were in the neighborhood, I snagged a chocolate chip cookie still soft from the oven—I'm always a sucker for chocolate chip cookies. I completed my serving with a glass of sweet tea and joined Janny under a big cottonwood tree. She pulled three chairs together for us, then set down her dishes on one, and went to see about Aurora.

An acrid scent of fall drifted down from the cottonwood leaves, still gold and full. The higher branches quivered in the wind, but at ground level, the air was still. I perched awkwardly on the small funeral chair, balancing the plate on my lap, my iced tea wedged in the grass at my feet.

My grandfather HT and his friend Armor were having a post-funeral exchange under a nearby tree. The word was that Armor still grew marijuana in an undisclosed patch to sell to his motorcycle buddies. Perhaps his knowing Cal Nettle wasn't such a stretch, then. Illegal substances like drugs and alcohol seemed to find each other.

Armor told a story of skunks in the still: how one had gotten into the whiskey mash and Cal's run had been delayed for hours while they figured out how to get the critter to move. "Finally used a mixture of day-old bacon and shrimp cat food to coax it out," Armor said. "We like to never got any hooch that week."

My grandfather had his own Cal story. "I remember one time he brewed a fine good batch and started sampling his own wares. Disappeared for three days. By the time Ruby Mae went hunting for him with a shotgun, there warn't but a single jar of white lightning left."

Janny returned and sat down next to me. She stirred her serving of enchilada casserole with a fork and picked at a sliver of black olive. For a moment she listened to the conversation between Armor and HT.

Then she turned to me and said in a quiet voice, "That whiskey still was only one side of Daddy. I remember the night he hid Easter eggs for us kids. One of the coonhounds got loose, gobbled down every last one. Momma told me Daddy was still dyeing replacement eggs at daybreak to hide for us kids. Easter was always his favorite time of year." She sighed. "He changed after my brother Lucas died."

Perhaps so. Would that bitterness be enough for a family member to turn against the old man, want him dead? I glanced sharply at Janny, evaluating, but her expression held nothing but the emptiness of loss.

Aurora returned and for a moment, Janny busied herself getting the little girl settled with her food. Aurora fussed that she didn't like green beans, and Janny bargained she could have a piece of cake if she ate them. Sounded like the negotiations I used to have with my mother when I was little and she was sober.

Howard and his wife Pietra approached. I felt sorry for Pietra, even as unpleasant as she was. An occasion like this must be an awful way to meet your mother-in-law for the first time. Their voices rose as they neared. Pietra's hair was in disarray, her hat shoved to one side.

"I intend to see your mother and pay my respects. You can't stop me!" She attempted to push past Howard.

"You're in no condition to see anybody. Go back to the car." Howard restrained her, his hands stiff and his face set.

"If I do, I'm leaving for good."

"Then go, damn it!"

Pieta pivoted and lurched toward the parked cars. When she reached their rental, she fumbled in her purse. The key scraped against the paint of the rental several times as she attempted to find the door lock.

I made a half motion to follow her. Liquor and temper—never a good combination But she climbed in, started the engine, and disappeared in a swirl of dust before I could follow through.

Howard raised his hands skyward in frustration and stopped in front of us. "Sorry you had to witness that. There's no reasoning with Pietra when she gets to drinking." He sounded disgruntled, unhappy.

His father's funeral had been tough on him, too. Although Howard and Janny seemed to be on speaking terms, he'd exchanged looks with his brother Ethan at the

funeral service, and they'd carefully arranged distance
between them ever since. So unresolved business there.

"Janny, Can I borrow your car?" Howard asked. "I need
to see about getting a room. Even though Pietra's leaving,
I want to stay over for the you-know..."

Janny reached in her purse, found her keys, and
handed them to her brother. He stalked off in the general
direction of her car.

"For the you-know-*what?*" I asked.

"The treasure hunt. Daddy didn't believe in banks. He
stashed money all over the property. Folded up in cracks in
the barn, hidden in wheel wells of some of the old farm
machinery. Momma says years ago he buried an old coffee
can filled with silver dollars in the back yard. The three of
us kids, or four if you count Aurora, are going hunting
tomorrow. Might as well be something good that comes out
of all of this."

"Janny, do you know who killed your father?" I asked.

She gave me a look of mistrust. "Don't start playing
police officer on me, Peg. This is my daddy's wake and
that's not something I care to speak about."

Maybe she was right, and I was being insensitive. Or
perhaps it was time to move on to more productive hunting
grounds. I gathered up my utensils. "I'll be circulating for
a while. Think on it, Janny."

She shrugged and turned to Aurora. "Here, darlin',
have a piece of this tasty fried chicken."

I scraped my plate in the trash and stacked the dish on
a side cart. Reverend Billy was talking to a group at the
end of the table and I considered a move in his direction.
Maybe a funeral was the wrong place to find romance, but
I'd seen stranger. Like on top of a beaver lodge, or alongside
a broken-down pickup truck, for instance.

So what if this man had children—worse things in the
world. I got along okay with Aurora, didn't I? Kids weren't
so bad, kind of cute, in fact.

Almost as though he'd read my intentions, Shepherd blocked me at the end of the dessert table. He nodded his head toward two strangers standing under a ponderosa pine at the edge of the yard. One a tall guy, resting easily on his feet like he worked out. The other stocky, like a knot of fireplace wood. The two stood out like vultures in a flock of sparrows. Their manner was edgy. The taller guy's jacket bulged with a concealed sidearm.

They stopped a young woman to ask something. Time to move. I hitched up my skirt to a walking length and accosted them as they reached the porch. "Mind if I ask what your business is here?"

"Yeah, we mind," said the tall one. "Step aside."

"I don't think so." I planted myself firmly in front of them. Sometimes it's nice to be six feet tall.

Shepherd reached my side, leaning heavily on the cane, the pain line between his brows pronounced. He lifted his jacket to show his own revolver. "Time to move along, gentlemen. This is a family service. No strangers invited."

"We're not strangers..." the stocky one began.

The tall one stopped him. "Never mind. We'll be back. You tell Ruby Mae that Aldo Nigglieri wants to talk to her. Soon."

The men turned on their heels, walked to a red Nissan parked on the street, and left. I got a partial plate number as they backed up so that I could check it later. Armor could laugh about skunks and Janny remember Easter egg hunts, but Cal Nettle's life contained this darkness as well.

Ethan walked back from the barn where he'd been tending the puppies. He looked after the two men. "What was that all about?"

"Ever see them before?" Shepherd asked.

"Once, talking to Daddy."

"What about?"

"Business, maybe. Seen 'em talking to Uncle Otis, too." Then like Janny, he changed the subject. "I want to

123

apologize for my uncle's behavior in the marsh. Wasn't no cause."

"That's personal business between Otis and me, son," Shepherd said. "More important is that you buried your father today, and I'm sorry for that. Only get one in this lifetime." He shook Ethan's hand and they hugged in that way men have, barely touching at the chest, each patting the other's back.

Reverend Billy directed his volunteers to clear the remaining plates, and the church group left soon after. When they did, the mood of the crowd lifted. Ethan hung two Coleman lanterns from the eaves of the house and picked up his guitar. He sat on the porch stair, tuning it, then strummed random chords. At the sound, Ruby Mae came onto the porch and settled into an old platform rocker to listen.

Ethan played the old country songs: "Walk the Line," "Behind Closed Doors," "Ghost Riders in the Sky." Then Howard jumped up on the porch. Ethan slammed his hand on the strings with a jangle of discordant sounds. The two men glared at each other.

Ruby Mae leaned down and touched Ethan's shoulder. "Please, for me."

Janny joined her two brothers and the music renewed. Howard's tenor and Janny's alto intertwined with Ethan's guitar. They sang the hill country classics, "Barbra Allen," "Down in the Valley," "Shenandoah." The voices and guitar intertwined with close harmony.

After one final verse, Ethan set down the guitar and addressed the listeners. "Thank you for coming," he said. "My daddy would have been proud to see all of his friends and family here." His voice broke. "We'd like to propose a toast to my daddy, and then ask Shepherd Malone to gift us with one last song."

He reached behind him on the porch and brought out a jug of clear liquid, and there was silence as glasses were filled. Shepherd held up a glass of water for the toast. "To Calhoun Nettle, to Cal." The words echoed through the crowd.

Then Shepherd limped to the porch and sat down on the top step. He reached into his pocket and pulled out a harmonica. First, he blew a few preliminary notes. Then he took a deep breath and played Taps.

The harmonica sang with emotion, a trailing vibrato with a slide that mourned and cried for all of us. Shepherd reached for one last note, held it, and then put the harmonica down.

A coyote up on the hill howled, and one hound responded with an answering bay. The lanterns shivered in the gathering wind. One by one, people paid their final respects to Ruby Mae and headed for home.

Tomorrow, our work would begin again. But tonight, Cal Nettle rested alone on the hill with only the wind for company.

CHAPTER FIFTEEN

Shepherd gave me a haggard look when I arrived at the office the next morning.

"How's that leg doing?" I asked.

He touched it and winced. "Not too good. Stressed it yesterday. Carrying death is heavy."

I looked to see if he was joking, but his face was serious.

He pulled up his pant leg—the skin around the incision was red and angry. "Infection, maybe." He inspected it dispassionately. "At least I had my tetanus shot last year. How recent is yours?"

"Current. Stop changing the subject. When do you see the doctor again?"

"He said to make a follow-up appointment. Been meaning to."

I picked up the phone receiver and handed it to him.

He gave me a sly look and pushed the phone my direction. "You first. Call your counselor."

I swallowed and dialed the number. Had the durned thing almost memorized by now. I thought to get the secretary, but the counselor's deep voice sounded through. I asked for an appointment, thinking it would be a week or more. She had an opening that afternoon, at two. I looked at Shepherd, grimaced, and took it. Might as well get it over with.

I hung up and handed the phone back to my partner. "Your turn. Tell the doc it's urgent."

He waggled his hand back and forth.

"Call," I ordered.

Shepherd's appointment wasn't until afternoon, either, so I left him and Ben in charge of the phones and went to investigate a break-in on the lower edge of town. We didn't have many burglaries in Mingus, the community being so small. Most likely it was a transient looking for beer money, but I went through the formalities anyway.

Then, since Su Casa was right down the hill, I called the station and took orders for lunch. Ben opted for fish tacos and Shepherd wanted the chili rellenos combo. I ordered my usual kitchen-sink burrito. When I returned to the station, we retired to the conference room to eat.

I laid napkins in my lap and ate the burrito with a fork.

"Quincy, you're hunched over that table like an old woman," Shepherd said.

"Stick a fork in it, Malone. Better'n spilling Picante sauce down the front." Today the burrito gods were with me and I didn't drop anything. That was good. I wanted to make the right kind of impression on the counselor. "Ben, you planted any grapes at the college vineyard yet?"

He wiped his chin. "Soon. Teacher says I'll make a good enologist."

"Grape vines." Shepherd snorted. "Buy your wine in a liquor store like civilized folks do."

"Careful, *balagaana*. You don't know who you be messing with." Ben reached for a jalapeno on my plate.

I grabbed it first and popped it in my mouth. I remembered too late why I set the pepper to one side when I'd unwrapped my burrito. I fanned at my mouth and grabbed for the water glass. It seemed wherever I turned I was running into unexpected heat.

***

At one o'clock, we left Ben in charge of the office. I drove Shepherd to his appointment first, to be sure he kept it. On the other hand, doing it that way meant Shepherd would be right there checking on my own actions when I returned to pick him up. Life gets complicated when you're keeping score.

Dr. Westcott's office was located in a medical complex at the edge of Cottonwood. A sign on the door said, "In Session, Please Wait," so I sat down on a worn wooden bench outside the door. I scrunched in my seat, squinting in the sun, hoping nobody would see me. Maybe they'd assume that I was here on official business, which I was, almost.

The door opened, and a stout woman in a bright coral suit exited. Dr. Westcott? She sniffed loudly and stuffed some tissues in her purse as she walked toward the parking lot. She was a client, then, not the doctor.

The door opened again and a petite East Indian woman in her sixties looked out. Her dark braided hair hung down past her waist. "You must be Pegasus Quincy."

Her voice was deep, with the cultured English accent I remembered from our phone conversations. As I towered over her to shake hands, the picture of the stout British matron vanished from my imagination like fall mist on Black Mountain.

"Please come in and have a seat," she said.

Her office was compact, painted in a soft green with light blue window sills. She touched a finger chime as she passed and a ripple of tone laced the air. A lavender fragrance lingered in the room as I entered.

On one wall hung a row of degrees: Ph.D., Licensed Psychologist, advanced training in hypnotherapy and existential counseling. If the credentials were intended to reassure me, they didn't. The love seat she gestured toward was low-slung and comfortable. I didn't feel low-slung and comfortable. I pulled up a green side chair and sat stiffly upright. The lady doctor did the same, and we angled each other, not facing exactly, but close.

"You don't look like I expected," I said.

She gave a soft musical giggle. "People often say that. My mother is English, born within the sound of the Bow Bells, but my father is from Mumbai. They made an interesting couple. I miss them, always. And you? I hear a southern flavor in your speech."

"Tennessee, mostly." I was never good with chitchat. Why didn't she get out the clipboard and start asking me psychologist questions? The clock ticked in the silence and I noted a box of tissues on the table. Did she expect me to cry? Not going to happen. I'd learned in grade school to stifle my tears—I'd rather be punched than be called a sissy.

She must have noticed my unease. "To business then. Although this is a mandatory referral, the only thing I need to report to your employer is that you attended these sessions. However, should you tell me you are intending to hurt yourself or planning to take the life of another, I would have to break confidentiality." She looked at me and I nodded my understanding.

"You shot and killed a man."

Ouch! Maybe we could go back to the chitchat.

"Yes," I said. "In the line of duty, I defended a citizen who was being held hostage."

"As I understand it, you actually were not on duty. You had been relieved at that point and were acting as a private citizen. Am I correct?"

She had me there. "Yes, but it related to a case I'd been working on."

"Fair enough. And how did you feel afterward?"

A small hourglass sat on the coffee table. I reversed it and watched the grains of sand dribble down like a life's blood draining away. "I don't know—numb, shocked, maybe?" I paused, watching for her reaction. There was none. The lady could be a good poker player. I tried for honesty: "Mostly, I was thankful."

"Thankful?"

Was that the wrong word to use? I backtracked. "I was gratified that I'd survived and he hadn't. What troops in combat must feel, I suppose."

That response seemed to satisfy her. I let out a breath I'd been holding. Had I passed the test yet?

Maybe not, for her next question was, "What do you expect to get out of this counseling?"

"My gun back." I made a joke of it, but she wasn't laughing. No sense of humor. Check. I replaced the smile with a solemn expression. My left eyelid started to twitch, and I raised a fingertip to quiet it.

"And that would certainly be a praiseworthy goal so that you'd be able to contribute to society with your work. But let's back up a moment. What social support do you have in your life?"

Social support. What was she looking for—Facebook, Twitter? I started to sweat and dampness trickled down my back. I hoped it wasn't staining her chair. "Social support...Okay, that would be my grandfather, HT. His housekeeper, Isabel. My clerk, Ben." I ticked them off on my fingers.

"Not your partner, Shepherd Malone?"

"Don't know him that well, he's a *new* partner."

"If you did, would you turn to him?"

"If I did what?" I temporized, scrambling for a good answer.

"Know him better." The woman was relentless.

What was she looking for? All I wanted was the magic word that would unlock the gun safe holding my weapon. I was tempted to lie and say that Shepherd and I got on fine, but we didn't. "He's an asshole who doesn't trust women cops." Maybe that would gain me some rapport, being that we were both women.

"Hmmm." She made a note on the pad in front of her.

I tried to see what she was writing. I'm good at reading upside down, but she angled the tablet so that I couldn't. Must have had clients like me before.

"Any bad dreams?"

"Some at first, but they've lessened." I wasn't lying, exactly. Their *frequency* had lessened, even if the intensity was worse. Sometimes I awoke drenched with sweat. But she didn't need to know that.

"What do you do for stress?" she asked.

"Well, I don't drink." That ought to get me a few points. A lot of cops I knew did. But I didn't meditate, either. And that probably would be her next question. I'd watched Life TV one day I was home sick with the flu. I knew the expected responses.

She surprised me, though. "You look physically fit. Run?"

"I jog. Helps after a hard day."

"Me, too." Again that musical giggle. "I like ultramarathons. Training for one in Hawaii this summer."

My respect for her ratcheted up. "The hundred kilometer race? Never run that far. Must be hard."

"Painful, mostly. Perseverance gets you there, and luck. Bad weather day, it's not going to happen."

The rest of the hour passed quickly. We talked about my mother in the nursing home. And my fear of the death which I knew would happen, but which I hoped wouldn't, anytime soon. And we spoke of my reluctance to rely on anyone.

I was just getting into the swing of things when she looked at her watch. "Time's up for today." She got out her appointment book. "When would you like to come in again?"

Not so fast. I'd done what was expected, put in some seat time in her precious office. It was her turn to deliver. "When do I get my gun back?"

"Soon. A few more sessions should do it."

Rats. But I made the appointment she seemed to think I needed for the following week. As I walked out her door, she touched my shoulder gently. "You did nice work today."

I hate to say it felt good, but it did. I chided myself. What was I looking for, some mother-figure approval? When I left the office, I passed a thin man on the waiting bench staring at his feet. Glad I wasn't crazy like he was.

***

Shepherd was standing in front of his doctor's office when I pulled into the medical center lot. He limped to the SUV and climbed in, his expression glum. "Damn doctor says I may have a MRSA infection. Put me on another antibiotic and if that doesn't work, I'll have to return to the hospital. That's where I *caught* the damn stuff. Why'd I want to go back for more?"

"Sorry," I said in a soothing voice, "I know you'll beat it, you're tough."

He looked at me like I was loco. "What's wrong with you, Quincy?"

"Never mind." So much for practicing loving kindness like the lady doc recommended. She didn't know Shepherd. "Back to the office?" I shifted the engine into gear.

"No, I'm done for today. Take me home and pick me up tomorrow morning at six."

"Right." The SUV groaned as we climbed the hills in the shadow of the mountain. "What's it like, Shepherd, to be so close to retirement? Think you'll miss work?"

"Never," he said. Then, "Every day. Both."

"What you going to do?"

"Sit around all day and watch soaps. What the hell you *think* I'm going to do?"

Touchy. Maybe I would be, too. Good thing I didn't have to face that one for another thirty years. I'd have a better attitude when I got there, though, that's for sure.

I turned into his drive, glad to be done with his depression. Maybe Fluffy's version of loving kindness would work better than mine. At least I could tell the counselor I had tried. He limped to the entrance, turned all three locks, opened the door, and bent to pet the cat. Then he moved inside and slammed the door.

I drove up the mountain to the Mingus office to write up the burglary report I'd taken earlier and to clean my desk before quitting for the day. Not like me. I must be spending too much time under Shepherd's influence.

That's when I got the call.

CHAPTER SIXTEEN

"Hello, this is Sally Ann. Remember me?" The voice on the phone sounded familiar.

"Sure I do..." I racked my brain.

"You don't. That's okay. Can't expect everybody to have a memory like mine. I live—lived—downstairs from Janny Nettle."

The lady in the CSI sweatshirt in Janny's apartment complex. It was all coming back to me. "What's up, Sally Ann?"

"I read Cal Nettle's obituary in the paper. Ronald— he's the meat manager down at FoodWay—gives me his papers when he's done with them. Jogged my recollections. I know something might be useful to you."

"Why don't you come up here to the office and let's discuss it."

"Can't. Cottonwood bus line doesn't run to Mingus. You have to come see me. This is important."

Finish the paperwork or go see Sally Ann? I debated for about five seconds.

***

Sally Ann waited for me on the bench outside her apartment and approached the SUV when I turned into the parking lot.

I rolled down the window. "Hey, there."

She shivered in the late afternoon wind. "Cold out here. Can I get in your patrol car?"

"Why not meet in your apartment?"

"Don't want folks to see me talking to you. Figured we could drive around for a while."

I clicked opened the door for her. She scrambled into the front seat, looking nervous. I drove down the road and into a vacant field. The body of the SUV tilted left and right as we crossed the weedy ground. The field was dark under Black Mountain's shadow, but across the valley, the Sedona red rocks still glowed hot in the setting sun. I jerked the vehicle to a stop in the middle of the field, with a clear view in all directions. A safe place to talk.

Sally Ann piled out and leaned against the SUV. "Got a smoke?" she asked. Her fingers jittered against the fender in a nervous tattoo.

"Don't smoke. What you want to tell me?"

"Don't informants usually get paid?" Her eyes were bright and expectant.

My wallet was so flat I couldn't feel it when I sat down. Maybe a limp twenty in there, I couldn't remember. "Depends on what you've got, Sally Ann. Your info has to be worth something." I lowered my voice to sound tough, playing the part she seemed to expect.

"I know who killed Cal Nettle. How's that?" She wiggled money-hungry fingers in my direction.

So that's how I paid my very first informant.

Sally Ann seemed disappointed there wasn't more than a twenty, but tucked it into her jeans pocket, and started her tale. "Some weeks ago, I was coming back from emptying my trash, minding my own business, you know, when Janny Nettle comes clipping down those steps to meet this old Ford pickup that comes banging into the parking lot. Window rolls down and Janny talks to the driver."

She looked up expectantly and I showed her the moths that were missing the twenty she'd conned out of me.

She sniffed. "Pretty cheap sheriff's office. Don't they pay you more than that?"

"Guess not. Recognize the driver?"

"This your story or mine?"

I gave her a go-ahead wave, and she continued. "I went back into my apartment with my empty trash can. I'm not nosy, you understand." She paused and gazed at the vista in front of us. "Right purty, isn't it. Reason I moved to Arizona."

How long was she going to draw this out? She had my money.

"Like I said, don't pry about visitors, not my nature. But I kept my front door ajar for air when I went back to the apartment. Hot you know, that afternoon sun beating down. Those two came and sat on this bench right there outside my apartment. Some of what they was saying caught my attention."

"Like what?"

"Guy asked Janny to help him dispose of some trash, said he had this 'heavy package' to lift. Janny argued, said she wouldn't. Must have changed her mind, though, because later on, she asked me to keep an ear out for Aurora.

"Janny didn't get back until real late and it was pitch black by that time. I'd already watched the evening news and put my face cream on—amazing what that stuff does for wrinkles. Didn't even think of the incident again until I read that obit. Wrote it up real nice, down at the paper." Her hand brushed the dust on the SUV, leaving a smear.

"The guy Janny talked to, know him?"

"Didn't see him, sun in my eyes when they drove up. And after, I never came out of my apartment."

"Recognize his voice?"

"It wasn't her brother, that Ethan. Know him. He gave me a ride once. Got dog hair all over my green print skirt. Took me forever to get it off."

"Anything distinctive about the voice?"

"Tweedy, reedy, what do you call it?"

"Tenor, maybe?" I asked.

"Like that opera guy? I listen to him on PBS sometimes. I watch those educational shows, you know, keep my brain active. Won't catch *me* watching Oprah. Bunch a junk, that's what she is."

My mind went to the Nettle home place and that duet between brother and sister. Howard Nettle would fit this woman's description with a certainty.

Sally Ann rambled on. "Oh! Now I remember. Someone else in the truck with the guy, a woman I think, wild hair flying around her face. She musta stayed in the truck, didn't hear her voice outside."

That might be Pietra, Howard's wife, or even Ruby Mae. "What else?"

"Well, isn't that enough? Them three was conspiring against that girl's poor father. You need to do something about that." When I was silent, she said, "Give me a ride downtown? Things to pick up at the grocery store."

I gave Sally Ann her ride, and she assured me she'd find a lift home. Her return driver better keep a tight hold on his smokes. Sally Ann was a pro.

***

The next morning I picked up Shepherd before sunrise. He seemed in a chipper mood and suggested we stop by the Flat Iron café for some breakfast before work. We parked the sheriff department SUV out front, nice and conspicuous, to slow down the early morning speeders.

The shopkeeper held open the door for us. Two sides of the triangle-shaped room were windowed and a small mini-

137

kitchen took up the third wall, so we had to forego our preferred back-to-the-wall seating arrangement.

Shepherd tried some of the gluten-free, multigrain waffles with real maple syrup. The owner even found some green tea bags, which pleased my partner. I settled for a chocolate-chip muffin, king-sized. Did I mention the coffee? Its aroma steamed the entire three-hundred-eighty-foot café. No wonder Shepherd liked this place. I was beginning to, as well.

Around bites of muffin, I told him about my conversation with Sally Ann.

"How much did she hit you up for?"

"Twenty."

"You got robbed. She'll talk for ten."

Great. Now I couldn't even pay the town snitch the right amount. "You know everybody in town, Shepherd?"

"Just about. Wait thirty years and you will, too."

Not likely you'd still find me here then. On the other hand, Shepherd had found enough of interest to stay. Looking that far into the future gave me a headache.

He finished the waffle, gave a satisfied belch. "Ah, that was good."

The café manager went to sweep the front step and Shepherd and I turned to the business of murder.

"I can't help thinking that Lucas's death ties into all of this," I said. "What do you remember about that explosion at the still?"

Shepherd sipped his tea thoughtfully. "I was the officer in charge, met the ambulance at the hospital. I heard Lucas breathe those raspy breaths. Lungs gone, the guy didn't have a chance." Shepherd twisted in his seat, uncomfortable at the memories. "Lucas asked me to tell Ethan goodbye. Not his daddy or his momma, just Ethan."

"That moonshine business tore the family apart."

Shepherd nodded. "The Nettles started out farming— sold honey, ran some milk cows, grew hay for sale, that sort of thing. But it was that whiskey business brought in the cash to support the family during the hard times. Law in these parts kept a blind eye, mostly." Shepherd stretched his stiff leg, easing the pain. "And times change. Now wineries cover those hills, all operating legally."

My coffee was cold and I helped myself to fresh from the pot on the counter.

"I'll dig out my notes on the case for you if you're interested," Shepherd said. "Couldn't hurt to give it another look."

He grabbed the breakfast receipt and I let him. Supervising partners get paid more than rookies. I put an extra bill under my coffee cup and we waved to the restaurant owner as we walked out to the SUV.

Later that morning, I called Janny Nettle and set up a meeting with us at our office the next day. Following my resolve to get along better with my partner, I even reviewed our interview strategies with him.

Was there a connection between Cal Nettle's death and the death of his son Lucas? Janny might know if we could get her to talk. And we intended to grill Janny on her part in ridding the town of the "heavy burden" that Sally Ann mentioned. Sooner or later, someone in that family had to break their silence, and I intended to be there when they did.

CHAPTER SEVENTEEN

The next day Janny arrived with Aurora. Shepherd set up the interview in his office since it was larger. We settled the little girl in the outer office with Ben. Soon I could hear muffled laughter as they bent over the computer, intent on Ben's video games. If Aurora could laugh, why couldn't she talk? I'd ask Dr. Westcott about that the next time I saw her.

Janny checked on Aurora one last time through the office door window and looked at me. "What can I tell you that I haven't already?"

I summarized my conversation with Sally Ann. "She says you were talking to somebody."

"Her word against mine." Her eyes snapped. "That busybody."

Shepherd didn't buy it. "No time to be lying now, Janny. Were you talking to your brother Howard that day?"

"So what if I was?"

"What about the woman with him?"

"What about her?" Janny countered.

"Was it Darbie?" he asked.

"Nah, she didn't have anything to do with..." Janny pressed her lips together.

"Who, then?"

Janny sat there, stone faced. Shepherd turned to me. Good cop, bad cop time. Although I wasn't sure which I was.

Sometimes it helped to tangent and then return to the matter at hand when the suspect was off guard. "I'm still curious about the accident at the still," I said. "Why did Howard leave the home place instead of staying to help?"

The distant past seemed a safer topic for Janny. "We'd had a bad storm, power still out, no phone, and the weather circled around, ready to hit us again. But Daddy was set on making that run. Said he had people waiting on him, important people."

She pulled in her arms and legs, scrunching into a tight ball. "The storm set everybody on edge. The lightning strikes were getting close—you could smell the sulfur in the air. Ethan and Howard were arguing about loading the truck—they never did get along. Lucas fussed with the equipment, said something was wrong. I went to find Daddy to fix it—he was out in the marsh, drunk as usual. I left my baby with the boys, for a second—just a second."

Her eyes filled with tears. "Daddy and I got back just as the still blew up. Nobody was watching Aurora like they were supposed to. And then I saw her on the ground near Lucas, the flames all around them. The fire was so intense! I tried to get closer, but I just couldn't bear the heat. Daddy and Ethan beat the fire back with gunnysacks so they could reach Lucas and my baby girl."

She was openly crying now. "By then it was too late. My poor baby was shrieking, and Lucas just lay there, quiet, like he didn't feel anything. Momma wanted to take him to the hospital, but Daddy refused. He said Lucas was a goner.

"Aurora was burned so bad, I didn't know what to do." Janny's face contorted. "Daddy stood in the way, blocked me from leaving. He said he needed the time to hide the still equipment. I picked up a two by four and rammed him hard in the stomach. He went down. I grabbed my baby girl and ran along the road. A neighbor gave me a ride to the emergency room. I recollect you were there, Shepherd?"

He nodded.

"And your Uncle Otis?" I asked.

"I don't know," Janny said. "He *should* have been at the still, attending the machinery. If he'd been there, maybe Lucas would still be alive. After the accident, Otis disappeared for two-three months. Momma said he went to the hill country visiting family. When he got back he and Daddy went out behind the barn, had a long talk."

"What did you do after that?"

Janny raised her hands defensively. "What *could* we do? Aurora was crippled; Lucas was dead. Daddy said the accident was Howard's fault, forbade him to set foot on the home place again." Her mouth twisted unpleasantly. "Brother Howard always caves when the going gets rough. His whole life, he's run away like that."

In Biblical times, the priest would send a goat into the wilderness carrying the sins of the people. Perhaps that was Howard's function within this broken family. In the anteroom outside our door, I heard Ben's encouragement and Aurora's squeals of delight as they played video games together. They were sunshine juxtaposed against the horror Janny had recounted.

Janny sat back in the chair, her arms crossed and her mouth set in a firm line. "I ain't got nothing else to say."

So much for circling back around to Sally Ann's story. Sometimes a diversion worked, sometimes it didn't. We got nothing further from Janny that day.

After the Nettles, mother and daughter, left, Shepherd and I reconvened to debrief. It was near lunchtime, but Janny's words had killed my appetite. "Tough, that explosion," I said.

"Family's been fractured ever since," Shepherd said. "What do you make of Janny's explanation?"

"Of the explosion? True as she saw it. Of the meeting outside the apartment? She may be lying."

"How so?" asked Shepherd.

"I still think Darbie is involved. She told me she served Cal apricot bars, and the medical lab found traces of apricots in his stomach. She's involved, somehow."

"You might be right. Why don't you nose around out where Darbie lives, see what you can find. Ben and me's going to hang some Halloween decorations. Holiday's coming."

Halloween. With its affinity for ghosts, Mingus embraced the holiday. All the buildings in town—shops, hotels, and bars were festooned with skulls and cobwebs. There was even a masquerade ball planned in the old Amory building.

I'd had fun as a kid trick-or-treating until neighbors poked fun at my height and said I was too big to be begging for candy. Then, at the after-school dances, the petite girls came as this fairy or that princess. I was the hobo or the Hulk until I finally just quit going. Maybe I could be designated cop for the night and skip the whole thing this year.

Shepherd must have been reading my mind. "I'll take over guard duty if you and Rory want to step out."

I threw him a suspicious look. "What do you know about Rory?"

"Small town, word gets around."

"Well, there's nothing *to* get around. He's a friend, that's all."

Out in the foyer, Ben sniggered.

"And you shut up, too." I stood. "I'll take a drive down by the river to scout out Darbie's neighbors. I should be back in time to deliver you to Miss Fluffy."

Ben laughed again, and I punched his shoulder as I left the station.

CHAPTER EIGHTEEN

Forty-degree temperature swings from night to daylight hours were common on Black Mountain in the fall. By the time the SUV reached the valley floor in Cottonwood, I had shrugged out of my jacket and turned on the air conditioning.

The dirt road to Darbie's trailer paralleled the Verde River and I stopped to walk for a bit along its bank. My shadow scattered the bottom-schooling minnows, and a green heron started from the reed bank as I drew close. Nearby, a golden eagle lifted from one tall sycamore, spiraling higher on the afternoon thermals. Would Darbie be moving from this peaceful spot, now that Cal Nettle was dead? Hard to foresee the twists that life takes.

I got back in the SUV and drove past Darbie's trailer. The first of her neighbors lived in a small cinder-block house, a couple and a young child outside enjoying the sunshine. The guy appeared to be in his early twenties, drug-skinny. He was tearing apart an old dirt bike as I entered the yard, parts scattered in a heap. He wiped greasy hands on ragged denim shorts and strutted over to see me. His face was just out of pimple stage, and the fringe on his upper lip almost made mustache grade. "Yeah?"

"We're checking the area for any strangers."

"Nothin' around here." His job as man of the family done, he strode back to his bike project.

His partner was friendlier. She sat in a worn nylon-webbed chair near the house, untangling orange Halloween lights. Her stringy brown hair escaped from a clip, obscuring heavily mascaraed eyes. On the straggly grass next to her was a toddler just learning to walk.

She gestured me closer. "I'm June and this here's little Mikey." The child tilted his face like a baby bird and she stuffed a piece of biscuit in his mouth.

I lowered myself into a second tattered chair, hoping I wouldn't break out the bottom. "Any unusual activity around here recently?"

"You mean with Darbie? I talk to her sometimes. She walks up and down the road for exercise, on account of the baby coming. Don't know what she saw in Cal Nettle, he's so *old*." She looked approvingly at her man, and he hiked up his pants for her.

"How'd you know it was Cal Nettle?"

"He drove that old '29 Ford pickup. Proud of that truck. Drives it in the parade on Memorial Day. But there was another, this beautiful silver car. Buddy, what was it?"

"2002 Trans Am, last production year." He went back to sorting parts.

"How often did you see the Trans Am?"

"Oh, three or four times over the last several months," June said. "Wasn't that about right, honey?"

He grunted at her.

"But never when Cal was here. First one, then the other, but never together. Always wondered if she had two of them on the string."

"Anyone else?"

"There was this homeless guy. Hoodie pulled down over his head, even on hot days. Small beady eyes. Reminded me of, who was that guy, Buddy?"

"Unabomber."

"Right. I called out to him, friendly like, but he'd never answer me. He'd just stop in front of Darbie's trailer and stare."

"How'd you know he was homeless?"

"He didn't seem to have a car. Would just appear and then vanish, the minute my back was turned. And he smelled. Pee-you."

"Rank? Like a skunk or something?"

She nodded. "I teased Darbie about him. I said if she was dealing drugs to give us some. She got real mad at me, said he was family." June's voice turned cranky. "Darbie said I was being nosy. I wasn't, was I, Buddy?"

"No, babe." He picked up a wrench and ratcheted off another part.

"Who's in the house across the street?" I asked.

"That's Martin Campbell. Comes down here from Canada every year. He's probably home right now. I saw his car pass about an hour ago, groceries in the back. He's nice. Always asks if there's anything he can bring. But Buddy, here, has everything I need." She beamed in his direction and he waggled his hips at her.

I gave her a card, added another for her boyfriend. She tucked them in the pocket of her short-shorts and I left.

When I pulled into the Campbell driveway, the smell of grilling meat drifted from the back yard. My stomach grumbled, reminding me it hadn't been fed recently. Maybe I could stop before I went back to the office—Somewhere there was a burger with my name on it.

I rang the bell and heard a couple of dogs bark. I waited a minute and walked behind the house. Two chocolate labs lay on a brick patio, attentive to their master cooking steaks on a small portable grill. Martin Campbell was in his sixties. Big, with a hefty gut, and sunburned, his face almost matching the color of his bright Hawaiian shirt.

When the dogs spotted me, they rose and he turned around. "Just a minute while I corral these pests." He grabbed their collars with a practiced hand and pushed them into a screened porch. When he returned, he volunteered to pour me a beer, which I declined and then offered me a seat, which I took.

"Saw you over at June and Buddy's place. Figured you'd be coming here next. Those two—babies having babies." He held out a big hand and we shook.

He turned the steaks once more and then collapsed into the lawn chair next to mine. He took a swig of beer and wiped his mouth with the back of his hand. "You here about Cal Nettle?"

Small town. Everybody knew everybody else's business. I wondered if folks talked about me that way in Mingus, a small town just like this one. Of course, they did. A sobering thought.

"What do you know about activities at Darbie's house?"

"You mean having two boyfriends? I don't approve, but I can understand. Cal, he had to be her father's age. But that third guy, he worried me, spying on Darbie like that."

"Spying?"

"Had these Army surplus binoculars. I flushed him out once down by the river, ran him off. I regret I didn't call you folks to nail him proper. He poisoned one of my dogs, after. Like to cost me a fortune in vet bills. Worth it, every penny, love those guys. But if he'd do that to a dog..."

"How'd you know it was him?"

"Day after it happened he was out here again. I accused him of it. He just looked at me with these soulless eyes. I've only seen that expression once before in my life."

"Another man?"

"No, a carcajou, a wolverine, you call them down here in the States." He settled his baseball cap more firmly on his balding head. "You'd never know it by how I look now, but in my younger days, I was a bush pilot up in the Yukon. Found one of those creatures in an abandoned trap up there. Absolutely fearless—one of them can take down a full-grown grizzly bear. Stared up at me with these black eyes, daring me to do something."

He finished his beer. Popped the top on another one and offered it my direction. I shook my head and he took a long drink himself.

"Learned my lesson, keep my dogs in while he's around. But I worry for Darbie."

"You think he might hurt her?"

"Could." He looked reflective. "Wolverine's a solitary creature. But one thing about them..."

"Yeah?"

"They don't allow other males in their territory. I've seen a wolverine tear a trap apart just to kill a rival male. *That's* the kind of man's been stalking Darbie Granger."

"You see him around again, you call me?" I gave him one of my cards.

"You can count on it." He stood, looked into the distance. "Beautiful here, beats that Canada snow all to heck and back. Wish I could stay here forever."

Thin bands of purple clouds intensified a deepening orange sky. Indeed, no prettier place on earth than the Verde Valley—except when murder was involved.

Darbie's trailer appeared vacant when I drove by. It couldn't be easy, being pregnant, living here on her own, now that her protector was dead. I shook my head and focused on more immediate matters: That burger I'd been thinking about all afternoon.

CHAPTER NINETEEN

The department SUV pulled into the drive-through order lane at FastBurger like a horse heading to the feed trough. I passed on the Halloween pumpkin shake in a special ghost cup, although I was tempted. Instead, I ordered a hamburger with all the trimmings to go, onion rings, a Diet Coke on the side.

I parked in the short-term slot beyond the drive-through reserved for drivers-in-a-hurry, like me. One napkin tucked under my chin, a few more wedged under my thigh, and I was ready. My fingers dug an onion ring out of the container as an appetizer. Then I took an enormous bite of the burger, wiping away the juice that spilled down my chin with the side of my hand. The grilled meat, the juicy tomato, and crisp lettuce were a satisfying greasy mouthful. I chased it with a gulp of soda, the liquid searing the back of my throat.

Three bites later I was done. Pure heaven. I tossed the wrappers on the floor and pulled out into the street.

An unwise motorist passed me, moving too fast. I blipped the lights and pulled him over. By the time I'd written a warning and chastised him for exceeding the speed limit, the sun had disappeared behind Black Mountain. I was late—too late—and I was Shepherd's ride home.

When I reached the Mingus station, he was standing at the front door, ready to rumble. He yanked open the SUV door. "Where you been? Smells like an onion factory in here." He balled the fast-food wrappers and tossed them in the back. "Least you could've brought me one," he grumbled.

I shrugged, unrepentant. "Next time."

I drove down the hill to Cottonwood, the SUV swaying through the curves. In front of the Dollar Store groups of teens congregated on the curb. They smoked cigarettes their parents probably didn't know about, telling stories their folks would be horrified to hear. I thought about the two teenage parents who lived on Darbie's road. Had their future lives been determined in a setting like this?

When Shepherd heard of the conversations I'd had with Darbie's neighbors, he decided it was time to have a formal visit with Darbie. While I drove, he called her on his cell to set up a meeting.

At his house, I helped carry in a box of files. Fluffy greeted me with an arched back and a hiss. She'd de-friended me in a matter of days. It had to be those chlorophyll treats.

***

Several days later Darbie Granger came to our office, accompanied by her attorney, Myra Banks. I'd seen Myra in court, and she looked even more formidable up close. Shepherd's mouth twisted as though he'd swallowed a lump of sour persimmon when they walked in. We met in the foyer: Shepherd and me facing Myra and Darbie. A stand-off.

Myra was in her late forties, short permed hair, wearing a spring-green suit that shouted money. Lawyering must be profitable.

She ignored me standing there and zoned in on Shepherd. "Irving Malone, heard they had shipped you up here. How have you been?"

"Fine," Shepherd grunted.

"No lasting effects from the divorce?" She patted his stomach. "Seem to have put on some weight there."

The curiously intimate gesture surprised me. Some back history Shepherd hadn't seen fit to share with me?

Shepherd retreated beyond her reach. "Let's get started. Know you bill by the minute."

"Are you still holding a grudge? Too bad that divorce was so expensive for you. Maybe you needed a better attorney."

Time for a distraction. I offered my hand to her. "Peg Quincy. Nice to meet you."

She appraised me with sharp eyes "I heard what happened at that shooting. Are you off probation yet? If the department is harassing you, call me. I think you've got grounds for a suit." With a practiced motion, she slipped a card out of her suit pocket and into my hand.

If Myra stirred up trouble on my behalf, the resulting bill would keep me in servitude until I retired. No, thanks, I'd handle my own battles, no matter what the price.

I introduced Darbie to my partner. Then we all trooped into our conference room. It wasn't fancy, just a government-surplus meeting table and six battered chairs, but it served the purpose.

Myra chose the head of the table and motioned Darbie to sit beside her on one long side. I sat opposite Darbie, where I could maintain good eye contact. That left Shepherd to deal with Myra down the length of the table.

The lawyer placed her Coach briefcase on the table with care and snapped open the latches. She removed one legal pad and three sharpened pencils. She lined them up precisely on the table, closed the briefcase and set it with her purse on the floor. Every action broadcast that this was a Person to be Reckoned With.

Darbie seemed uneasy, her eyes marred by dark smudges beneath them. The young woman was close to bringing a new life into the world, and yet here we talked about death. If Cal Nettle were looking down from above, what would he think about Darbie's new role as a murder suspect? Too bad we couldn't get his version of what happened. It would make our work a lot simpler.

Myra whispered to her client and then looked down her reading glasses at Shepherd. "Coffee, black. And herbal tea for my client."

We sat in uneasy silence until Ben brought in the mugs and then left, shutting the door behind him.

Myra sipped her coffee, found it to her liking, and lowered the mug. "Proceed," she ordered.

Shepherd set a micro-recorder on the table and clicked it on. "For the record, we are here for an informal interview with Darbie Granger. Also present in the room are Shepherd Malone and Peg Quincy from the sheriff's office and attorney for Miss Granger, Myra Banks. The date is—"

Myra interrupted. "I'd like a copy of the tape when this interview is finished. And I expect that you can have it transcribed for the permanent records."

Shepherd's jaw knotted. "So noted." He finished the opening remarks and began the interview. First, he asked Darbie the basics, establishing her place of domicile, time in the area, and occupation. Then his questioning turned more personal. "Darbie, tell us about your relationship with the deceased, Calhoun Nettle."

"Don't answer that," Myra interjected.

Darbie clamped her lips together, her eyes wide.

Shepherd began again. "Did Calhoun Nettle visit you at your trailer several times over the past several months?"

Myra objected before Darbie could respond.

Shepherd scowled. "Come on, Myra. This isn't a deposition. We're just trying to establish some timelines here."

"Sorry, Shep. Save it for the jury."

Their bickering reminded me of my parents. Enough. I leaned across the table. "Darbie, has Howard Nettle been visiting you, too?"

She looked at me, surprised. "How'd you know that?"

"He was seen driving down your road in his Trans Am."

"That stupid neighbor. I *told* her to mind her own business."

Myra touched Darbie's arm. Darbie shut up.

I sneaked in another question. "Was Howard Nettle your lover, Darbie?"

"How could you think that? I loved *Cal*, not his son!"

"Then why—"

Myra stood up. "This interview is *over*. Darbie, it's time to leave."

Darbie frowned at her attorney. "No, I want to answer her question." She leaned forward to address me directly. "Howard was teaching me how to shoot."

"To shoot?" Shepherd was dubious.

Darbie started to cry, hiccupping loudly. I shoved a box of tissues her direction. She pulled several and blew her nose, a satisfying honk. She pulled a new tissue from the box and patted at her eyes. Then she wadded all the tissues into a defensive wall in front of her.

"I was terrified," she said. "I tried to tell Cal about Otis, but he wouldn't listen to me. So I called Janny and she called Howard. He drove up from Phoenix and brought a revolver for my protection. We went down by the river to plink at tin cans. I got pretty good. Even learned how to clean the darned thing."

"You needed help because Otis was stalking you." I wanted to clarify that fact on the recording.

The tears flowed down Darbie's cheeks. "I'd never forgive myself if anything happened to this baby. It's all I have left of Cal." Her hand rested protectively on her stomach.

She flashed those brilliant green eyes at me. "That Otis Stroud comes near me, I'll blow his head off, so help me I will. There, I said it, and I'm not sorry."

Myra grabbed for the recorder to erase the incriminating threat her client had just made, but Shepherd beat her to it. Holding the recorder away from the attorney's grasp, he spoke into it. "This concludes the interview with Darbie Granger," and clicked it off.

He grinned widely. "I'll make sure you get a copy, Myra."

The attorney stuffed her three pencils and one legal pad back in her briefcase. "We're done here." She stood and Darbie did, too, but not before taking one last slurp of her tea.

Myra exited the building, her nose quivering at some offensive smell. Darbie followed close behind like an obedient duckling. But we had her statement.

Shepherd laughed, the first time I had seen the man in a happy mood since his foot got caught in the bear trap. "That'll be a tale for the next department meeting," he said. "Myra Banks meets her match in Peg Quincy. Good work, getting that suspect to talk."

Ben arrived to clear the cups. "That your new girlfriend, Shepherd? She seems to have taken a shine to you."

Shepherd's laugh choked in mid-chuckle. "I'd tote popsicles to penguins before I'd so much as treat Myra Banks to a glass of stale creek water."

I poked his arm. "Heard those cold-weather birds like the orange kind best. Better stock up."

Shepherd reddened. "Can't be wasting time here. Work to do." He left the room.

Ben and I looked at each other and hooted. The moment broke the tension of the past weeks. It took us back to how it had been before Shepherd Malone arrived, before the murder of Cal Nettle.

I followed Ben into our small kitchen and ran soapy water over the mugs and spoons.

"But that's not all," Ben said, rinsing and stacking silverware in the drainer. "Guess who's paying Darbie's legal fees."

"Well, I know for sure it's not Ruby Mae. Those two ladies do *not* get along." I drained the sink water and dried my hands, still mulling it over. "Janny is broke and Ethan is busy with his dogs..."

"So, that just leaves Howard Nettle." Ben was triumphant about his discovery.

"And you got this information how? You better not be hacking into any computers." Ben had nearly died the last time he did that, meddling in the affairs of town elders.

"No, didn't have to. My new girlfriend works in the attorney's file room, told me all about it."

A new girlfriend. That was welcome news. Ben had been miserable when his old flame, Vanessa Heaton, and her family left town.

But his statement opened up some interesting complications to the case. It seemed that Howard might be stepping into his father's role of Darbie's protector. How long had that been going on? Howard didn't appear to be one for patricide. On the other hand, most murders were committed by someone close to the victim. I drifted into my partner's office to discuss this new development.

Shepherd agreed with my conclusions. "We need to get Mr. Howard Nettle's take on this."

"On it." And this time I meant it. Speed was essential if I were to question Howard before Myra Banks tainted his testimony.

I liked Howard, but could I trust him? Janny had declared Howard was terrified of guns. Now, Darbie claimed Howard was giving her shooting lessons. They didn't seem to be describing the same man.

This Nettle clan could draw a nugget of half-truths into a fine wire that looped around itself until you lost the end of it. Reminded me of some of my relatives back in the hill country. Reminded me of *me*, too, now that I thought about it.

Time to visit Howard, my cousin three times removed, and get his version of the story. The *true* version, whatever that might be. I pulled out my cell phone and dialed his number.

CHAPTER TWENTY

The weather turned colder with a wind kicking up as I drove down the hill to meet with Howard Nettle. He had rented a cabin at Dead Horse Ranch State Park, close to Tavasci Marsh. Maybe he needed some peace and quiet after Pietra and the Nettle family problems.

The one-room log cabins at the park were arranged in a semi-circle, each cabin named for a wild creature. Howard's cabin sign read "Fox," and he sat waiting for me in a retro metal lawn chair out front.

I pulled over a second chair, which rocked on its S-bar supports as I settled into it. "How you doing after the funeral, Howard?"

He rubbed at a furrow between his eyes. "Still have regrets about those last days. I never got to talk to my dad, never got to the bottom of why he asked me to leave in the first place. Now I never will."

Beyond Howard, the open door revealed a small room paneled in knotty pine. Howard's sleeping bag was spread on top of a green vinyl mattress, his belongings scattered across the floor.

"The cabin's primitive," he admitted, noticing my gaze. "I could do without those two a.m. trips to the central bathrooms. But it's cheap."

"Where's Pietra?"

"Drove back to Phoenix. Doesn't like 'the sticks.' That's what she calls the Verde Valley." His mouth turned down. "Probably not news to you that we're having marriage problems."

"Hope things work out." I touched his hand. "Death sometimes brings out the worst in people."

"Especially people like my wife." His expression was sad.

Overhead a tall mesquite scraped branches against the metal cabin roof, and the wind scattered yellow cottonwood leaves onto the pavement in front of us.

"You know that we talked to Darbie," I said.

Howard nodded. "She called me as soon as she got rid of Myra. My hiring of that attorney may not have been such a great idea."

"Expensive, anyway. You got that kind of money?"

Howard raised his palms skyward and we shared a look of recognition. Myra Banks could turn out to be more of a roadblock than a protection.

Some boys played a game of kickball in the cul-de-sac in front of us, screaming and shouting. Howard frowned. "They just moved into the cabin next door. Can hardly hear myself think. Want to take a walk?"

"Sure, why not."

Howard pulled the cabin door closed and set the lock. We hiked down the main camp drive and then turned left on Flycatcher Road. The route climbed a hill and then dead-ended at a small parking lot. There, hundreds of gold and orange butterflies covered a patch of blooming rabbit bush.

"That's like a paradise to me." Howard pointed. "What do you see there?"

"Monarch butterflies?"

"Good eye. Actually, those are a close cousin called Queens. But see the Buckeyes, with those mock eyes on the wings, and over there, a Painted Lady."

Then he pointed to a cluster of butterflies with wings of a brown-and-orange mosaic and identified them as Variegated Fritillaries.

"You a butterfly person?" I asked.

"A lepidopterist? Wanted to be when I was a kid," Howard said, "but my daddy said a real man didn't study bugs, so I took a business major instead. Look where it got me, riding ostriches. I should have stayed with the butterflies." His tone was bitter.

"It's not too late."

"Yeah, I'm free as a bird, now that Daddy's not here." His eyes held a haunted look. "...Except for Pietra and her father."

It appeared that even his father's death brought no sense of freedom to Howard. On the other hand, perhaps he didn't seek it, either. Maybe Howard was one of those people who needed the chains of limitation to feel safe.

We walked toward the far side of Tavasci Marsh with the Tuzigoot Indian Ruins silhouetted on the hilltop opposite. A small plane rose steeply from the Cottonwood airport, its motor whine rising as it banked against the swift winds aloft. If the airport had not been so close, Cal Nettle's body may not have been discovered for a long time.

Perhaps that's what his murderer intended. And yet, here on the other side of the marsh, quiet reigned. Only a kestrel observed us from a cottonwood snag and shrieked as we entered a tamarisk bosque near the marsh.

Howard broke off a stem of desert marigold and twisted it in his fingers. "This was my hangout when I was a kid. Maybe that's why I wanted to stay at the campgrounds. The closest I could get to Tavasci Marsh."

"Bring back memories?"

159

"Lucas and Ethan had this special bond," Howard explained. "They did everything together and didn't want me tagging along. So I'd disappear into this marsh for hours at a time. I found peace here."

But it seemed there was little peace for any of the Nettle family since the father's death. "What's your connection with Darbie Granger?" I asked.

It sounded abrupt, even to my ears, but Howard was still in the past. "We went to high school together. I always had a crush on her. Never had the nerve to ask her out. Wanted to, but hell, I knew with Lucas sweet on her, I didn't have a chance."

I pressed the issue. "And *now* you do?" With his marriage on the rocks, maybe he dreamed of reigniting an old flame. Others had tried that remedy. Sometimes it even worked.

Howard had the grace to look embarrassed but didn't respond, so I pushed to define the present relationship. "Your sister Janny says you're scared of guns, but here you are helping Darbie."

A shadow passed over his face. "A lot has changed since I left home. Janny never understood me. None of them did."

"That might be," I said. At the same time, it seemed that members of this Nettle clan spent a lot of time and energy keeping their thoughts secret. "So how *are* you different now?"

"In a way, my helping Darbie was a pay-it-forward for running away when the still exploded."

"Say more."

"Well, *somebody* had to stick up for her when Daddy refused to keep her safe."

"A somebody like you."

"Yeah, like me." Howard's mouth twisted as he rationalized his present-day actions. "Maybe Daddy didn't want to hear what she said about Otis. That whiskey still was all-important to him. And even now, Otis is the one that keeps it running.

"That still." Howard kicked up a cloud of grasshoppers that spread out in a fan ahead of us as we hiked the trail. "It's killed all of us in a way."

"What do you mean?"

"I'd always been afraid of fire," he explained. "When I looked back from the truck cab and saw that fireball of explosion, all I could think about was that load of pure alcohol sitting right behind me. I bolted out of there, intending to park the truck in a safe zone. But then I just kept going. I've been running ever since."

He paused before a four-wing salt bush, its blooms golden in the fall sunlight, and crushed a few in his fingers. "I've thought about that moment a thousand times, wishing I could change it. I was the coward that caused my own brother's death."

"Nothing you could do at that point," I said, but it seemed he couldn't hear me, intent on fulfilling the family's need for a person they could blame for the tragedy.

We reached the edge of the marsh, and the air turned dank and humid, with standing pools of water on either side of the path. Desert cicadas gave way to crickets. Golden butterflies winked in and out of the sun like tossed coins in the tall marsh reeds. Sulphurs, Howard called them.

The trail reached a dead end, and Howard said, "Used to be an observation platform up ahead, under water now because of the beaver activity. Otis used to blow the beaver dams clear to smithereens with sticks of dynamite, the lodges, too. Then he'd laugh. I'll never forget that laugh of his."

"Did he kill your father, Howard?"

"Otis? Nah, why would he? The old man was his meal ticket with that whiskey still. Easy money."

"Did you?"

That question gave him pause. "In my mind, I wished Daddy gone, a dozen times over. He'd turned mean and bitter when he drank. But he was still my father." He ground his boot heel into the mud. "You find out who did it? I'll pound the first nail in his coffin."

We walked out of the marshland, then, back to the high desert campgrounds. The breeze evaporated the sweat off my arms when we reached the top of the hill. I left Howard at his cabin and drove back to Mingus.

Did he tell me the truth, that he had no part in his father's death? Hard to know with this family. They clung together like scared children. And even after all these years in exile, Howard was part of that tribe.

Secrets can bind a family together as tightly as love can.

CHAPTER TWENTY-ONE

That afternoon at the station, my phone rang.

"This is Billy Gerald," a baritone voice said.

"Who?"

"Reverend Billy. We met at Calhoun Nettle's funeral."

Ah, that was right. Tall, handsome, three kids. Which meant a mixed bag. Sometimes family ties were complicated. I hadn't thought of the man since the burial service so his next words were unexpected.

"I'm wondering if you have a date for the Halloween Night Dance in Mingus. If not, would you go with me?"

I hesitated. I've never had a good experience at formal dances—from junior high on I remember standing by the refreshment table pretending to have a good time, while the cute, *short* cheerleader types danced every dance.

On the other hand, I had sympathy for the man. Reentering the dating game had to be tough after his wife's death. Maybe that's why I ignored the tiny voice in the back of my mind that said this would be a really bad idea.

Maybe this dance would be different.

We scheduled a time for Billy to pick me up. I'd have to scramble for a costume. No hobo or Hulk this time around.

Two minutes later, I had another phone call. "This is Rory Stevens. I was wondering what you're doing Saturday night."

A year with a dearth of male companionship and now two offers in the same hour. I stopped Rory before he went any further. "'Fraid I'm tied up. Reverend Billy asked me to the Halloween Dance here in Mingus."

"And you accepted." Rory made it a statement of fact. "Okay, I should have asked sooner. On to Plan B. If you go, and if I'm there, will you dance with me?"

I liked that. A good loser, not giving up. I said I would and clicked off, thinking it all settled.

Shepherd called me into the conference room to help him hang a white board. He had the markers out, and I wondered if the next step would be a color-coded work schedule. Seemed like overkill with only two of us in the office, three if you counted Ben.

"Hold the board still while I check it with the level." He talked around a mouthful of screws as he adjusted one corner a fraction of an inch, checked again. "Rory call about the dance? Said he was going to."

What, was Shepherd eavesdropping? I explained that Reverend Billy had beaten Rory out by a nose.

Shepherd revved a cordless drill once, twice, then placed a screw precisely in each corner of the white board. "Billy Gerald. Are you sure? I heard that he..."

I interrupted, not wanting Shepherd of all people to second-guess my decision. "You done? Can I stop holding this now?" I released my hold on the white board and stepped back. "I know all about him. Janny Nettle told me. He's widowed, three kids."

"Yeah, right, that must be it," Shepherd said. But his voice sounded troubled, as though there was something more he wanted to say. Instead, he stepped back to inspect his handiwork and then lined up the board markers in a precise line.

"I wanted to talk to you about your meeting with Howard Nettle. What'd you find out?" he asked.

"I think the whole family is covering for each other."

"Could be. What do we know so far?" He wrote the names on the white board as I ticked them off.

"Darbie says Howard's not her lover."

Shepherd wrote Howard and Darbie in black letters, then drew a line between with a diagonal line crossing it. "What else?"

"She says Otis was stalking her, but that Cal wasn't at her house night he died."

A zigzag line between Darbie and Otis signaling a conflicted relationship, another diagonal-crossed one for Cal, indicating her denial of the meeting.

"I think she's telling the truth about Otis," I said. "About her relationship with father and son? I'm not sure."

Shepherd nodded. "Darbie seems to attract the Nettle men, and Howard might not be immune. What's Ruby Mae's part in this?" He wrote her name in red block letters, drew double lines to each of her relatives on the board indicating intense bonds, a zig-zag line to Darbie for a conflicted one.

"Ruby Mae will do whatever's needed to protect her kids. If that meant lying about Darbie's whereabouts, she'd not hesitate," I said.

"Or framing Darbie for something she didn't do. I wouldn't put it past our Ruby Mae, either."

"And that's not all," I said. "I know you like Ethan, but he's right in the middle of this, too. He lost the big brother he idolized. If Cal had something to do with eldest son Lucas's death, Ethan becomes a prime suspect for the murder of their father. And don't forget he got in a fight with his father over the dog's mistreatment."

"I still think Ethan's innocent," Shepherd said. But he added Ethan's name in tan marker, with a cartoon picture of a coonhound next to it.

"Howard, on the other hand, would do anything to get back into the family. He had every right to blame Cal for his exile. If Darbie pressed him hard enough, maybe he'd act." He drew a big circle around Howard's name.

"And then there's Janny, the peacekeeper." I picked up a marker and added her name to the confused tangle of relationships growing on the board.

Shepherd reviewed the artwork. "What's the weakest link?"

I drew a heart next to Janny's name with an "A" in the center of it. "Aurora, but she's mute, not saying anything. At least *she's* not lying."

"You might want to talk to that counselor buddy of yours about her. Been recently?"

Shepherd was a worse nag than HT. "I'm scheduled this week. I'll ask her what she thinks." Smart lady like that should have some ideas. I chunked the marker in the tray.

Shepherd nudged it into line with the others. "Any word on the whereabouts of Otis?"

"None. The BOLO's out. I've put a notice on the Post Office bulletin board and talked to his buddies at the biker bar. Nobody's seen him. He's totally vanished. Maybe gone back to Tennessee?"

"I don't think so," Shepherd said. "Ruby Mae's protected him all these years—her brother is family. And the Verde Valley is home now, not some place back east. Keep turning over rocks. Something will slither out, sooner or later."

I wished I had his patience. I liked this family. After all the tragedy they'd experienced, they at least deserved closure on Cal's murder. "What about those two guys at the wake? I got a partial on the license plate, anyway."

"Go for it. See what you find out." Shepherd wandered back to his office.

I ran the plate and got three possibles for the red Nissan. Two were local to our Verde Valley, but the third was registered to Nigglieri Shipping and Export in

Phoenix. That had to be the Aldo Nigglieri the two men at the funeral had mentioned.

I poked my nose in Shepherd's door. "In the mood for a road trip?"

Shepherd pointed to his leg elevated on a footstool. "Doc doesn't want me sitting in a car too long. But I'll drive you to the motor pool on the way home and you can check out some wheels."

I called the Nigglieri Company and made an appointment for the next morning. A half-hour later Shepherd drove me over to Camp Verde and I checked out an unmarked for the Phoenix drive. I wanted this trip to be low-key, without the official announcement that the Sheriff's department SUV would make. Besides, Shepherd needed the SUV himself. He told me so.

I put his comments about Reverend Billy out of my mind along with Rory's Plan B. Little did I know that both men would return to haunt me on All Hallows Eve.

***

As I traveled the two hours from Mingus to the Valley of the Sun, I dropped four thousand feet in elevation and the temperatures outside rose another thirty degrees. This time of year, the annual rye grass sprouted tiny green shoots on the Phoenix golf courses, and the winter inversion layer of smog hadn't settled in yet. It was the best time of year in Phoenix, the reason why millions of people lived there and millions more visited.

When I stopped for a break at Sunset Rest Stop on I-17 before heading into the city, I shed my winter jacket and rolled up my sleeves. The last time I'd been to Phoenix, I'd been investigating the death of a young drifter and it had been blazing hot. Now, although it was October, the sun was still warm. I lowered a window to enjoy the balmy desert weather as I drove down Black Canyon and from there onto the widening freeways of the metropolitan area.

I checked my watch. Did I have time for a quick stop before I took care of cop business? Usually this time of year an ad hoc Halloween costume store set up shop on the north side of the city.

I was in luck. About five minutes later, I saw a billboard sign of a vampire and a zombie superimposed with the words, "Halloween costumes." I took the next exit and backtracked along the frontage road to the store. Maybe they had something that would fit me.

I realized when I walked in the door that I should have changed into civvies. The young woman behind the counter hastily sprayed some breath freshener in her mouth, and a stock boy jerked upright, staring in my direction.

I tried to set them at ease. "Looking for costumes is all. Anything for someone my size?"

"How tall?" The clerk wore chalk-white makeup and black lipstick. She had a spider-web tattoo streaking down one forearm. Halloween could be a year-long holiday for her.

"Six feet," I said. "No Statue of Liberty costumes, no Hulk."

"Got it. What about a princess? You'd make a great princess."

I shuddered and she took the hint. "Come with me and let's see what we can do."

We walked to the back of the store and she scraped hangers along a factory-pipe clothes rack. She blitzed past the usual—barmaid, pirate queen, Hillary Clinton. Finally, she stopped and reached for shiny blue stretch pants covered with stars. A red sequined T-shirt. Even had the gold cuffs.

"That'll do," I said. "Got a gold star for my hair?"

"In the jewelry counter."

We walked to the front where I picked out something shiny.

Rory Stevens was all raw energy, earthy and sexy. Billy? Formal, spiritual, and *tall*. I was attracted to both and wished that I could combine the best traits of each—meld Rory's lust for adventure with Billy's height and presence. Yes, that would do it—the perfect man.

I smiled with anticipation as I left the store, ready for action on Saturday night. Reverend Billy might have no idea who he was dealing with. But I did.

#

I hit the usual midweek jam entering the outskirts of the Phoenix metropolitan area. Traffic dragged to a standstill at Union Hills on the I-17 and crept along in blocked lanes for twenty minutes until we passed a wrecker clearing off a fender-bender. Then cars speeded up to seventy-five only to slow to thirty again as they reached the Stack interchange. Freeway hydraulics at work.

Railroad tracks used to divide towns into residential and business districts. Now freeways served the same purpose. Beyond the Buckeye curve on the south I-10, the freeway passed through a collection of industrial parks. If a person was looking for a pallet of Kraft boxes, a supplier of specialty hardwoods, or a wholesale outlet for patio furniture, they could find it on the South Side.

The Nigglieri firm listed an address off Broadway. I signaled for the exit lane there and drove farther south into the industrial area. South Mountain with its forest of electronic communication towers formed a distant jagged horizon as I reached my final destination.

When I pulled into the parking lot for the Nigglieri Export Company, a reserved spot for Aldo Nigglieri, Company President, marked the front entrance. And situated right across the street was Big Al's Used Car Lot, home of the famous ostrich. There was even a plywood cut-out of the giant bird propped at the entrance. The lot was empty of customers—maybe the ostrich was on vacation.

No wonder Howard felt obliged to return and mollify his wife and his father-in-law. Happy my last name wasn't Nettle. Glad I didn't have to work for somebody named Big Al.

The reception area was furnished in cheap carpet, fake wood paneling, and no-nonsense metal desks. Two security cameras focused on the counter and the front door. A red light on each indicated it was connected to electricity.

I didn't make any assumptions about something actually happening behind the lenses. Companies often put up dummy mounts as a deterrent to crime. But part of me wondered exactly what it was that they exported or imported. Security cameras usually protected valuables, not a cheaply furnished office like this one.

Giving my name to the receptionist, I sat down to wait for Aldo Nigglieri. When he strode through the half-door to the side of the counter, I stood.

"Morning, officer. What can we do for you?"

Aldo Nigglieri was stocky, with a square face and thinning gray hair, maybe early sixties. His white long-sleeved shirt was rolled to the elbows exposing black forearm hair a gorilla could take pride in. Aldo's bone-shaking grip crushed my fingers.

He reopened the half-door behind the receptionist and escorted me into his inner sanctum. There, he waved me to a chair and sat down behind another metal desk, not much larger than the receptionist's.

Nigglieri puffed on a thick black cigar and blew acrid smoke my direction. "You don't mind if I smoke."

It wasn't a question. The man was just checking to see if intimidation worked. It didn't.

I showed him my badge. "Deputy Peg Quincy, from Mingus, up north. What sort of business do you do here, Mr. Nigglieri?"

"A little of this, a little of that." His voice was deep and gravelly.

"You own the car lot across the street?"

"I do. You in the market for a used car?" He took another puff and set the cigar down in an expensive cut-glass ashtray at odds with the cheap furnishings of the office.

His dark eyes were still. Something stirred behind the mask of civility, intelligent, yet implacable. Something I wouldn't want to encounter late at night on a deserted street.

"Who's your manager over there?" I pointed at the lot across the street.

"Howard Nettle. Up in your neck of the woods right now." He waited and his quiet stare said, but you know that.

I let the silence intermingle with the cigar smoke for a moment.

He broke the stalemate. "I'm a busy man. What can I do for you this morning, Peg Quincy? Is that Miss or Mrs.?"

I ignored the implied question. "Make that Officer Quincy. Who else works for you?"

"From the Verde Valley?" He lifted a hand and counted off on stubby fingers. "Otis Stroud. Ethan Nettle once in a while. Probably a few others that I can't remember. Used to deal with Cal Nettle. Understand he's not around anymore."

"Two of your men were at the funeral."

He nodded. "Wanted to be sure Nettle was actually dead. Slippery bastard."

"You don't sound sad that he's gone."

"Should I? Man didn't meet his obligations. Now his family owes." He lifted the cigar, rotated it between his fingers examining it.

"Owes what?"

"That's between them and me. Not a police matter."

171

"Is, if it breaks the law."

He made a sweeping gesture with his hands. "Look around you. I'm an honest business man, trying to earn a living. Don't need any police harassment, especially from out-of-town cops." He tilted his weight in the chair and it squealed in protest. "Got a warrant?"

"I can get one."

"Not without probable, and you got bupkis on me. Look Officer..." He leaned toward me and stared at my chest, ostensibly reading my name tag. "...Quincy, my advice is to drive back to that little town of yours. And when you get there, tell my good-for-nothing son-in-law Howard Nettle to get his skinny ass back here where it belongs. My Pietra, crying her eyes out."

He stood and held out his hand. I didn't take it.

"Next time, call first," he said, dropping his arm. "Need a guard dog for this place. Keep out the riff-raff."

"We'll be in touch." I didn't bother to leave a card. I knew he knew where to find me. He knew I knew.

I wrote down the license numbers of the cars in the parking lot, just to have the final say. Nigglieri watched out his office window and gave me a salute when I looked up.

I got back in the unmarked and headed to the freeway. I rolled down all the windows, trying to rid my uniform of the stench of Nigglieri's cigar. I'd just met my first mob boss, and his dead eyes scared the hell out of me.

Whatever Cal Nettle had been meddling in wasn't finished.

CHAPTER TWENTY-TWO

Mingus had been making Halloween preparations for weeks. The store windows held enough dangling skeletons to double the town's population. Isabel had been out to the town cemetery cleaning the graves in anticipation of the Day of the Dead Festival on November first. Many of the Hispanic miners had been part of her extended family.

But the images of death also held a somber message for me. Sometimes when I walked the streets, I sensed the presence of unquiet spirits in the miles of abandoned mining tunnels honeycombing the mountain beneath my feet. Too many explosions and cave-ins occurred down there, bodies never recovered.

I had my own unquiet ghost, the man I had killed. Most of the time the memory of that shooting lurked below the surface, but the Halloween symbols brought his death to the forefront again. I wondered if that haunting image would ever leave me. I'd have to ask the shrink.

The morning of Halloween dawned angry, with the horizon clouds tinged with red. The weather bureau predicted sleety rain and possible snow by midnight. Our little town was located in a hollow of the mountain that collected fog—Sometimes we got socked in so bad you couldn't see across the street. The goblins and ghosts, both young and ancient, would be happy tonight.

That afternoon in the station our phones were silent, perhaps in anticipation of the chaos we'd be chasing later.

Even the javelinas, our "wild pigs," would join the ruckus, gobbling down the pumpkins that teenagers smashed to the ground. This evening also held the Halloween Dance— would Wonder Woman be ready?

Shepherd, bundled in a heavy parka with his cane leaned against his folding chair, sat outside the station door with a huge bowl of candy, greeting the early trick-or-treaters. I wandered out to snag some chocolate.

"Here, take a piece of licorice." He offered one.

"I hate licorice." He just wanted to get rid of the stuff— the kids hated it, too. Brushing his hand aside, I dug down for some Hershey's miniatures.

I had a system for Halloween candy. Always buy what I wanted to eat. That way, if the kids were scarce that year, I had a feast.

When I was a kid, the best candy appeared on rainy nights when folks felt sorry for me. Most of the good stuff didn't make it home, and in the morning I had a huge chocolate hangover. Nevertheless, I hoped the storm would hold off until the little kids made their rounds. They didn't need to feel the cold like I had.

Janny and Aurora stopped by to show off the little girl's costume. She was dressed as an angel, with a fuzzy halo and gauzy wings that bounced as she skipped up the sidewalk toward us. Halting in front of Shepherd's large frame, she carefully picked a red lollipop from his offerings.

"Momma's keeping her tonight," Janny said, "so I can go to the dance." She unwrapped a Tootsie-roll and popped it in her mouth. "You be there?" she asked Shepherd.

"Wouldn't miss it," he said, sneaking another lollipop in Aurora's trick-or-treat pillowcase. "Even Peg is coming. She's got a date with the Reverend Billy."

Janny looked at me and her eyebrow lifted. Then her attention flew to Aurora, several stores up the hill. "See you then," Janny said, giving me a wave as she rushed to catch up with her little girl at the next shop. The kid was going to make a haul. Good thing she had a big bag to hold her loot.

I spent the rest of the afternoon on foot patrol, weaving in and out of the trick-or-treaters on Main Street. I kept a sharp eye for Otis Stroud. That man needed to be sent away for a long, long time.

***

The dance started at eight, and I was still fussing with my hair when I heard a knock at the door. Thinking it might be late trick-or-treaters, I put on the star tiara and pounded down the stairs in my stocking feet. I opened the door to see Reverend Billy, dressed in a formal suit. He held a corsage box in one hand and balanced nervously, one foot in front of the other.

Super Woman stared at Mr. Traditional. "It's a *costume* dance," I pointed out.

"I don't believe in masquerading as something I'm not," he said firmly. He shoved the corsage box my direction.

Good thing I hadn't chosen to go as a witch. I considered changing to street clothes and then decided against it. This was Halloween and even cops deserved a little down time. "Wait a minute while I get my shoes," I said.

I grabbed the box and pounded up the stairs in my blue star-spangled tights. When I opened the box and spotted the orchid, my heart sunk. Wonder Woman, with a wrist-strap corsage.

Then I laughed. I slipped it on my arm, squeezed toes into the highest stiletto heels in my closet and tottered downstairs. Reverend Billy could join in the fun of it, or not. Either way, I planned to let my hair down tonight.

\#

When we arrived at the Armory Hall, Shepherd sat at the door collecting tickets. He still wore his cop uniform. Smart move. Get overtime pay that way. He took Billy's money and stamped both our hands with a purple pumpkin. He paused at the sight of my orchid and looked up at me.

Wonder Woman shrugged back.

The hall had black-and-orange crepe paper streamers running from each corner to a glittery dance ball hanging from the middle of the ceiling. Chairs lined the sides of the hall and apples floated in a barrel of water.

The band warmed up on the front podium, two fiddles, and a bass. A classical guitar leaned against one wall, and a drum kit fanned out along the back of the stage—high hat, cymbals, and snares. The set included a nice bass drum.

I'd always wanted to be a drummer. But my mother wouldn't hear of it—instead, I got piano lessons until my teacher fired me—told my mother not to waste her money. But I could still learn the drums, maybe, someday. Bet the Mingus ghosts wouldn't mind.

Janny, dressed in a peasant wench costume, touched my star tiara. "Cool outfit. Why aren't you in disguise, Billy?"

He stared down at her cleavage. "Too late to get one," he murmured. That should have been my first warning. Never trust a man who looks—especially one who lies, too.

Something furry banged against my knee and I glanced down to see Ben's dog, Bitzer. He had a red-blinking LED light tied to his wagging tail and silver-epaulets on his shoulders. Ah, disguised as the video game's General Pepper.

Ben grabbed the leash. "Hi Peg." An early-twenties brunette with long straight hair joined him, and he put a companionable arm around her shoulder. His friend from the attorney's office?

"This is my date, Ashley." Ben was dressed in a square box labeled "Bar of Soap" and Ashley was a mirage of pink tulle with a rope around one bare shoulder, a shower pouf.

Next to arrive was a figure dressed in black, with glowing red horns on his head. Reverend Billy stroked his throat and grimaced as Rory Stevens headed our direction. I wondered whether Rory had chosen the costume on purpose, just to needle my date.

The Imp stopped in front of me and his eyes sparkled. "Nice corsage. How's the weather up there?"

I jammed his instep with my spike heel. Had to give it to him, he didn't even wince. Must be that SEALs training.

Rory turned to my date. "Reverend Billy. Nice to see you here. You the chaperone?"

Before Billy could respond, Rory spun into motion again. "Catch you later for that dance you promised me." He gave Ben a high-five slap, then crossed the floor to visit with HT.

The band started with a slow one, a waltz, and Billy led me out onto the floor. His moves were stiff. Probably the man hadn't been dancing since he'd courted his wife. But he gave it a good try, shuffling me around the floor with a one-two-three box step.

Darbie Granger and Howard Nettle passed us, an elegant couple in medieval velvet. Then the room swirled in a kaleidoscope of colors as others took the floor. The ball overhead glittered and twinkled.

The next two dances were fast ones. We sat on the sidelines, Billy becoming more and more restless. Finally, he muttered, "Going for some punch," and disappeared.

A burly lumberjack with a three-day beard and a rubber ax invited me to dance. I joined him on the floor for some free-form moves that passed for an oldies rock and roll number. Out of breath, I returned to my chair and scanned the hall for my date, Billy. He was over at the punch table with his arm around a can-can dancer in a ruffled red skirt. When he bent close to whisper something, she tilted her head and laughed.

What was Billy pulling here? He was *my* date. A flush of irritation began at my throat and spread to my cheeks. I rose.

HT dropped into the chair next to me and pulled me back down. He pointed the opposite direction. "You're in for a treat. Watch this," he said as the floor cleared.

Ethan Nettle climbed up on the stage, costumed in a red velvet shirt, with a Zorro mask and a flat black hat. He picked up the guitar and sat in a chair, tuning it softly until satisfied. Then sat there waiting. The crowd stilled.

To the side of the room, Isabel appeared in glamorous black, wearing an elegant ivory comb and lace mantilla. She walked purposefully to the center of the room and struck a pose with hands arced over her head. Then she clapped three times, with authority, and began a passionate flamenco, keeping perfect time to Ethan's guitar.

Circular wrist movements lent strength to her graceful hands as Isabel struck the dramatic poses. Her back arched as she lifted through rapid heel work, tapping out the rhythm. The flamenco dance became a shared experience, sucking the very air out of the room with its energy.

Finally, Isabel halted, motionless in the same beginning pose, alone in the center of the dance floor. The audience breathed out a collective sigh of release and then exploded into thunderous applause.

An orange baseball-capped man stood at the side, watching Ethan play. Otis Stroud! His slouch straightened as the man caught my gaze and he bolted out an emergency exit door. Jerking into cop mode, I dashed after him.

But within a block, my ankle turned, betrayed by my high heels. I grabbed at a trash can for support, but it crashed to the street, dumping me on the cracked sidewalk. I slapped the wet cement in frustration as Otis vanished into the fog as easily as a miner's ghost.

Reluctantly, I abandoned the chase and limped back to the hall. Reverend Billy leaned against the far wall, in attendance to a Maid Marion. Enough was enough. Time to call him out. I stalked in his direction, brushing fog-damp hair out of my eyes.

But fate intervened in the form of a tall, skinny woman in her late thirties who appeared in the doorway. "Where is he? I know he's here!"

The room hushed with anticipation. The band, sensing something wrong, stopped playing with an awkward fiddle squawk.

Spotting me and Billy, the woman strode over with a purposeful step. She reached up and slapped my face. "You home wrecker."

Then she turned to Billy. "They told me you'd be here, you lying minister of God. I'm on my sick bed, close to death and you're out consorting with sinners." She glared at me.

Billy spread his hands in supplication. "Please, Agnes. It's not what it looks like."

"You better believe it's not. Here, I don't want this anymore, you—you—devil's spawn." She extended a shaking hand in front of her, yanking and pulling at her ring finger. "Our engagement is *over*."

A sparkle arced in the air as she threw her ring to the floor. She turned on her heel and stamped out the door. Billy shot a look of indecision in my direction. Then he snatched up the ring and dashed after her.

The dance ball gyrated slowly over my head, its promise of enchantment shattered. People murmured to each other, heads close, and someone half-pointed at me, alone in the middle of the hall. A ripple of laughter spread through the crowd.

All of a sudden, I was back at a Jr. High dance, crushed by the smirks of popular girls. My cheeks burned, and I started to shake. If only they'd stop *looking* at me—I yearned for a bag to shove over my head so I could disappear.

There was a hand on my shoulder and I flinched.

"Time for that dance you promised me." It was Rory Stevens.

"No...Don't want to...Tired." I stumbled over excuses.

He took my hand in a firm grip. "Breathe."

I took in a shuddering breath.

"Now take off your shoes."

"What?"

"Work with me here, Peg. We're going to do a fantastic West Coast Swing. You need good footing."

I slipped out of the high heels and handed them to Janny, standing nearby. Then I followed Rory onto the floor. The band took the cue and swung into a loud rendition of "My Give-a-Damn is Busted."

We anchored and whipped. Then we pushed-and-pulled in a slot that got longer and more extravagant. Rory did a right side pass and I followed with a swivel.

I got this crazy grin on my face—Wonder Woman was back! The crowd parted to give us room and shouted approval when the song ended.

Rory stayed by my side the rest of the evening, a courtier in black with red glowing horns. Shepherd brought me a cup of punch and stayed to talk a while. Ben pulled me out on the floor for a spirited salsa. Even HT and Isabel came over to give me a hug. Family surrounded me, at a time when I needed them the most.

When the Halloween Dance was over, I walked to the door with Rory, my heels in one hand. The night was bitter and the wind howled. Billy had never returned and it would be a cold, slippery walk home.

"Give you a lift?" Rory asked.

I thought of his small sports car and the agony of trying to fit in, once more, where I didn't belong. I started to say no.

"Plan B," he said. "Borrowed my roommate's Hummer."

So I rode home with plenty of legroom on All Hallow's Eve, accompanied a guy who understood me. I didn't slip once. Not even when he followed me into the studio apartment and stayed for a while.

For once, my ghost gave me a holiday.

Chapter twenty-three

I took the rest of the weekend off and walked up to HT's house for Sunday dinner. I asked Isabel if I could help, but she just laughed. Must have known my disaster-prone proclivities in the kitchen.

HT shared the paper with me in the living room while we waited for her to finish. He got the sports page; I propped my feet on the coffee table and read the funny papers. They made more sense, sometimes, than the front sections did.

We assembled at the table, and after grace, Isabel passed a soup tureen filled with lamb stew fragrant with bay and cinnamon. Dinner rolls, so warm that the butter melted and ran off onto the plate. I took a bite, flaky and sweet.

"Saw Howard with Darbie at the dance," HT commented, passing homemade cherry jam. "Making free since his wife has gone back to Phoenix."

"That Pietra's a witch," Isabel hissed.

"A witch? Are you sure?" I asked.

"I can tell. Evil woman, not good at a funeral." Isabel was definite in her judgment.

I had to agree. "Did you see Otis at the dance?"

HT nodded. "Yeah, saw him there watching Ethan play. Surprised Shepherd didn't arrest him. Or that you didn't. Seems to me that you work at that sheriff's department, too?"

His voice was teasing, and I swatted at his arm with my hand. "Believe me, I tried." I rubbed my ankle, sore from the tumble I'd taken.

"Not surprising he escaped, though," HT allowed. "Man's had a lot of practice slipping and sliding in that bootlegging business."

That brought up bad memories for me. "Would he kill Cal Nettle?" I asked. It was always the question at the back of my mind.

"Otis has a dark side. Always on the outskirts of the family, never quite fit in, even if he was a brother to Ruby Mae."

Isabel brought a sweet potato pie from the kitchen and cut slices for us. "That Billy preacher. Making a scene like that. You deserve better, Pegasus." Her soft accent gave my name a melodic lilt.

Before I could respond, Ben entered. "Sorry I'm late. Leave some pie for me?" His teenage energy filled the room, and the moment passed.

After dinner, I sat with them on the front porch for a bit and then went for a hill climb up Black Mountain. Exercise was my answer to stress. Someday I'd be able to laugh about what happened at the dance, but not yet.

***

I'd planned to arrive at the office early Monday morning, but when I climbed out of bed, the temperature in my studio apartment hovered south of forty degrees, cold even for November in Mingus. I put in a call for a heating repair service, but by the time the furnace guy arrived, the morning was half over.

He delivered the bad news that the thermocouple had arced. Had to order a new one, be a couple of days, he said. I shivered. The weather bureau was predicting temperatures in the teens that night.

When I finally arrived at work, I stood for a moment under the ceiling vent, soaking up the warm air. Good to be in a place where the heater worked. I thought I'd get some nasty comments from early-bird Shepherd for my lateness, but his door was closed.

Ben was dithery with excitement. He put one hand over his heart. "I'm in love, I'm almost positive. Now I know what Bill Gates felt when he met Melinda. Pure bliss."

"Ashley?" I remembered his date in pink tulle at the dance.

Ben waved his hand in dismissal. "Adolescent infatuation, a flash in the night. This is the real deal, the love of my life, sitting right in there." He pointed to Shepherd's office.

I dropped my coat on a chair and knocked on Shepherd's door. I couldn't wait to see this perfect woman.

"Enter," Shepherd said.

The young woman held out a confident hand. "Hello, I'm Sheryl Malone, Shepherd's daughter."

Bare traces remained of the little girl in the photo at Shepherd's house. This grown-up Sheryl wore a micro black leather skirt with knee high boots and fishnet stockings. Her salmon-colored T-shirt had been slashed in strategic places, and she wore enough metal-filled piercings to trigger airport security devices. She topped it off with spiky, lavender-tipped hair.

Shepherd stirred uneasily in his chair. "Sheryl just arrived. She's going to spend some time. Her mother and she..."

"My *mother* is a bitch and I knew I'd be much happier living here with my dad." She turned to smile at him.

"How long are you staying?" I asked.

"As long as I want to."

My partner would have fun with this girl-child.

"Sheryl, would you go out into the waiting area for a moment while I talk to Peg? Police business."

She grabbed her backpack and sashayed out to bedazzle Ben. Shepherd closed the door behind her and slumped in his chair. "I haven't talked to her mother in years, and Sheryl shows up half an hour ago in this rattle-trap Volkswagen. Said she hadn't slept since the day before yesterday. Made it here on uppers, she says." He rubbed an agitated hand across his face. "What am I going to do?"

I suppressed a smile. "Go learn how to be a dad again. Ben and I will take care of things here."

My partner shifted to disaster-planning mode. "I'll leave the SUV with you—Put out another Be-On-The-Lookout for Otis—Work the angle with little Aurora—Talk to Ruby Mae again but don't lean too hard—Don't touch that mess down in Phoenix with the Nigglieri bunch until I get back—And what about that appointment with your counselor?" He paused for breath.

"We'll be fine."

"And check in every hour. Text me."

"We'll be fine."

Shepherd went to retrieve his daughter. When they departed, Ben's dazed expression focused on the closing door.

Time to reassert my own control. First I switched off my cell phone. I'd report to Shepherd when I had something to say, not before. Then I poured a leisurely cup of coffee and sauntered back into my office. I sat down and propped my feet up on my desk.

"Print me up another desk sign," I called out to my assistant. Pegasus Quincy, Super Cop, was at the helm once more.

Only after I finished my coffee, did I write down Shepherd's new to-do list before I forgot it. Then I got to work.

The sheriff's office in Camp Verde said they'd issue another Be-On-The-Lookout for Otis Stroud. I knew the chances of locating him were slim. He'd evaded the first

BOLO and probably would this one as well. The guy slid in and out of view like a snapping turtle in dank marsh water.

Next, I called Dr. Westcott. She agreed to let Janny and Aurora take my appointment that afternoon. If the mother approved, the counselor said I could sit in. Another one of Shepherd's to-do's crossed off.

I'd been dreading the upcoming visit to see the counselor, but now I had something new to report. Rather than rehashing all the stuff I'd talked about last week, I could focus on Aurora's problem. The way I saw it, that showed I had compassion and concern for my fellow humans, an obvious sign of a well-balanced and responsible adult, a person capable of handling a weapon once more. Besides, I liked the little kid and maybe this could help her, too.

Janny was excited about the appointment and assured me I could attend. "Since Aurora likes you, it's fine by me. Never been to a shrink before. Not going to cost us anything, is it?"

"Not a red cent," I assured her. The sheriff's department could pay the counseling charges. Be worth it if we could get some good info out of it. "You might bring Aurora's stuffed rabbit," I suggested, "Help her feel safe."

CHAPTER TWENTY-FOUR

At two that afternoon, the doctor welcomed us into her office. She crouched with a graceful gesture in front of Aurora. "What a lovely rabbit. May I pet its ears?"

Aurora nodded, and the doctor's small brown hand stroked the fur. She seated me at the corner of the room to observe and then introduced Aurora to a dollhouse where she could play while therapist and parent conferred. Dr. Westcott had Janny sign the necessary permission forms, and Janny gave her the background about the explosion at the whiskey still.

The therapist sat for a moment, digesting the information. "It sounds like what your little girl may have is selective mutism. It is a condition that sometimes occurs in cases of childhood trauma as extreme as what you describe."

"Does that mean she won't ever talk again?" Janny asked.

"By the time a child reaches teenage years, they can remember very little that happened before age three, and memories of any trauma happening in those early years would be difficult to retrieve. But she's young enough now that we may have a chance to heal the emotional injury while she still remembers parts of it." Dr. Westcott smiled at Janny in a reassuring manner.

It seemed like a tall order, but I trusted the therapist. She'd done okay by me, and I sensed she'd be able to connect with Aurora.

The doctor told Janny that she'd need to establish some mental anchors so that Aurora could feel safe during the session. "Can you think of a time before the accident when Aurora was happy and talking?"

"She loved to sit in the rocker with her Grandma Ruby Mae."

"A great image," Dr. Westcott said. "We can use that one. Now we need to bookend the trauma with a safe experience on the other end. Can you give me an example of a time *after* the accident when Aurora felt safe?"

"I always sing 'Over the Rainbow' to her and tuck her bunny under her arm before I turn out the lights," Janny said.

"Wonderful. Does she have a special name for the rabbit?"

"She calls it Sunny."

"Sunny it is. What we're going to do is put Aurora in a trance."

"Does that mean you are going to hypnotize her?" Janny asked.

"In a way, yes, using guided imagery. Children love to use their imaginations. We'll sandwich the trauma between these safe memories you've given me, and possibly get her to remember what happened during the explosion. Then we'll plant some healing images before we bring her back to the present."

Dr. Westcott pulled a small rocking chair opposite her own chair. "Aurora, bring Sunny and come sit here close to me."

The little girl glanced at her mother, got a nod of reassurance, and sat across from the doctor in the little rocking chair.

"Now, hold onto Sunny and just relax a little. Wiggle your arms and legs like me." The doctor wiggled her fingers and Aurora copied her, giggling a little. Then the therapist induced the trance. Aurora's eyelids drooped and at last closed. Her grip on the rabbit softened. She put her thumb in her mouth and rocked the chair back and forth.

The counselor's voice got softer and more distant. "Aurora, we're going for a journey. You'll be very safe. You have Sunny along and your mother is in the room. Are you ready?"

The little girl nodded her head without opening her eyes, clutching the stuffed rabbit, and stroking its ear.

"First, imagine a big tree with leaves the size of dinner plates. Can you see that?"

Head nod.

"Now this tree has a hole in the trunk and you are able to climb inside the tree, very quietly. Go ahead and do that now." She paused for a moment. "Are you inside?"

Aurora nodded, shifting a little in her seat as she followed the counselor's direction.

"Inside the tree you discover a set of stairs going down, down, down into the ground. You descend the stairs and they open onto a meadow filled with flowers..."

She quieted to allow the little girl to make the imaginary journey. "In the meadow you see your Granny sitting in a rocker. She invites you and Sunny to rock with her. Feel the chair, rocking back and forth, back and forth..."

Aurora's feet pushed her own tiny rocker in cadence with the counselor's words.

"In front of the rocking chair is a TV screen. You're going to watch a show about something that happened a very long time ago. You can make the picture change, anytime you want to, by just pushing a button. Are you ready, Aurora?"

Again the little girl nodded, leaning forward in the rocker, her eyes still closed.

"The movie is starting, at the distillery before the bad fire. You were there with Ethan and Lucas. Tell us what you see."

The whisper was hoarse but recognizable from a voice unused for years. "Mommy goes to find Grampa. I stay, be quiet, not get in trouble."

She squirmed in the remembering, and Janny reached to touch her daughter. The doctor intercepted her hand, put a finger to her lips to silence her so that the child would not be pulled out of the trance.

"I didn't get into trouble, mommy, I didn't!" Her voice rose in an anguished shriek.

"Turn the dimmer on the movie, Aurora," the counselor instructed. "Is it getting smaller? It's only a picture, it can't hurt you now."

Aurora made a twisting motion with her hand and then pointed. "Otis!"

"What's he doing?"

"Bad. Turned wheels when Lucas gone. I try fix, but Lucas mad. No, no!"

The little girl's head jerked from side to side and her arms gripped the chair as she remembered the fire and the explosion. "Lucas, where are you?" She cried out, as if in pain.

The doctor intervened. "Aurora, push the button now! Turn off the show."

Aurora clicked her finger down sharply and gave a huge sigh.

"The fire is gone, all gone," Dr. Westcott said in a soothing voice. Aurora's breathing slowed as she rocked in the chair.

"Now, I want you to imagine you are ready for sleep and your mother is right here next to you. Nothing can hurt you. You are safe in bed with Sunny Bunny beside you."

The doctor picked up the stuffed toy where Aurora had dropped it and tucked it in under the little girl's arm. Aurora stroked it and lay her head down on its fur, the tension in her own body releasing.

Dr. Westcott then reversed the original trance story, bringing Aurora up the stairs in the magic tree and out into the imaginary sunlight once more.

"You'll wake up feeling strong and happy, Aurora," she said. "You can talk, whenever you choose to. You can draw pictures about the accident, anytime you want to. Do you understand that?"

Eyes still closed, Aurora nodded.

Then the therapist's voice got louder and more distinct. "I'm going to count backward, from five to one, and as I get closer to one you will start to hear the sounds around you, here in the room. Five... four...three...we're almost back home safe with your mother, Aurora. Two...one. I want you to wiggle your toes and fingers and, when you are ready, open your eyes."

Aurora wiggled her fingers and toes as instructed, and then opened her eyes and looked for Janny. She reached for her mother. "Mommy," she said, in a croaky voice.

Janny's eyes filled with tears as she pulled Aurora close. "Baby girl," she said. "You did just fine."

Dr. Westcott cautioned that the ability to speak would return in fits and starts, but that Aurora had made a good beginning. She asked Janny to give her a call about scheduling another appointment after she'd seen Aurora's progress over the next week.

Then, the counselor looked at me, as if to say, you're next. I nodded, indicating I'd call her to reschedule.

Janny wiped tears from her eyes as we walked into the sunlight outside the office. "Thank you, Peg. You helped this happen." She gave me a big hug before she left for the Nettle home with Aurora sitting close beside her in the old blue car.

I was shaken by the suddenness of progress in the counselor's office and yet encouraged. Perhaps Aurora's recovery would unlock some secrets this family had held close all these years. Her release from trauma might allow her to identify who in the family hated Cal Nettle enough to kill him. I brushed aside the problem of payment for the counselor's session—Shepherd could deal with that, he was the senior partner.

I stood on the sidewalk watching Janny's old car disappear down the road and Dr. Westcott's door opened once more.

"Oh, I hoped I could catch her. The little girl left this." Dr. Westcott held the soft yellow rabbit in her hands.

I reached for it. "I'll return it. Thanks for all you did in there."

"It's not me, it is the healing universe. Something that you could use a little of yourself, Peg."

The softness I'd felt toward the woman vanished. The *universe* had nothing to do with it. I didn't need healing. All I needed was my weapon back and I'd be just fine.

CHAPTER TWENTY-FIVE

When Shepherd walked through the station door the next morning, a cloud of fumes followed him. Sheryl's old Volkswagen huffed away in the distance.

"How's the reunion with Sheryl working out?" I asked.

"She stayed up until three a.m. playing video games with some guy online. Woke me up with her chatter. When I put my foot down and told her to go to bed, she asked for black coffee, strong." Shepherd's expression was glum. "Didn't have any in the house, knows I drink green tea. So she left to find a Starbucks."

I glanced over at Ben, who smiled like a cat who's found the mother lode of cream.

"Come into my office and fill me in on what's been happening here," Shepherd said.

I topped off my cup with Jamaica Blue Mountain coffee and walked into his office. Before I sat down, I slammed the door to forestall Ben's finely tuned ear—he didn't need any more ammunition in his quest to romance Sheryl Malone.

"I don't know what to do with her," Shepherd grumbled.

"Considered the New Directions Ranch? Get her involved with the horses out there. They can always use volunteers." Regina Smith ran a remediation clinic for troubled teens using Equine Assisted Therapy. Maybe a half-ton horse could temper the rebellious Sheryl.

"Good idea. Maybe Ben could show her around the valley a little—Sheryl and I seem to be getting on each other's nerves."

Or perhaps father and daughter were too much alike. I switched to business and told him about the events at the counselor's office.

"Glad to hear that little girl is on the mend. I've worried about her in these years since the accident. The son, Lucas, knew the risks, but Aurora was only three or so when it happened. Just a baby."

I wondered what Sheryl was like at that age. It was difficult to picture the teen-vamp that so captivated Ben as an innocent toddler.

"Thought I'd drop out to the Nettle place this morning and return Aurora's rabbit," I said. "Maybe catch Janny before she leaves for work."

"Good idea. Then you can go out and write a few tickets this afternoon." Shepherd pushed his cane out of the way, opened his desk drawer and pulled out his crossword puzzle book.

If I wrote any more traffic tickets, the Chamber of Commerce would tar and feather me. They said ticket writing was bad for business. Perhaps they were right. Didn't like them myself.

***

A cold breeze chilled the SUV's interior on the way down the hill to the Nettle house, and I rolled the window back up. It might reach high sixties by afternoon, with just a brush of wind to clear the air from the forest service burns.

Wildfires had cut a huge hole in the center of the state several years ago. Now we had to contend with fires intentionally lit by range management crews on days when the conditions were right. After a few of these fires had gotten away from the Forest Service when the wind kicked up, they stopped calling them "controlled" burns. Now the correct term was "proscribed" burns. Either way, the fires filled our normally blue skies with smoke. The price we paid for living in the juniper-pine forests.

When I pulled into the Nettle yard, the coonhounds set up a howl from the kennels in back. Ruby Mae met me at the top of the porch stairs, purse tucked under her arm.

"You go talk to Janny. I've got business, *important* business with the Reverend Billy." She marched with a determined step to her old blue Chevy, gunned the engine, and disappeared in a billowing cloud of dust. I walked over to the trailer and knocked on the door.

Janny opened it with a hair dryer in her hand. "Just getting ready for work," she said. "Come in."

I handed her the rabbit.

"Thanks! I about didn't get Aurora to sleep last night without that stuffed rodent."

The trailer she was sharing with Ethan was tiny but neat. Even so, quarters must be tight with three of them living there. I wondered when Janny would be moving out. She seemed pretty independent, not ready to go back to living under her mother's thumb for any length of time. On the other hand, not paying apartment rent meant more money for Aurora's surgery. Janny seemed pragmatic about matters like that.

"Baby is talking a little more, thanks to you," Janny said. "But the big change is with her art work—take a look at what she did this morning." She handed me a stack of drawings. "Be with you in a sec."

She disappeared into the tiny bathroom and a hair dryer shrieked on the high setting. I sat on the narrow couch and thumbed through Aurora's art work. Sheet after sheet of paper was covered with pictures: Ethan and the puppies, pictures of her mother and of Ruby Mae.

Then Aurora's drawings regressed to a more primitive style. The pencil lines became blacker, more broken, with images outlined in jerky strokes. Amazing, the likenesses she captured, even so. A portrait of her grandfather, Cal. Then one of a younger Ethan standing next to a man that had to be her Uncle Lucas. I studied the picture for a moment, two brothers now separated by an eternity.

Then I examined the final drawing in the collection. It was creased and wrinkled, as though it had been crumpled and straightened again. A dark figure, Otis it looked like, fiddling with the dials on the distillery, flames exploding behind him. And a broken body at the side of the drawing— was that Lucas? Angry strokes had ripped gashes in the paper.

Janny reappeared in her work uniform. "Is my name tag straight? I never can tell. One time I wore it upside down most of the day. Luckily a customer caught it, not my boss."

She patted her chest and then sat down and looked at the picture in my hand. "Momma was fit to be tied when she saw that one. Looks like Daddy lied about what happened. Howard's a snake, running away like he did, but maybe my Uncle Otis had more to do with that explosion than Howard did."

I considered her statement. Was Otis responsible for Lucas's death? And if Cal discovered Otis was at fault, might Otis kill him as well?

"Did Aurora draw any others?"

"No, that was the last one. She cried and wadded that one up, so I put her paper and pencils away for a while."

"Poor kid. She's been through a lot." I put the drawing aside. "Has Otis been around recently?"

Janny hesitated. "No, haven't seen him around at all. Dogs tell us when anyone comes in the yard."

Which meant Otis was probably high-tailing it out the back as I drove in the front. But the man couldn't hide forever in this small valley. Somebody would spot him.

"What did Ruby Mae want with Reverend Billy?" I asked, my voice tightening.

Janny shot me a sympathetic look. "The man's a rotten louse for what he did to you at the dance, but Momma trusts him. She needs a lawyer, wants him to recommend one."

I snorted. "I thought she had better sense than that. A lawyer for what?"

"When we were treasure hunting, we found Daddy's Last Will, hidden under the floorboards of the barn. Handwritten, which is still legal, they tell me. This homestead was his, left by his daddy to him, and in his will he gave it to Ethan, Howard and me, divided three ways. He skipped Momma entirely."

"Is she upset, you kids inheriting like that?"

"Momma knows we'll take care of her, that's not the problem."

"What is?"

"Daddy left *two* wills, both dated the same day. The second will leaves everything to *all* his kids, including the soon-to-be-born Cal, Jr. I passed that copy along to Darbie last night. So I'm in Momma's doghouse, too."

"Ruby Mae's going to contest it?"

"You better believe it. Claims Daddy wasn't in his right mind. Says nobody is going to take this place away from her family." She scooped up the drawings and placed them on a side table. "But Darbie's baby is going to be my little brother. So in a way, Darbie's family, too."

"Would you miss this place, if it sold?"

"If it meant Aurora's hand could be fixed, I'd do it tomorrow. But leaving might be harder for Momma. All us kids were born right here. Momma said she just popped us right out with Daddy pacing outside the door." Janny laughed ruefully. "When I had Aurora, I needed a four-star hospital suite with all the known drugs possible."

Janny hadn't ever mentioned Aurora's daddy and I hadn't asked. She wasn't wearing a wedding ring and it was her business, I figured. Janny's method of childbirth was exactly what I'd choose, too, if I ever had kids, which I didn't plan to.

"Janny, how's your mother doing after Cal's death?"

She was quiet for a moment, her face pensive. "Momma walks up to the grave every morning and talks to him. I bet he got a ration this morning after she found out about the two wills." Janny stood and straightened her skirt. "Gotta scoot. They can't run that store without me."

I followed her out of the trailer, and she pointed to the barn. "Go say hello to Aurora and Ethan. They're visiting the puppies."

The pups had outgrown the whelping box. Ethan had broken it down and moved the coonhound family to a fenced-in area of the barn. Puppies shoved and pushed in a swirling auburn tapestry while Aurora sat on the floor creating barriers for them to pile over. Ethan leaned against a wall watching.

He looked my way as I entered. "Join the fun."

I stepped over the barrier, and squatted, then changed my mind and sat on the floor like Aurora. A Family Liaison Officer needed some flexibility. The pups rushed toward me, tumbling and falling in a joyous, jerky procession. They glowed deep red in the sunlight through the open door, still stocky-bodied but big-pawed with the promise of future growth.

"How old, now?" I asked Ethan.

"Going on eight weeks. At ten I'll begin some basic obedience and scent training."

Their faces were wrinkly, with loose skin yet to fill out, giving them the appearance of old men with droopy eyes. Baby tails whipsawed from side to side, and young bodies wavered like toddlers just learning to walk.

"Sold them yet?"

"Most are promised. One or two still available. You in the market?"

A puppy in my apartment with its steep stairs and small back yard? I shook my head regretfully. "No place to housebreak one."

"Need to speak to you outside," he said, cocking his head toward the door. "Aurora, you watch the puppies for us, okay, kiddo?"

She cuddled one of the pups and smiled up at him. "Okay," she said, her voice still rough.

"That-a-girl." He gave her a thumbs-up.

We both stepped over the fencing into the yard. I brushed dust and puppy slobber from my pants. The late fall sun spattered the tree branches with shafts of light. We moved to the porch where I sat on the top step.

"What's up, Ethan?"

"Janny told you about the two wills?"

I nodded. "What was your father *thinking*? Surely he knew that would cause problems."

"He didn't consider he'd die so soon." Ethan squinted up at the milky sky signaling the end of Indian summer. "He promised one thing to Momma," he said, "and another to Darbie. Probably figured he tear up one will, just didn't know which one yet."

"Your folks fought that day he left..."

"I heard china breaking, Momma screaming at him. Set the hounds to baying something awful." Ethan picked up a stick and drew in the dust, lines crossing one another like jack straws.

"Think he was getting ready to leave for good?"

"He was close, only staying on because of the property sale. But Momma's the jealous sort, even though they'd stopped sleeping in the same bed. Claimed it was his snoring. Sometimes, I'd find him out in the barn sleeping in the back of that old truck."

199

"Ethan, I could use some help here. You think your mother might have killed your father?"

He shuddered. "Think she would have liked to at times, he aggravated her so. But I'm figuring somebody else got to him first."

"You thinking that somebody might be Otis?"

"I can't talk about him. Momma forbids it." Ethan swallowed hard.

It was difficult to understand this man-boy. He was so good with animals and little kids, so awkward with adults. If the home place were sold, how would he fare in a town, even one as small as Cottonwood or Mingus?

"What about your younger brother Howard?" I asked. "Might there have been conflict left over from when he was banished?"

"Stupid. Why'd he run like that when Lucas, when my big brother..." Ethan struggled to find the right words. "Howard should of stood up to Daddy once and for all."

"Does Howard have it in him to kill your father?"

"Daddy ragged on him terrible, called him a sissy and worse. And that was when Daddy was sober. Drunk, you stayed out of his way, you didn't want to get hurt. But now Howard's running with that bad crowd in Phoenix. Could be he's learned a street lesson or two down there, maybe how to get rid of somebody in a hurry."

That could be. I wondered about the other sibling. "Janny?"

"She blamed Daddy for the damage to Aurora's hand. Said the baby would be fine if he'd been there to help instead of out drinking in the marsh." Ethan rubbed a hand over his jaw. "She had years after the accident to kill him, though. Didn't."

Ethan seemed ready to talk and I pushed a little further. "What about Darbie Granger, your father's other wife?"

"She's pretty. Needed a man, found one. Found two, if you count Howard and Daddy both."

"Would she have murdered your father?"

He latched onto that suggestion. "Maybe it *was* Darbie, if my daddy was leaving her. She looks mild-mannered, but underneath is one stubborn-willed woman. She could do it, I reckon."

I got the sense he'd rather have it be Darbie than Ruby Mae or Janny or even Otis. In his eyes, Darbie wasn't family. Still, that didn't make her a killer.

"You forgot one," he said, looking at me with eyes of a most innocent blue.

"I did, that. Did *you* kill your father, Ethan Nettle?"

"No, ma'am, I did not." He paused. "Of course, us Nettles have a habit of lying when it suits us. Which do you think I am, Ms. Quincy, truth or lie?"

I scanned his face, pondering the question.

Then Reckless bounded around the house, breaking the moment. He planted his front paws on my chest leaving muddy prints on my fresh uniform shirt.

"Reckless, down!" Ethan grabbed at his collar, rubbing the dog's ears to mollify his words. Then he looked up at me. "I need to ask you something, law woman."

"I'm listening."

"I got the pups spoken for, and Momma needs the older hounds here. But I worry about Reckless. He likes you. If I had to go away somewhere for a spell, would you take care of him?"

"Go away? Where?"

"Never mind. Would you?"

Not satisfied with my nod, he repeated his request. "Promise me. Swear it."

"I promise," I said. At least it would be only temporary, and the dog *was* housebroken. I hoped, though, that I'd never have to keep that vow.

I'd become unwisely tangled with this Nettle clan, way too close to be impartial. Ethan knew more of the story than he revealed. Would he decide to tell me before it was too late?

CHAPTER TWENTY-SIX

The next afternoon I wrote parking tickets as an excuse to get out of the office. I'd rather do that than patrol for moving violations. I didn't believe in speed traps—figured tourists could read speed limit signs the same as the rest of us. Although sometimes they chose not to, putting the little kids who were walking home from school at risk.

My cell phone vibrated against my thigh, and I pulled it out of my pocket. I was still getting used to my new smart phone. It was a memory hog, especially when I forgot to charge it. I scowled. Only two bars of battery left this afternoon.

The call was from Rory Stevens. "Want to go out and celebrate? Scores just posted. I made the promotion to detective."

"Great news." I was pleased for him. He'd told me the test was a hard one. "What time?"

"Pick you up about six-thirty. We can do wine flights at Grapes."

It was nearly five. Time enough to write one more parking ticket and then quit for the day. I walked down the street looking for a likely target.

A fancy black Lincoln parked in a handicapped slot. No handicapped plates. No temporary wheelchair tag hung on the rear view mirror. I opened my ticket pad and started to write the citation.

"Hello officer," a man behind me said. "Glad I caught you before you started, don't want to waste your time."

I turned and he flashed a professionally-whitened smile at me. Expensive suit, sapphire pinky ring, coiffed silver hair—A politician? "Do you have a permit to park in a handicapped space, sir?"

"Just parked a moment to locate a hotel room."

"Find one?"

"Would you believe they're all full?"

I kept writing.

"I can make this simpler for both of us," he said. "Let's shake on it."

At the tone of his voice, I looked up.

He extended his hand, a fifty folded between thumb and forefinger. "Chalk it up as a misunderstanding. I'm new to your fine city."

Not a politician, then. Just a really dumb Joe-Citizen.

"Know what the fine is for attempted bribery in this state?" I tore off the ticket and handed it to him with a smile. He grabbed the paper, his face contorted. The fifty disappeared into his pocket.

As I walked off, the Lincoln jammed into gear and fished-tailed into the street. Good thing there wasn't a semi coming the other direction. We had some of those big rigs drive through town, but they followed the laws of our fair metropolis, didn't park in handicapped spots.

***

It was almost five-thirty when I opened the studio apartment door and pounded up the stairs to change. The challenge of living in a studio was limited closet space. Or maybe not such a problem—I didn't have much of a wardrobe.

Rory had already seen my green first-date blouse, and Wonder Woman had made too much of an impression at the dance to reappear. Maybe the pink dress? No, too feminine for a second date, or was this the third?

Darn! I was turning into my cousin Suzy. By the time she had dressed and undressed six times, her waiting date had fallen asleep on the living room couch. I wasn't that bad yet, and anyway I didn't have six date outfits. Rory would have to settle for the white silk shirt and black pants. Cool, sophisticated, who was I kidding?

I swiped again at the puppy smudges on my uniform, undressed, and tossed it in the dry-cleaning pile. Perhaps those professionals could work their usual magic on the red earth stains.

When the water was hot, I showered, dressed, and was brushing the braid-waves out of my hair when Rory knocked downstairs. I stuck my feet into compromise, mid-heel slingbacks, grabbed a turquoise pashmina shawl, and waltzed down to greet him. I could get used to this.

He held a corsage box in his hand, and he must have seen my face fall. "No," he said, "not a wrist corsage. This is different." He placed the box in my hands.

I opened it to find a small spray of plumeria on a hair comb, tiny white blossoms with soft apricot centers. I buried my nose to catch their sweet airy fragrance. Then I freed them from their green shredded-paper nest, put the box on the entry table and turned to the hall mirror.

"May I?" Rory's skillful fingers pulled back my hair and placed the comb over my left ear. Then he kissed the ear for good measure. "Plumeria for new beginnings."

"From Hawaii?"

"From my grandmother down in Florida. She owns a nursery. Says hi."

Now he was talking to family. I liked it, and I didn't like it. I'd rushed headlong into my one attempt at marriage, and it bombed. Keep-it-physical was my new motto with guys. I wanted this relationship with Rory to last. Maybe I was wrong, but marriage signaled the opposite for me. I refused to go down that twisty path anytime soon.

Rory led me to the Hummer and opened the passenger door. When he got in on his side, I asked, "Borrowing cars from your roommate again?"

He mumbled something I didn't catch as he started the car and drove down the street. A black cat streaked in front of the Hummer, and he braked sharply. "Halloween reject," he joked. "Hope you're not superstitious."

Friday the Thirteenth, black cats, even lucky socks— I'd known cops that believed in them all. Worst I'd ever met was a fellow student in the Police Academy who swore not to shower until he passed Physical Quals. He failed three times. By then he smelled so bad we started avoiding him in the lunchroom. Finally, we couldn't stand it and threw him in a shower. Left him to drip dry on a towel hook. He passed the Quals next day.

Rory pulled up in front of the restaurant. I opened my own door before he could walk around. I didn't want to advertise to the whole town I was out on a date, but perhaps they knew anyway.

The hostess smiled at Rory when we approached her stand. "We've reserved your special place, sir." She led us to the same booth we'd had on our first date.

Rory made a sweeping gesture. "Lady's choice. Which side you want?"

We were celebrating his accomplishments. I gifted him the street-front view and sat with my back to the door. I trusted him to be watchful, but the switch in positions still made me uneasy.

Rory grabbed the wine list away from me and signaled the waitress. "Bring us something extraordinary."

Soon she returned with a wine stand filled with ice and a bottle of champagne. Crooked between her fingers were two flutes. "Sir?" She set the flutes on the table, then handed Rory a towel and the champagne bottle.

"Let's see if I can do this properly." He removed the wire muselet from the cork and set it on the table. Then he put the towel over the cork and wiggled it back and forth. It released with a hiss of air. "I like flying corks," he said, "but not in a crowded place. Might hurt somebody."

He handed the bottle to the server, who poured champagne into each flute and set them in front of us.

"To your promotion," I said, lifting one.

"To your beauty," he responded, lifting the other and touching mine.

The speakers overhead played the sound track from *Momma Mia* while I studied the bubbles rising from the base of the flute. The evening was off to a wonderful start.

"Rory..." I began.

A hand clasped my shoulder and I jumped.

"Sorry. Saw you and had to come say hello."

I twisted to see Ben standing behind me. Next to him, resplendent in an off-the-shoulder magenta blouse and matching skirt was Sheryl Malone.

"Join you?" Ben nudged me over on the booth seat and Sheryl scooted in next to Rory.

"Sheryl," Ben said, "this is Rory Stevens from the Prescott sheriff's department. And you know Peg."

Sheryl nodded at me and turned in the booth to give Rory a megawatt smile.

"Heard you leased the Hummer," Ben said. "How you like it?"

Rory's gaze avoided mine, and he rubbed the back of his neck.

I sat up straighter. He'd *leased* it? He told me it was his roommate's.

Sheryl chimed in. "A Hummer? That wide-track red beauty out front?"

Rory beamed at her attention. "Actually the color is called atomic orange."

"And you *customized* it." She semaphored admiration through long eyelashes.

If Rory'd been a flamingo, he'd be preening atomic-orange feathers.

Sheryl stuck out her little finger and sampled Rory's champagne. He moved it out of her reach. Then she put her arm through his in a companionable fashion.

Next to me, Ben's knee started jigging.

Sheryl snuggled closer to Rory, her lavender-tipped hair brushing his cheek. "Take me for a ride sometime?" she purred.

Ben made odd noises in his throat.

Rory leaned slightly away from Sheryl, tugging his top shirt button as though it had become too tight. Perhaps wanting to break free from this treacherous sand, he changed topics and dug himself in deeper. "Ben," he said, "great pair costumes at the dance."

Sheryl removed her arm from Rory's and glowered. "What costumes? What dance?"

"The Halloween Dance," Rory said helpfully.

Sheryl's eyes skewered Ben. "Why wasn't I invited?"

"Because you weren't here yet. *Thanks*, Rory." Ben jumped to his feet and grabbed Sheryl's arm. "Our table's ready."

Sheryl departed in a shimmer of magenta. A red-faced Ben flung a payback comment before he followed her. "Peg, ask him about the call to the fiancée."

In the silence that followed, I let it all sink in. The Reverend Billy's fiancée had found out about his taking me to the dance because someone called her. I was getting a good idea who that somebody might be.

Rory avoided my eyes, circling his champagne flute in a puddle of moisture on the tabletop.

The waitress paused beside us. "Are we ready to order yet, or do we need more time?"

The stormy silence hung between us.

"Right. I'll come back," she said, and left.

Rory still wouldn't meet my eyes.

"Would this fiancée be named Agnes? And would her affianced be the Reverend Billy?" I kept my voice level with effort. "You got something to tell me, Rory Stevens?"

"It's not what you think."

"What am I thinking? Enlighten me, since you know so much."

"Billy was engaged. I thought Shepherd told you."

"And why would he? Shepherd is my friend, unlike some other people." My voice raised and heads turned. I lowered my tone and hissed through clenched teeth, "Who told you to stick your nose in my business, anyway?"

"Let me explain."

"You're real good at that. You and your precious Plan B. Do you know how *awful* I felt?" My stomach clenched in a knot. "People laughed at me."

"That's not true, I..."

"Did you laugh? Did you have a grand time with your little joke?" I brushed fierce tears out of my eyes, and my cheek muscles tightened.

"I didn't set you up, Peg. That guy's a jerk. I thought you had more sense than that."

"So now you're calling me stupid, too."

"I tried to help. How about saying, thank you? I didn't hear you say thank you."

"I didn't need to be rescued like some stray dog—And what about that Hummer? That wasn't your roommate's car at all. You *lied* to me."

He gripped the table edge. "What I drive is my business, not yours. And I didn't lie to you."

"Just didn't bother to tell me the whole truth. You're worse than Billy."

He jerked to his feet, and a champagne flute crashed to the floor. "I've heard enough."

"Good, because I'm leaving! I can find my own way home."

We stood glaring at each other. With head held high, I grabbed my purse and shawl. I marched through the restaurant and out into the night.

Rory didn't follow me.

My righteous anger kept me warm as I stomped down the first block, but by the time I reached my apartment, I was cooler. Not cool enough to forgive Rory Stevens, though. That would take longer.

He was wrong. Absolutely, positively wrong.

CHAPTER TWENTY-SEVEN

A few days later, Shepherd motioned me into his office.

"Heard you got into a fight at Grapes Restaurant the other night." He frowned. "Remember you're living in a small town. People notice."

My chin jutted out, and I rocked back on my heels. "So what?"

"You're the law, whether you're in uniform or not."

"Not your business." We'd been down this road before, with Shepherd assuming he could rule every corner of my life.

He sighed. "Probably my fault as much as anybody's."

"Meaning?"

"Peg, hear me out."

I closed his office door and sat down.

"You may not want to hear this." Shepherd clicked his pen in and out. Then, "Rory Stevens has fallen in love with you."

"What?" It was the last thing I expected. I shook my head in denial. This relationship between Rory and me was *physical.* That's all. I didn't need complications. And anyway, if Rory felt that way, why didn't he call and apologize? *I* was the injured party here.

"Why do you think he leased that Hummer?" Shepherd pressed on to make his point. "He loved that yellow Z3 Beamer he used to drive. But he loves you more."

211

"I don't want to be beholden to anybody," I said, "especially someone who lies."

"We *all* lie. When we want to save face, when we get backed into a corner, when we want to avoid conflict..."

"Yeah, I get all that." I wasn't in the mood to wax philosophical. My feelings were wounded. Rory Stevens owed me. "So why'd he pull that stunt with Reverend Billy?"

"Call it a young man's folly. Perhaps he saw a way to gain advantage over a rival and took it. Didn't expect that you'd get caught in the middle of it."

I wasn't ready to concede yet. I wanted flowers and candy. And groveling. A *lot* of groveling. "I'll think about it," I muttered. "Anything else?"

"No, that's it. Oh, wait, here's something you might be interested in." He activated his computer screen and pulled up the court log for Anasazi County. "There's going to be a will contest in the Nettle family estate. You know anything about that?"

I told him about the two wills, one leaving everything to the Nettle kids, the other adding Darbie Granger's unborn son, Cal, Jr.

"That's got to put Ruby Mae in a snit," Shepherd said. "She the one filing?"

"Probably," I said. "Janny says her mother is satisfied with her kids getting the property, just doesn't want Darbie laying claim to it."

"Understandable."

"Who are the attorneys involved?" I asked.

"Myra Banks for Darbie."

"That figures. Myra has been involved since the beginning. What about the other side?"

Shepherd peered at the screen. "Don't recognize the name. A James Wightman out of Phoenix. Wonder where Ruby Mae heard of him?"

I fidgeted a bit. Didn't want to share the Reverend Billy connection that I'd discovered. "Are probate hearings public? Can anybody attend?"

"Why? You want to go?"

"Might," I said. "Give us some insights into the family. I'm still looking for an angle on Cal Nettle's death."

"Friday morning, 10 a.m., it says. Take the SUV. I'll have my daughter Sheryl squire me around if that VW doesn't self-destruct first."

"How're she and Ben getting on?" I nodded toward my assistant in the reception area.

"Too well. Did you know he went out and bought a motorcycle?"

That fact had escaped me. I tuned out the guttural roar of so many Harley motorcycle groups passing through town on their way to swoop down the mountain hairpins. One more wouldn't make much of an impression.

"Not only that," Shepherd said. "He's teaching her how to drive the damn thing."

"Helmets, I hope."

"I insisted on that. They're headed out to the New Directions Horse Ranch this afternoon to do some volunteering."

"If that doesn't work, maybe they can try Out of Africa. Sheryl can feed raw meat to the lions and tigers."

Shepherd chuckled. "Yeah, she'd fit right in. How'd I end up with a daughter like that? Not in *my* gene pool, I'll tell you."

I wasn't so sure.

***

The morning of the Nettle probate hearing, a massive low-pressure system settled over the Four Corners area of the Southwest, pulling the jet stream lower. What that meant for us in Mingus was rapidly dropping temperatures and lots of moisture.

I had my second cup of coffee at the apartment and put out some dry cat food for the stray that frequented the balcony. I grabbed my phone off the dresser—I'd forgotten to charge it, but I'd plug it in tonight—and headed out the door.

Right on schedule, the clouds arrived, dark with snow potential. The storm descended in a rush of stinging sleet. I pulled my windbreaker close and ducked my chin under its collar for the short walk to the station

Ben arrived just after me, pink-cheeked and triumphant on his new bike, a bright-red Ducati. It was more maneuverable than a Harley Davidson, he explained, and cool in the chick department. I didn't have to ask which chick. It felt good to be on an even ground again with Ben after he apologized for his part in the Grapes affair.

My status with Rory was still up in the air. I'd called him but only reached his voice mail. I left a non-committal message, but he hadn't responded. Would he be driving Tweetie-Bird yellow or atomic orange, next time we met? I missed the man but didn't know how to bridge this chasm.

When Shepherd arrived, I took the department SUV and left for the courthouse. The sleet shifted to hard rain around Cottonwood and I headed east on Highway 260 with the windshield wipers on max speed.

The icy rain pelted the vehicle in hard, unforgiving sheets as I drove the thirty minutes to the Courthouse Complex near I-17. High winds buffeted the car's framework, and I canted the steering wheel to keep the tires on the road. The temperature hovered near freezing according to the digital readout on the dash—black ice conditions, that ice coating so transparent that it took the color of the black asphalt beneath it. The highway patrol officers would have their hands full today.

I signaled at the light and drove past the wildlife park toward the municipal complex and then turned right into the courthouse parking lot. The building was five stories high and held not only the courthouse but also a branch of the county jail. Being so close to Out of Africa, the favorite joke of both inmates and guards was who would be the big cats' next supper.

The courthouse building itself was state-of-the-art, which meant bathrooms with showers for the judges' chambers, and theatre-style chairs instead of wooden benches for spectator galleries. The building also housed a cafeteria for those awaiting jury selection, which was a definite step up from the vending machines in the main sheriff's office in Camp Verde.

A frigid wind blasted me as I opened the SUV door. The guard at the security entrance to the courthouse watched with an impassive expression as I emptied my pockets and walked through the metal detector. Then he directed me down the hall to Judge Compton's Probate Courtroom.

There were no windows in the room, and glass slits marked each side of the door. I shrugged out of my wet jacket and hung it on the back of my chair to dry.

The Probate Court was like most courtrooms—lots of walnut paneling, and inconspicuous surveillance cameras in the ceiling corners. We hadn't needed cameras like this when I was a kid. Hadn't needed the bulletproof judge's bench or security screening, either. Times had changed over the past decades to include a general disrespect for institutions and increased gun violence.

The bailiff appeared with a water pitcher and glass for the judge. The court reporter brought in her equipment and set up in the well, ready to record the proceedings.

In front of the bar railing, Ruby Mae, her son Ethan, and a silver-haired man occupied the table nearest the jury box. It was my traffic-ticket customer from the other day. I hoped the fifty-dollar briber was a better persuader of juries than cops, or Ruby Mae would be frittering away the Nettle fortune, what there was left of it.

She wore gray wool slacks and a bright pink V-necked sweater over a white blouse. Ethan was dressed in a somber brown suit, the same one he'd worn to his father's funeral.

Myra Banks sat at the defendant's table and next to her, Darbie Granger, wearing a subdued two-piece blue maternity outfit. She looked very pregnant.

"Scoot over." Janny Nettle appeared at my shoulder.

"Terrible weather," I said, moving over for her and draping my jacket over the next chair. "Where's Aurora?"

"My brother Howard's babysitting. Momma doesn't want him anywhere near Darbie. Momma's still not talking to me either after I gave that other will to Darbie, so I'm sitting here in the spectators' area. Wouldn't miss this show for anything."

She pointed toward Darbie. "Looks like an overripe watermelon, doesn't she? Stubborn, too. Wants to have the baby natural."

"That the attorney Reverend Billy suggested?" I asked.

Janny nodded. "He's some big-wig from Phoenix. Not sure how he'll get on with Judge Compton—his honor doesn't like being talked down to. But that attorney's a fine looking man, isn't he?"

I withheld my judgment on that one. I'd had my fill of fine looking men. "How do you think the judge will rule?"

"I heard that the judge's daughter is pregnant with his first grandchild," Janny said. "I'm betting on Darbie."

We stood when Judge Compton entered from his chamber. He was a small man with short brown hair and heavy glasses, wearing the black robes of office. As he mounted the bench he appeared to grow in height. Justice does that.

We sat and waited for him to begin.

"Look, people, I'd like to tell you I'm late for my golf game, but that would be a lie, and judges never lie." He waited for our polite laughter. "Truth is, I'd like to finish up early and get us all home before this weather gets worse. Blowing up a real gale out there." He rocked back and forth in his chair to get comfortable. "This hearing will be an informal one. First Respondent, introduce yourself to the court."

Ruby Mae's attorney rose. "If it pleases the court, Mr. James Wightman, from the Phoenix probate firm of Smith, Branson, and Wightman, representing Ms. Ruby Mae Nettle and the Nettle family." He made a gesture to his right and then sat.

"Heard of you. Good firm. And for the Second Respondent?"

Myra rose. "Myra Banks, your honor. My client, Darbie Granger."

"Ms. Banks." The judge took off his glasses and looked at her sternly. "The last time you were here, I held your client in contempt of court. Nothing like that planned today, I presume?"

"No, your honor." Myra looked thoroughly penitent.

"Good, then we can begin."

Myra sat.

The Judge summarized. "First the court received the petition allowing the will brought forth by the Nettle family. Then we received a petition for a second will from Darbie Granger. My clerk was smart enough to realize what was happening, and I've taken the liberty of combining these two matters into one case. We're here today to decide which Last Will and Testament of Calhoun Nettle will prevail. Mr. Wightman, you're up."

The faithful-father, loyal-husband flag went up the pole again as Attorney Wightman presented a glowing picture of Ruby Mae's spouse. Wasn't what I'd heard about Cal, but then, attorneys do stretch the truth occasionally.

Myra Banks stood to describe Darbie Granger as a poor single mom, beloved by Cal Nettle who intended to provide for her unborn son. I could hear the violins playing.

I wondered which story the judge would believe, but he showed a poker face. They must teach that in judge school.

He asked both sides whether they believed the two wills had been signed by Calhoun Nettle.

"We do, your honor," said Mr. Wightman.

"We also so stipulate," said Myra.

"As both sides agree to the validity of the wills, and as we do not know which was written last, I need to ask more questions of both respondents." The judge templed his fingers. "Let me get the relationships straight. Myra Banks, does your client Darbie Granger agree that Ruby Mae Nettle is the lawful wife of one Calhoun Nettle?"

"Yes, your honor," Myra said.

Darbie stood indignantly. "But he didn't love her, your honor. He was going to marry *me*." Myra pulled her down quickly and the judge nodded his approval. Score one point for Myra.

Then the judge turned to Mr. Wightman. "Does your client acknowledge that Darbie Granger is pregnant and that the probable father may be the recently deceased Calhoun Nettle?"

I expected an explosion out of Ruby Mae, but she sat there stolidly, her arms crossed. Wightman bent over and conferred with her. "Yes, your honor," he responded, "we so acknowledge."

That was a surprise. Although Cal's patrimony seemed to be common knowledge, I hadn't expected Ruby Mae to confirm it.

The hearing continued, examining the relationships Cal had with both women. Darbie squirmed in her seat and Ruby Mae shot several looks her direction. At first, I thought the glances were hostile, but then I wasn't so sure. Finally, Darbie whispered to Myra and the attorney stood.

"Your honor, my client requests a small recess."

The judge looked up. "Granted."

Darbie made an awkward dash for the side door that led to the restrooms.

Janny jumped to her feet. "I'm going to see what's happening."

While they were away, I checked my phone. I had a message from Melda, the dispatcher. The weather bureau warned of freezing temperatures and increasing chances for ice and high winds. They recommended all persons stay off the road. Would have been nice to know that earlier. Minus one point for the meteorologist.

Darbie retook her chair at her attorney's table, and Janny dropped into the seat beside me. She leaned over to whisper in my ear. "Darbie thinks she's having false labor pains. I told her she should have delayed this hearing, but she wouldn't listen to me. Wanted to get it all settled before Cal, Jr. arrived."

The hearing plodded along as both attorneys presented arguments why their side should prevail. Finally, the judge signaled a halt. "Enough. Let's see if all parties can't compromise on this. Set another hearing date with the clerk and come back to me with an agreement. No sense in piling up attorney's fees if we don't need to."

The attorneys stood and gathered their papers in preparation for departure. The lights flickered once. Then we lost all power, and the courtroom turned inky black.

A woman's scream echoed from the front of the courtroom.

CHAPTER TWENTY-EIGHT

The power flickered to life in the courtroom. Myra stood. "Your honor, my client has gone into labor. Do I have the court's permission to call 911?"

The judge waved his assent. "Of course, please call."

Myra's fingers got busy.

"You don't look well, young lady. Would you like to lie down in my chambers until the paramedics arrive?" The judge looked around the courtroom. "Is there a doctor or nurse present?" For a moment, no one raised their hand.

Then, Ruby Mae stood. "Guess I'm it. Birthed my own four at home. Midwifed others."

"Ms. Granger, you okay with that?" the judge asked.

Darbie nodded and then clutched at her stomach as another contraction shivered through her.

"Bailiff, clear the courtroom. Ms. Granger, to my chambers."

Ruby Mae looked our direction. "Janny? You get down here. Peg Quincy? You, too."

We braced the tide leaving the courtroom and joined her in the front.

Myra made an attempt to stay with her client, but Ruby Mae stopped her. "Ever had a baby?"

Myra shook her head.

"Didn't think so. Go back to your fancy office." Then she looked at her own attorney. "No sense in paying your high fees either if you're just standing around. I'll talk to you tomorrow." With that, she dismissed both of them.

Ruby Mae had plans for her son Ethan, as well. "Go down to the cafeteria. Get a bag of salt, a big pan, see if they've got some fresh tablecloths, not been used. Bring all those up here. And stop at Security. We need an unopened box of those blue gloves. Finally a good use for those nasty things."

We trooped into the judge's chamber. Next to the desk, a backless couch stood against the wall. A door opened to a bathroom beyond. The room was spacious but made for attorney conferences, not for delivering babies.

"My office is at your disposal," the judge said. "What can I do for you?"

"How about some whiskey?" Ruby Mae asked.

He looked startled. "Why, yes, I keep some for medicinal purposes." He opened a bottom drawer and withdrew a nearly full bottle of Chivas Regal. "Should I give some to Ms. Granger?" He pulled out a glass.

"Fool! That's to sterilize the scissors. I assume you have some?"

He reddened and pulled a pair from a desk drawer.

Ruby Mae made her next demand. "Need a first aid kit. You got one in here someplace?"

"Yes, behind the door, there."

"Well, reach it down to me. Don't have all day," she barked.

The good judge and Ruby Mae bristled at each other. Wouldn't bode well for a possible delivery. We needed an unruffled midwife. "Sir, I'm an officer of the law. I'll keep track of things here, if you'd like to retire outside."

Handing Ruby Mae the first aid kit, Judge Compton retreated from the field of battle.

Darbie collapsed in a chair, and Ruby Mae knelt down beside her. She took the girl's hand and looked into her eyes. "Ms. Granger—Darbie—I didn't ask for this and neither did you. But that baby you're carrying? The last thing that Cal left on this earth. I'd not harm his child. You understand that?"

Darbie nodded, holding back tears.

"Good. Then we can begin."

Janny had flopped in another chair, her eyebrows squinched up, arms crossed tightly.

Ruby Mae looked into her pale face. "Janny, you got a watch?"

"On my phone."

"There's a likely chance that Darbie won't deliver that baby before the ambulance arrives. So I want the two of you to walk around the courtroom while we get ready in here. Be good exercise for both of you. Use that smart phone thing of yours to time the next contraction."

When they had left, Ruby Mae turned to me. "You squeamish?"

I shook my head. I'd not witnessed childbirth before, but I helped my uncle deliver a calf once back home. And I'd been first on the scene for several traffic accidents, which meant blood, crying people, and chaos before the medical help arrived. Surely, one baby's arrival couldn't be worse than that.

"Babies are messy," Ruby Mae said. So we layered the judge's couch for the birthing. First the shower curtain from his bathroom. Then newspapers from a vending machine in the hall. Ethan brought in the supplies from the cafeteria, and we placed one of the clean tablecloths on the layer of newspapers. Finally, towels from the judge's shower went on top.

Ruby Mae pawed through the judge's locker and discovered a shirt fresh from the laundry, paper-banded and clean. "Baby wear," she said triumphantly, holding up the package. "Empty that big drawer from the desk for a temporary bassinet."

On the desk top, the first aid kit containing gauze and adhesive tape joined the box of gloves, hand sanitizer, and the scissors soaking in the glass of the judge's favorite whiskey. Ruby Mae pulled off her pink sweater and rolled up her sleeves.

We were as ready as we'd ever be.

I'd transferred the 911 operator to my phone when Myra Banks left, and now I checked in with him. "Ambulance on the way," he said. "I have Doctor Elizabeth Johnson on the phone. She's the Ob-Gyn doctor on call at the hospital."

An easy voice with an Oklahoma drawl came on the phone. "Hi, this is Liz Johnson. Who'm I talking to?"

"Peg Quincy, Deputy Sheriff."

"Hi Peg. Who else is there?"

"Darbie Granger, the pregnant lady, and her friend Janny Nettle. They're out walking in the next room. And Ruby Mae Nettle, Janny's mother, is here with me." I put the phone on speaker and Ruby Mae said hi.

"Anybody there know about birthing babies?"

Ruby Mae cited her experience and explained the preparations we'd made.

"That's good. How far along is our new mother?"

We heard a gasp from the other room. Another labor pain. I looked at my watch. Seven minutes from the last one. I notified Liz and told her this was Darbie's first child.

"They tell me the ambulance is about ten minutes out, so we should be fine," Liz said. "Important thing is to keep the mother as calm as possible. Keep me posted on the contractions. I'm standing by."

I set the phone on the desk, still on speaker. There was a hurried knock at the door and I opened to a white-faced Janny.

"Her water broke. What do we do now?"

"Time to get to work." Ruby Mae's tone was quiet as she slipped into midwife role. She first brushed Darbie's sweaty hair out of her eyes with an experienced hand and then assessed her daughter. "Janny, you okay? I can't take care of two of you."

"Let me sit still for a moment." Janny shrunk into the chair.

Ruby Mae turned to me. "Guess you're my assistant on this one. Help Darbie up onto this couch and let's get her prepped."

I settled the girl on the couch and took off her shoes—five-inch spike heels, what was she *thinking* of? Ruby Mae washed her hands in the bathroom. She brought wet soapy cloths, removed Darbie's underwear, and cleaned her inner thighs with gentle hands.

The lights flickered again and the phone crackled to life. "Liz here. How we doing?"

Ruby Mae leaned over. "Water broke, but she's doing just fine, aren't you Darbie?"

"I think so." Darbie's voice was hesitant, a little scared.

"Good," the voice from the phone said. "I have years of experience delivering babies just like yours. Right now, though, I want to talk to Ruby Mae privately. Why don't you chat with your friend Janny, and we'll be right back to you."

Darbie moaned, a keening sound that knifed through the air.

"Janny, look in that first aid kit," Ruby Mae directed. "See if there's any aspirin, she can have that, and a sip of water."

Then she grabbed my phone, hustled me into the courtroom, and closed the door behind us. "Okay, go ahead, Liz."

"Let me put the police dispatcher back on for you."

We leaned near the phone's speaker.

"A delivery truck slid on that glare ice," the dispatcher said. "The ambulance couldn't stop and slammed into it. We contacted our backup ambulance in Camp Verde, but their EMTs are out on another call. You're on your own for now."

The lights dimmed again. If the power went out, we'd lose light *and* heat, with a new baby on the way. I caught my breath. The lights flickered once and the power resumed.

Ruby Mae seemed buoyed by the dispatcher's news. "Cal always made strong babies, and this one will be fine, too. You with me, Peg? Be fun."

I wasn't convinced, but I was game. Anyway, that baby wasn't asking our permission to come into this world. We returned to the judge's chambers.

"Time to check the cervix," Ruby Mae said. "You ever seen one before? Darbie, what about you? I can use a mirror if you want to look."

The girl grunted "no," as another contraction shuddered through her.

Ruby Mae looked at Janny. "What's the time on that one?"

"Five minutes."

"Wash up, Peg," Ruby Mae instructed, "and put on some gloves. Clean that flashlight of yours with the hand sanitizer. Then come over here and we'll take a look. Need a speculum to do it proper, but we'll manage."

She washed her own hands again and put on gloves. "Scoot your knees up, Darbie."

I held the flashlight so that Ruby Mae could examine her. "Hold that flash a little closer," she instructed. "See, that bulge in back?"

Looked all pink to me, but apparently, Ruby Mae saw something she liked.

In the quiet minutes between contractions, we prepared the bassinet. We heated the salt in the Judge's microwave and put it in the drawer like a hot water bottle under the folded towels.

As the contractions got shorter, Ruby Mae's manner became brusque. "Darbie, next contraction, start to push. Janny give her a sip of water, get her ready."

The lights went out again with a clunk of lost power. Janny dropped the glass and it broke against the cabinet.

She screamed. "Momma, I can't see. It's dark. I can't breathe..."

Ruby Mae's reassuring voice filled the darkness. "Peg, come here, hold Darbie's hand while I see to Janny."

Darbie clutched at me like a drowning swimmer.

Ruby Mae turned to her daughter, crooning. "You're doing fine, baby. Just breathe. Where's your purse?"

The door opened and Ethan appeared with a flashlight, directing erratic beams of light across the room.

"Direct that thing to the floor," Ruby Mae said. "Give this mother-to-be some privacy."

The beam turned downward, its beam glinting off the broken glass and creating silhouettes of Ruby Mae and Janny against the wall.

"Ethan, take your sister outside." She shoved Janny's purse at him. "Find her inhaler in that mess of junk she carries in there. And leave us that extra light."

Ruby Mae directed Ethan's flashlight at me. "You okay, Peg? Can't lose my best assistant over a power failure." She bent awkwardly, gathered up the larger glass fragments, and piled them on the desk.

"I'm fine. What happened to Janny?"

"Been scared of the dark since they diagnosed asthma in childhood. When she loses light in an enclosed space, she panics, freezes up, like. Ethan knows what to do. He'll watch her."

Ruby Mae switched off the flashlight and the room blackened like the far side of a very dark field. "Don't need light while we're just sitting here. We'll save the batteries until that baby-child arrives. Plenty of light from your phone, Peg, if we need it."

I picked up the judge's phone, but it was dead. Then I glanced at my phone on the judge's desk and remembered the charger sitting on my dresser. Not a chance in hell we'd have enough juice. But I couldn't turn it off, or we'd lose connection with Liz at the hospital.

"Ruby Mae, you got a phone?" I asked.

"At the house, same number for years. Didn't see no reason to get one of those carry-around things."

"Darbie, you?"

"Couldn't pay my phone bill. Company turned me off. I meant to go see them..."

Her words echoed in a darkness that grew colder with no power to heat the room. Ruby Mae wrapped her sweater around Darbie. I pulled out the last tablecloth and we piled that around her, as well. Ruby Mae started shivering, and I did, too. The temperature rapidly chilled. If the power didn't come back on soon, we'd be in a bad way.

"You still there?" Liz asked, her voice booming eerily from my cell phone into the dark room.

"We're doing fine," I said, not sure how much longer our connection would hold with my draining battery.

Again there was silence until Darbie broached the subject everyone had been avoiding, the father of this soon-to-be-born child. "Ruby Mae, what was Cal like when he was younger?"

Ruby Mae paused, remembering. "He was this big strapping guy, so handsome. We met at a church social, I was only fourteen. My own daddy disapproved, said Cal wasn't a Christian.

"So the next Sunday, Cal went and got baptized. Weather so cold there was ice on the pond. He just marched right in and dipped in that freezing water. Told me later I was lucky all his equipment still intact, that's how we made four healthy babies together. We had thirty good years. I miss him."

"I miss him, too," Darbie said. She sniffled a little.

"Not your business to miss *my* husband." Ruby Mae's voice stiffened and I was afraid the temporary truce between the two of them would disintegrate. But the baby had other plans.

Darbie writhed in pain, and Ruby Mae flicked on Ethan's flashlight again. In its light, Darbie's lower belly bulged out. The baby was crowning.

"One last push," Ruby Mae said, "and then let this baby come out to greet us."

Ruby Mae jerked to her feet to attend to Darbie and slipped in the spilled water. She grabbed at the side of the couch and went down, landing hard. The flashlight skidded under the chair as she shrieked with pain.

"Damn wet floor!" Then she moaned. "My wrist."

I grabbed for the light and flicked it on. Ruby Mae lay on the floor, blood dripping in a widening pool around her hand. Too much blood, like the mortal wound of the dying man I had killed. It was my worst nightmare, exploding to life once more.

But Ruby Mae couldn't die, not here. I wouldn't let that happen.

"Darbie, hang on," I said, as my mind zoomed into emergency mode.

Propping the flash on the table, I reached for a washcloth and wrapped it around Ruby Mae's wound. Then I grabbed bandages and gauze from the first aid kit and made a field wrap.

"Nothing broken," Ruby Mae said, "except my stupid pride. I knew that shattered glass was down there. Shoulda been more careful. You doing okay, Peg?"

I was fine. What did she mean?

"You'll have to take over," she explained. "I'm contaminated, can't be anywhere near that baby. I'll talk you through it." She gave me a little shove. "Go on now."

The baby's head appeared face down and Ruby Mae instructed me to gently turn it sideways when it was entirely out.

"Do we reach for the shoulders now?" I asked.

"That baby knows what to do. You just cradle the head steady. New babies are slippery."

Darbie gave one final, easy push and that baby entered the world. I cradled the infant in my hands and placed it on Darbie's stomach.

"Clean the mucus from the mouth," Ruby Mae instructed.

I did and the little one let out a blustery cry. Ruby Mae held the flash closer and we examined the baby. Ten fingers, ten toes. But no...

Ruby Mae chuckled. "Thought you were having a boy child, Darbie. What you got here is a little girl."

I tied two strips of gauze tightly around the birth cord about three inches apart. Pulled the sterilized scissors from the doctor's whiskey and cut the cord between the ties. Wrapped the cord close to the infant's belly with the gauze. Then I bundled the child in the judge's fine white shirt and gave it to Darbie.

"See if she'll feed a little," Ruby Mae said." Contractions will help the placenta separate."

The afterbirth came soon then. I captured it in the big pan and set it aside.

Ruby Mae turned to me. "Tear off a piece of tape and let's identify this girl-child for the world. What's your new daughter's name?" she asked Darbie.

Darbie looked up with big eyes. "I want to call her Ruby Jannell. Cal would have liked that."

Ruby for the grandmother, Jannell for the new stepsister, Janny.

Fatigue passed over Ruby Mae's face, and then a melancholy smile. "Yes, I think he would have. Write it down, Peg. Ruby Janell Granger."

I tore off two strips of tape, affixed one to the other making a small bracelet with sticky ends. Checking my watch, I wrote the name on the tape along with the date and time and attached it around the little baby's ankle. She kicked at me as I touched her heel, strong-willed like the other Nettle children. For an instant, I felt Cal Nettle's ghostly presence in the room, and then it vanished.

"That's it," Ruby Mae said, wiping at her forehead with her bandaged hand, wincing at the pain.

I heard applause from the phone, still live on the desk. "Well done," said Liz. "Get that little girl-baby over here to the hospital. We'll take good care of her."

The lights blinked back on, flickered, held. With a rush, the heater blasted warm air into the room. I stripped off the gloves and held my fingers to the vent, feeling the welcome heat. At that moment, my phone crackled into powerless silence. But we'd made it!

Cold air blasted in when I opened the door to the courtroom.

Ethan looked at me anxiously from where he and Janny had been huddled together. "Are they..."

"You've got a new little sister," I said. "And Darbie's doing fine."

Hard, pelting snow blasted the outside windows as I walked beyond him into the outer hallway. Amidst the gathered court workers, was a familiar face, Rory Stevens.

He looked uncertain of my welcome, but first held out his hand and then widened his arms. "Heya, lady. Hear you had a time of it in there. Congratulations."

"Thanks for coming." I walked into his embrace and held onto him for a long minute. There were still issues between us, but they could wait.

Outside the window, arcing red lights created sword stabs through the snow. The replacement ambulance had arrived. "It took them forever to clear that accident off the highway," one EMT said. "Where's our new mother?"

I never knew what passed between Ruby Mac and Darbie in those few moments before the ambulance arrived. But when the EMT crew reappeared with Darbie, her baby was swaddled in Ruby Mae's bright pink sweater.

Rory and I walked to the front door, his hand steady under my arm. Then he wrapped his jacket around me for the plunge into the blinding snowstorm. When I peered into the white blizzard, an atomic orange Hummer came into view.

"Let me offer you a ride home," Rory said. "You can pick up the sheriff's SUV in the morning."

Sounded like a plan. My adrenalin drained away in the safety of the big Hummer. Rory cranked the heat to high, and I leaned back against the leather seat. It was good to have a friend.

CHAPTER TWENTY-NINE

Late that night I awoke to the sound of my cell phone buzzing on the night table. I fumbled for it in the darkness. "Hello?"

First some heavy breathing, then: "Eleanor?" The only person who called me that was my grandfather and this wasn't him. I should have hung up—haven't gotten a harassing phone call for a while—but for some reason, I stayed on the line, curious.

"Who're you trying to reach?" I said, hoping it was a wrong number.

"Eleanor Pegasus Quincy?"

"What do you want?" The voice sounded familiar, yet different, as though someone was trying to disguise their voice.

"Leave well enough alone. Don't mess in what you don't understand." The tone was guttural and rough.

I broke the connection and threw the phone away from me, rejecting the slimeball that had called and the message along with it. The phone hit the wall with a satisfying thump and bounced on the carpet.

Thoroughly awake now, I retrieved it and thumbed down for the caller ID. "Restricted." How had they gotten my cell number? And my full name? Few people knew that, not even Shepherd.

My heart was pounding, my nerves on high alert, but I was angry now, not frightened. How dare they call me, here at home when I was sleeping? I checked all the outside door locks. With everything secure, I stepped out onto the balcony to sample the night air. The neighborhood was quiet in the early pre-dawn darkness, yet something hummed in my primitive reptile brain.

Was the caller male or female? I couldn't tell with the disguising. But the message conveyed a danger, like a whiff of smoke in a dark forest.

The door slammed shut behind me, caught by a draft of wind. I yanked it back open, went in, and locked it behind me. Dropping to the couch, I pulled a throw over my feet intending to rest a moment…

***

The next morning, I awoke to a stiff neck and sunlight bursting in the window. Indian summer had returned to Mingus. Shopkeepers swept the last of the snowmelt off sidewalks and the gutters dripped a steady tattoo. Overhead skies were a deep blue, oblivious to the damage they had spewed forth only a day before.

Shepherd was in his office when I arrived, playing solitaire. Sheryl must have driven him up from Cottonwood because the SUV was still at the courthouse. I remembered that with a guilty start. I stopped by his office to explain, but he was ahead of me.

"Heard you had a bit of excitement yesterday," he said. "Congratulations on your first baby birthing."

"You deliver any?"

"Half a dozen, over the years. But nothing like that first one. Welcome to a very elite club."

And then, cutting into my glow of achievement, the business side of Shepherd emerged. "What'd you learn in that time you spent with the family? We any closer to finding Cal Nettle's killer?"

His comments stopped me short. A good reminder for me to keep my mind on death as well as life. I told him about the early morning call.

"You got gun clearance from your counselor yet?" His tone was direct as he honed in on the dangerous reality of an unarmed law officer.

I'd avoided returning to the counselor, I'd admit that. I'd used my last session to help Aurora, but that meant a delay in getting my own objectives met. "Another appointment this afternoon," I promised.

"Get it done. *Now.* If you can't back me up, I'll find somebody who can."

Shepherd had a steel core that I was beginning to appreciate. Push him so far and he morphed into an emotionless machine, all empathy banked. Maybe that's what was needed to be a good sheriff's deputy, but I hadn't been able to achieve that Zen state yet. Still trying.

The door burst open. Ben arrived, dressed in biking leathers, two helmets in hand. "Rory called me. Great job yesterday." He high-five-ed me. "You ready to pick up the SUV?"

What was Rory doing, spreading *my* news? I felt a momentary irritation and then reassured myself that it was the department grapevine working at full tilt.

Shepherd reached behind him for his coat. "Take this, keep you warm."

I started to protest, but he dangled it in front of him, impatient. "Here."

So I bundled in his heavy padded coat, found a pair of gloves in the pocket, put them on, too. I was dressed for the ice storm yesterday, and it was already fifty degrees outside when we walked to the bike. Ben pounded the bulky helmet on my head and I adjusted the chin strap.

"Thanks for the ride," I said, my voice reverberating within the helmet's echo chamber.

He'd already mounted the bike, pushed up his face plate, and steadied the frame. "Watch that exhaust pipe," he warned. "It'll burn your calf right through that pant leg."

I climbed on behind him and wriggled to adjust my weight.

Ben must have sensed my inexperience, for he gave beginner instructions. "When I lean the cycle into the curves, you do, too. Pretend you're an extension of the bike."

"Come on, Ben, let's get going. I'm sweating a river in this gear."

The Ducati had a poor excuse for a sissy bar, some six inches of laddered chrome behind me, but it was better than nothing. I gripped Ben's skinny waist, kicked the pegs down for my feet and we were off, bouncing onto the street.

The bellow of the engine rebounded from the glass and metal storefronts as we roared down Main Street and through the zigzags toward Cottonwood. I leaned and swooped through the curves imitating the angle of Ben's back. In the rush of road wind, curves blurred in front of us and the side of the road disappeared down into the steep drop-off to our right. I closed my eyes and hung on.

This motorcycle experience was unique. Not just a hundred-eighty effect like a convertible, but a total three-sixty-degree sensation. Different from riding horses, too, with the roar and heat of the engine beneath me. The environment rushed in from all directions.

But cold! The open air flattened my clothes to my body and jerked my helmeted head backward. The frozen wind seeped through my gloves and crept up my legs and under Shepherd's coat. How did Ben stand it, in front there, with no protection as the wind blasted against him? I leaned close, unashamedly absorbing his body heat.

He slowed in Cottonwood. I closed my eyes again and identified where we were by smells: The hot grease odor of the burger joints, the diesel fuel in each service station, the seared-bleach aroma of the laundromat.

Once out of town on the flat, Ben hit an open stretch without traffic. He gunned it, and the engine growled in response while the creosote and cactus whizzed by. The bike speed approached a hundred miles an hour. I experienced a rush I'd never felt before, a sensation of raw, addictive speed.

All too soon we reached the courthouse turn off. Ben downshifted through a series of gears and put on his turn signal. We pulled in the parking lot and he coasted to a halt next to the SUV. Putting down the kickstand, he dismounted first and then steadied the bike as I followed. I stomped my numbed feet and doffed my helmet, still feeling the vibration in my crotch.

Ben grinned at me. "Like it?"

The wind tears in my eyes dried as I beamed at him. All kinds of Zen experiences.

I went into the courthouse to retrieve the jacket I'd left on the back of a spectator seat when all the excitement started yesterday. I paused at the doorway, reliving the birthing from the day before. I'd brought new life into the world, right here. Did doctors feel this heightened awareness of life when they walked into the delivery room the day after they'd assisted a birth?

The room wasn't empty. Rory stood there with my jacket in his hands. "They called the sheriff's office in Prescott and said the jacket was here. Thought I'd retrieve it in case you forgot."

My euphoria crashed to earth at the possessive tone in his voice. There it was, another man trying to own me. "Why would I forget my own jacket?" I snapped. "And why did they call *you,* and not me?"

"Yeah, sure. I just thought..."

"Thanks," I said, snatching the jacket out of his hands.

Rory straightened as the words hung uneasily between us. "Hey, see you around, right?" He turned on his heel and left the room before I could say anything.

An all-too-familiar sensation of being trapped descended on me as I returned to the parking lot. First Shepherd's comments about how Rory felt, and now this interchange. Rory's words and actions hemmed me into a relationship I wasn't ready for. He was a friend, nothing more.

I rolled down a window to smell the air on the drive back to Mingus, but the magic had disappeared like yesterday's snow. Cradled in the steel cocoon of the SUV without the heart-thumping vibrations and the throaty roar of the motorcycle engine between my legs, I felt half alive, isolated from the world around me.

The digital thermometer on the dash showed fifty-nine degrees and climbing as I approached Mingus. The roadside ditches contained rapidly shrinking puddles of melt, and only patches of snow remained in the hill shadows. The parched air sucked up the remaining damp, leaving behind possible fuel for late season fires. Feast or famine, our high desert partnership with water.

I shook my feeling of loneliness and turned into HT's driveway. It was near lunchtime, and I craved a connection to family. I found it, but not in the form I was expecting.

CHAPTER THIRTY

Isabel yelled something about tracking dirt into her kitchen and HT hollered in something in response. They were fighting.

I waited for a break in the action and knocked.

"Come in!" HT shouted.

He sat at the kitchen table, unlacing his work boots. "Sorry, Isabel, I just never thought."

"That's the problem. You never think before you come tromping through here with those boots." Isabel's dark eyes snapped with irritation. "I just cleaned this floor."

Clearly in the wrong, and ready for lunch, he tried to make amends. "It's not that dirty. Here, look." He swept an offending clod of dirt under his chair with one big hand.

Was this what a committed relationship was all about, this bickering? If so, I was glad that Rory Stevens and I were not going there anytime soon. I grabbed the offending footwear and chunked them outside the door. I hated conflict, and I was hungry, too. Did I smell a tamale pie fresh out of the oven?

"Peg!" Isabel rushed over to hug me. "What am I going to do with this grandfather of yours? Here, sit. I'll fix you some lunch. You can stay, yes?"

The argument over, HT and Isabel quietly bantered back and forth, including me in their conversation. Isabel set a place for me and heaped a portion of tamale pie on my plate. I poured ice tea for myself and the two of them, and she said grace before we began. I dipped a sopapilla in honey and swallowed the morsel, feeling the warmth of their love. The ice in my veins thawed just a little.

Isabel touched my cheek. "After that baby yesterday— You doing okay?"

At her gentleness, unexpected tears blurred my vision. I wished I could share my great new experiences with my mother, and that would not happen, ever again. I squeezed Isabel's hand, accepting her concern.

"I'm fine. Glad to be here." I was. At the same time, I worried about emotions too close to the surface. That wasn't safe, especially for a cop.

***

Later that afternoon I arrived at Dr. Westcott's office for my counseling appointment. The bench outside her office door was vacant and I sat down to contemplate my sins, of which there were many. None that I planned to share with her. I breathed in and out, trying to practice Shepherd's Zen.

Dr. Westcott opened the door and broke into my reverie. "Peg, welcome. I'm ready for you."

Her office looked just the way it had last week, only larger because Janny and Aurora's energy wasn't there. I took a seat on the couch instead of my usual hard chair to show the therapist how calm I was.

Dr. Westcott smiled. "How is little Aurora doing?"

"Better. Talking a little, drawing. Some of the scary memories are coming back, but she's able to share them now, thanks to you."

"Glad to hear it. Be sure to ask Janny to bring her back in if she feels it could help. I left a message, but she hasn't returned it."

Not surprising, knowing Janny. She had the same distrust for authority that I had. Funny that I became a cop with all that bottled up inside me.

It was time to get down to business. I looked directly at Dr. Westcott. "How does this go? Want me to talk about my problems?"

"You have problems?"

I backtracked rapidly. "No, no problems, I'm fine. No flashbacks, no nightmares. I'm completely recovered."

"Is that so?" She examined me closely.

Was I telling the truth? Maybe shading it a little. But the recent events had overshadowed the death that I had caused. It seemed to have happened to someone else, a long time ago. "I'd do it again, if I had to. That's my job, what I was trained for."

Choosing to perch on this too-soft couch was a mistake. I jammed a pillow behind me, wiggling uneasily. I looked at the clock. Only thirty more minutes to go. I could do this thing.

She went for the jugular. "Is this the right job for you, Peg?"

What a strange question. Of course, it was. Or was it? I took a risk and shared what I held locked inside me. "Sometimes I'm confused. I see the law and it's supposed to be black or white, good guys or criminals. But a lot of people straddle that line, and sometimes step over. Dishonest cops, good bad-guys."

"Are you speaking from experience?"

"Dishonest cops? I'm sure there are a few." Cyrus Marsh, the deputy I'd replaced in Mingus might fit that category.

I thought a bit more. "Bad guys that I like? Yes, some." Nigglieri in Phoenix might fit that category. I didn't like him, exactly, but respected the man's implacable strength. "It's not always as easy as the training manuals tell you."

"No, it's not," Dr. Westcott agreed and went on to her next question. "What would you do, if you had to deal with a similar crisis situation in the future?"

In a deadly weapon confrontation, there was only one possible response. "Neutralize the guilty, protect the innocent."

"What if you can't tell the difference between the two?"

"Then maybe it's time for me to step down and take up needlework." I made a joke of it, but leaving the force was something I thought about late at night. Maybe other cops did, too. Maybe Shepherd did.

"Perhaps that doubt makes you human," the therapist suggested.

What did she want me to say? That I regretted what happened? A blush started at my collarbone and rose. My breath came and went in short jerks.

"Slow, Peg. Breathe. Let it happen."

Let what happen? I was fine, just fine. And then suddenly I wasn't.

I started to sob. And then howl. The tears dribbled down my cheeks and off my chin. Suddenly the tissue box was there in my hand and I grabbed a couple, stabbed at my offending eyes. And then started wailing again, my whole body shaking with the effort.

Ten minutes later, it was over. My breathing evened out and the room spun back into view. I felt lighter, as though a heavy pack had been lifted from aching shoulders.

Dr. Westcott reached behind her for a paper on her desk. She scribbled her signature at the bottom and handed it to me. "Give this to your commanding officer. You're cleared for regular duty."

She looked at me with searching eyes. "You did good work, today, Pegasus. But when the time comes that those questions need re-examining, call me. You've got my number." Again she gave that musical giggle. It was so out of place with a professional demeanor, but so much a part of who she was, totally unselfconscious and at peace with herself. In the career I'd chosen, I couldn't afford to be that free. Maybe that was a good thing.

I left clutching the precious paper. I drove to the sheriff's department in Camp Verde to retrieve my Glock. Get Shepherd off my back, do the job I was paid to do. My mind settled back into a comfortable law enforcement mode as I planned my next actions.

But Dr. Westcott's question echoed in my mind: "What if you can't tell the difference between the innocent and the guilty?" Was I doing that with the Nettle clan, turning a blind eye to a killer that still roamed free?

***

The next few days passed quietly. The air got warmer and drier, but the forest service proscribed burns clouded our blue skies. Howard was still camping at Dead Horse Ranch State Park, but I imagined he'd be going back to Phoenix soon. Couldn't keep Pietra waiting forever. Darbie and baby were doing fine in the hospital—The doctors kept mother and child a few extra days because of the circumstances of birth.

Shepherd went back to working his crossword puzzles and I pounded the streets giving out traffic tickets and catching speeders. At least my old friend Glock was strapped nice and heavy at my waist. But always, the unsolved murder of Cal Nettle haunted over us.

Then one morning I arrived at the station to find both Ben and Shepherd wearing glum faces. "What happened? Your favorite football team lose?" I asked.

As one, they replied, "Sheryl left last night."

"And she took Fluffy," Shepherd added. "Going back to live with her mom. Says it's too boring out here."

I patted Shepherd's arm. "You'll survive. Be glad you had the economy tour and not the round-the-world extended cruise."

I turned to Ben. "And there's always Ashley."

He brightened considerably.

"Shepherd, Sheryl's growing into an independent woman, like you want her to be. Keep your door open— she'll be back."

"Probably so," he admitted. He pulled out his keys. "Need to do a patrol of the shopping district this morning. Want to ride along?"

Whereas I did foot patrol, Shepherd always chose the vehicle. He claimed it gave him a perspective on the town from the higher viewpoint. I said he was getting old, didn't like to climb the hills with his bad leg. Maybe both of us were right.

He cruised slowly down Main Street, made the turn onto Hull, then the sharp hairpin going the other direction, his eyes watchful. Finally, he pulled into a parking space in front of the First National Bank. I waited for him to open the door, but he just sat there. "Situation I want to check out," he said. "Wait a bit."

Fine with me. I settled back in my seat, watching the town opening up for business. Moms and dads shivering in their late summer wear, adjusting to our mountain heights. Little kids racing ahead in T-shirts and shorts, ignoring the morning cold.

"Got some local news for you."

"What's that?" I asked.

"The Nettle family's copy of Cal's Last Will and Testament has been withdrawn. Darbie's version has been admitted to probate. Ruby Mae's the executor."

Maybe that was the unspoken agreement I had witnessed at the hospital. In a way, it healed the chasm between the two families. "Smart move. Ruby Mae can sell the property on her own terms, make sure the price is right for the kids. Don't know as her and Darbie will ever be friends, but they've got that common bond of Cal's new daughter. Ruby Mae won't let go of that."

A car raced up the street, about ten miles over the speed limit. It would be gone before we could pull out, and Shepherd let it pass. "Cal knew he was dying. Wonder if he hoped that healing between the two women would happen?"

"Could be," I said, "but I doubt he knew the baby would be born in the judge's chamber. And Cal didn't have to die like he did."

Shepherd didn't seem to be in a hurry to move on, so I reviewed the progress, such as it was, in the murder investigation. "I could visit the snitch Sally Ann again, but since Janny moved back home, not much is new there. I've re-interviewed all of Darbie's neighbors, but they didn't see or hear anything other than visits by Howard and Cal, and of course, Otis snooping around."

"Think he was your mystery caller the other night?"

"Could be. If he calls again when I'm more awake I'll try to find out."

"Case getting pretty cold at this point," Shepherd admitted, "but keep working on it. I'm still thinking the answer is right out there with Ruby Mae's beaten biscuits. Family members are always the likeliest candidates in a murder case."

He jerked upright. "There. See that?"

A young kid picking pockets, right under our noses. "Yours or mine?" I asked.

He gestured magnanimously, and I piled out of the cruiser. By the time I rounded the corner, the boy had disappeared, and I jogged back to the car, breathing heavy.

"Lost him," I said, climbing into the car. "Kid's fast."

"Maybe you just need a better perspective on the situation," Shepherd commented. "I'll visit his parents tonight when they get home from work. Find out why little

Jimmy Hackett ain't in school instead of out here giving us problems." He cranked up the engine, checked his rear view mirror, and pulled into traffic.

As we drove into the station parking lot, I said, "I'll be gone this afternoon. Looking for a new place to live."

"Apartment not suiting you?"

"Too small. Might be getting a dog."

"One of Ethan's pups? Be good for you. Thinking of doing something like that myself. Quiet around my house without Fluffy there. I checked at the animal shelter. Maybe I'll be a foster mom."

"What? You don't quite fit the image of a stay-at-home mom."

He gave me the finger. "They're looking for somebody to help with the pregnant cats. Assist the birth of the kittens and then return the whole litter for adoption when they're old enough. Be something I can do short-term."

"Still looking ahead to retirement? What you going to do, Shepherd?"

"Don't know. I've worked all my life. It's worrisome," he admitted. "I'll figure something out. I can always compose crossword puzzles." He gave me a wry smile. "Keep your cell phone close. We've had some Otis sightings in town, but nothing definite. Be careful."

"Agreed."

After lunch, Ben and Shepherd left to go motorcycle riding. I was glad to see them depart. It would take both their minds off Sheryl's departure.

After they left, the Crime Lab technician called. "Sorry we didn't get back to you sooner on that murder weapon— we've been running some tests."

"Was it the battling board?"

"That what it's called? No fingerprints, it had been in the water too long. A dead end, anyway."

"What do you mean?"

"Well, that red oak stick didn't fit the indentation at all. But we took a plaster cast of the wound before we released the body..."

"What do you think caused the death blow?"

"Well, the weapon was oak, all right. We found some fibers in the wound. But *white* oak, not red. And weathered, like it had been out in the rain too many nights. Maybe a four-by-four."

The loose railing on the Nettle porch! It had been there right in front of me the whole time and I didn't see it.

I gave a hasty thank you to the tech guy and hung up. I wanted a closer look at Ruby Mae's porch, and I wanted it right now.

The office phone rang again. I hesitated. The ringing stopped. Good, maybe they'd just leave a message. Then it started again as though somebody had an urgent call. I jerked up the receiver. "Peg Quincy, sheriff's office."

"Took your sweet time, deputy."

I recognized the raspy, oily voice immediately. My midnight caller was back. "What you want, Otis?"

A throaty chuckle. "Thought you recognized me. I know who killed Cal Nettle. You interested?"

"Come in and let's talk."

"No, you come here. To the still. Come soon, or I'll be gone and you'll never know who did it." He hung up.

I dialed Shepherd's cell, but no answer. He was probably swooping through one of those tight mountain curves out of cell phone coverage.

Hindsight says I should have called for backup, waited for reinforcements. But this was *my* district now. I grabbed the keys and ran out the door. The light bar flashed blue fire as the SUV accelerated down the hill. Tavasci Marsh and Otis Stroud waited for me.

CHAPTER THIRTY-ONE

When I reached the Nettle home place, the sun had gone behind Black Mountain, throwing dark shadows across the rough landscape. I halted in the drive, anticipating the rush of coonhounds, but the yard was silent. Opening the door of the SUV, I hailed the house. "Ethan, Ruby Mae, anyone home?"

A blue jay screeched on the hill and a raven high in a yellow pine cawed in response. I touched the Glock for reassurance and jogged past the barn down the quarter mile to the whiskey still, squelching through puddles of pungent marsh water.

Otis waited for me, squatting on his haunches by the reassembled whiskey still machinery. He rose as I drew near. "Out of breath, deputy? Want a drink?" He saluted me with the jug in his hand.

"Don't do anything drastic, Otis. Just want to talk, that's all."

"I'm here. Talk." He took a drink and dropped the jug to the ground.

I leaned against a juniper snag to slow my breathing. My hand touched the holster at my side. Hearing a sound, I glanced behind me. It was the opening that Otis needed.

"Throw that gun over here."

I looked back to see two barrels of a sawed-off shotgun pointed my direction. Would Otis use it? I calculated my draw time. He'd probably beat me, and his look said he wouldn't hesitate.

I lay my Glock on the ground.

"Now kick it over here."

I did, scanning the marshlands behind him for any chance of assistance. Saw none. Might as well ride it through to see what happened.

Otis picked up the Glock and stuffed it in his waistband. Then he pulled some zip ties from his pocket.

"Turn around, deputy, and get on your knees. Let's do this proper." He bound my arms behind me, yanked them tight. "Now you know how it feels, being tied like a steer." He gestured derisively. "Swamp's right there. Swim if you want to, won't stop you."

Stubbornly, I didn't quit, couldn't quit. I needed answers. "How'd you know my name when you called?" I asked. "That took me back some."

Otis leaned against the still and chuckled. "Your office personnel files."

He took in my puzzled expression and explained. "The guy you took over from there in Mingus?"

"Cyrus Marsh."

"I delivered a payoff of hooch to him every Saturday after midnight. He gave me a key to the office so he didn't have to wait up. You could say I've been visiting after hours. Followed your whole investigation on Cal Nettle, step by step. By the way, your note taking could use some improvement. Doesn't match up to Shepherd's."

Otis was loquacious, but not drunk enough on the white lightning to lose focus. Still, if I found a way to deflect his attention, there might still be a chance.

My fingers grew numb against the flex ties, but my mind moved with increasing speed. What had Shepherd said about the first accident, something about Lucas and

Darbie? Maybe the still explosion and Cal Nettle's death fit together, somehow. This man would know.

"Otis, you called me out here to talk. So start at the beginning. What happened at the fire when Lucas died? Why weren't you there watching the whiskey still that night?"

"Long time ago. Doesn't fit here."

"Lucas steal your girl?" I taunted him. "That why you abandoned him?"

"Didn't abandon anyone. Lucas's own damn fault he got killed." His eyes focused on me. "Not so fast, deputy. I want a guarantee of safe passage out of here. Tired of running."

"Done." I was lying, but worth the try. "Now tell me what happened."

"What the hell. *You're* not leaving here anyway." He squatted down beside me, fixed me with that malevolent stare. "All right, it was me. I fixed those valves so they'd blow. Just wanted to back Lucas off a bit, teach him a lesson. If he'd been watching the machinery instead of payin' attention to that damn brat, he would've noticed the pressure was rising."

"Why'd Lucas need a lesson? Darbie Granger prefer him over you?"

"You shut up! Darbie wasn't for the likes of him. She was *mine*. Lucas didn't listen. He never listened."

I remembered the neighbor of Darbie and his story about the Wolverine. Otis considered Darbie *his*. He'd been crazy-obsessed over those brilliant green eyes.

"You kill Cal Nettle, too?" I asked. "Be good reason to: He took your truck, he got Darbie pregnant."

Otis's eyes wavered. "Don't know if you'll believe me, but here's the truth. The kids did it."

"The kids?"

"Howard, Janny, Ethan—three of 'em together. Saw them dumping Cal in the swamp, right over there."

"You liar!" Ethan exploded from the path behind me.

Howard was close behind him. "Peg, are you all right? Ethan and I saw your SUV, but not you. Figured you might be out here."

"Stay back," I warned. "Otis is serious about that shotgun."

"That's right, boys. Have two weapons, in fact, thanks to Ms. Quincy, here." Otis waved the shotgun in a purposeful arc. "This ain't your fight."

"We didn't kill Daddy," Ethan protested. "It was an accident. That's what you told me, Otis. Daddy was drinking, tripped over my dog Reckless, and hit his head on the porch rail."

"*Sure* he did," Otis mocked him. "And here's the rest of the story. I sat there, watched him bleed. Pushed that little Elvis pillow against his face to be sure he wasn't coming back. The man was after Darbie, taking *my* truck to do his courting. Couldn't have that, now could I?" He dropped the shotgun and drew my gun. Weaving back and forth on unsteady legs, he tried to keep us all covered.

"You let Daddy die!" Ethan screamed, darting for the man.

I scrambled to my feet, arms still caught behind me. The situation was about to explode—I had to stop it if I could.

But Howard pushed Ethan to one side. "No, brother, this one's mine." He grabbed at Otis, his face contorted with rage. "You're not going to hurt Darbie anymore!"

His shoulder slammed Otis in the chest, and the man grunted. They staggered backward toward the marsh, locked in a tight embrace. Otis broke free and jabbed the heel of his hand into Howard's face. There was a sickening thud of bone against flesh.

Howard clawed back at his uncle's eyes. Otis screamed and retreated, his heel sinking into the mud. He brought up the pistol to hit Howard and the two men struggled for possession of it. A shot rang out and Otis spun backward. He landed face down in the shallow water of the swamp.

I took a step toward them and tripped. My forehead hit a rock, hard, as I landed. Ethan planted a foot in the middle of my back, pinning me to the earth.

There was muffled splashing, and then the voice above me said, "Leave be, Howard. He's gone."

I lost consciousness.

CHAPTER THIRTY-TWO

When I awoke, my hands were free, but I was alone. Alone, except for the body of Otis Stroud, floating face down in the dank water near the bank.

I staggered into the murk and pulled Otis to shore. Then I turned him over and tried mouth-to-mouth resuscitation. How long does it take a man to drown? Four minutes? I'd been out for that, and more.

Would he have lived if someone had turned him so that he could breathe, as I had done for Shepherd when he caught his leg in the bear trap? I would never know. Otis Stroud was dead.

I called the sheriff's department for assistance. Once more, I stood watch over a dead body in Tavasci Marsh. My head ached and I was shivering uncontrollably when the first officers arrived on the scene.

The yellow barrier tape marked Tavasci Marsh, garish against the fall hues of the cat tails and swamp reeds. After the coroner pronounced the death, they loaded what remained of Otis Stroud onto a stretcher board and started the hike down the path to the house. Further inquiry would follow. It always did.

I left the forensic team gathering evidence and walked back toward the Nettle homestead. The silence of the marsh enveloped me. A red-winged blackbird called and a frog splashed in the water as I traced the uneven path out of the marshy land. My legs were shaky and my throat tight. I stumbled and slowed to steady myself.

Shepherd waited at the edge of the marsh. "Nasty bump on your forehead, Peg." He touched my arm briefly. "You need a visit to the emergency room?"

I shook my head.

"Let me give you a ride home, then."

He helped me into the SUV and Ben followed behind us on his Ducati. Shepherd took the curves and hollows of the dirt road at a slow pace, but I felt each jarring bump of the wheels as they hit the ruts. I closed my eyes to stem tears that this new death in the swamp released.

Shepherd's low voice recounted his version of the story. "Ethan came staggering back to the house just as we all arrived. He said he found Otis holding you at gunpoint, that he struggled with Otis and the gun went off. It seems pretty cut and dried. Ethan'll probably get manslaughter, if that…"

His droning words formed a comfortable buzz as I leaned my aching head back against the headrest. I'd been vague in my initial statement to the investigating officer, laying the blame on my head wound. Before I signed my official statement, I needed to talk to Ethan Nettle in person.

And I had to find out where Howard had gone. I might have a concussion, but there was no doubt in my mind I'd had *two* rescuers tonight in Tavasci Marsh, not one.

***

My partner suggested I take a day off to recuperate, and I spent most of it in bed at HT's house. Isabel fussed over me and I let her. It had been a while since I'd had any true mothering.

253

That evening, Shepherd dropped by to check on me. I was basking in the last of the afternoon sun on the porch. I had bundled against the cold, and rocked in the old swing as I tried to comprehend what had happened out there at Tavasci Marsh.

Shepherd dropped into the porch swing beside me. He awkwardly adjusted the afghan I had pulled around my shoulders. "Figured you might need an update on the town," he said.

Not likely. I got an hourly report from Isabel, who mainlined the town grapevine. Just this morning she reported that Ruby Mae turned the coonhounds loose on the paparazzi and threatened to use her shotgun if they didn't get off her land.

But partners needed to be humored. "What's the latest?"

"You hear that with the forensics on the porch rail, Myra Banks will likely get the death of Cal Nettle deemed an accident? Everybody knew he was a heavy drinker, no question about that. 'Course the kids shouldn't have dumped his body in the swamp, but they panicked. Understandable." Shepherd nodded with satisfaction. He liked tidy endings.

Who was paying Myra? I didn't ask but had a good idea.

As though that ended the matter, Shepherd's conversation shifted to the mundane happenings at the station, Ben's problems at school, the traffic bust he made on Ash Street. Conspicuously absent were questions about the death of Otis Stroud, and the whereabouts of the other Nettle brother, Howard.

"When you coming back?" he asked. "Station's quiet without you."

Closest he'd ever come to admitting he needed me there.

"Soon."

***

The next day I arranged to visit Ethan Nettle in the county jail where he was being held pending arraignment in the death of Otis Stroud. The sheriff's office was hounding me for my official statement and I needed to talk to him first. It was time to straighten matters between us.

Ethan faced me through the scarred Plexiglas of the visiting room communication window. He picked up his phone and I picked up mine.

"How you doing, law woman?" He looked tired, strained, in his prison orange.

"Okay. And you Ethan?"

He shrugged. "Been better. Miss the dogs."

"Family in to see you?"

He brightened. "Janny brought Aurora. Little kid showed me some of her drawings. Rainbows, trees, houses."

Normal seven-year-old drawings. Something good coming out of this then. "Maybe that shrink stuff works," I said.

"Yeah, maybe. Janny says Aurora's scheduled for surgery next month. Doc's putting it on credit. The check's in the mail." He forced a laugh at his feeble joke.

He leaned forward and pressed his forehead against the barrier. His voice echoed hollow in the prison phone. "Can I trust you? We're family, like."

I hesitated a minute. "Depends on what you tell me, Ethan. I'm listening."

That seemed to satisfy him. He started awkwardly. "It's like this. I'll never amount to anything, I know that. What does it matter whether I have a prison record or not? Be out soon, anyway, according to Myra."

I could see where this was heading. "What about Howard?"

He cut me off. "My brother has a shot of making something of himself. Might even be a big legislator someday. Jail record would be the end of all that."

"But..."

"Family's got to stick together. Otis's death was an accident, that's all." His Adam's apple bobbed as he swallowed.

"Ethan, you sure you want to do this?"

In the dim light of the prison conference room, his blue eyes stared through at me. "It's my life, Peg. Let me live it as I choose."

After I left Ethan, I drove out to the campgrounds at Dead Horse Ranch State Park. The Fox cabin was vacant, the door banging in the wind.

Was Howard a coward, then, letting his brother serve the sentence for his own misdeed? I comforted myself thinking that all actions have consequences. Choosing to return to Big Al's world might be Howard's own prison sentence, one that could last a lifetime.

CHAPTER THIRTY-THREE

After several sleepless nights, I gave my statement in the case, confirming the fight between Ethan and Otis was self-defense. I chose not to mention Howard's presence.

On the basis of his confession, Ethan got indicted for manslaughter in the death of Otis Stroud. Thanks to the good efforts of Myra Banks, he was out on bail. Armor was making book at the biker bar that he'd get a year or less.

Shepherd lent me a weapon until mine was returned. He didn't press me for details about what happened at Tavasci Marsh, and I didn't volunteer.

Everything was settled, or so I thought until Ruby Mae requested that I visit the Nettle place.

***

The big dogs were locked up when I swung the SUV into the yard, but Reckless greeted me as I opened the vehicle door. I leaned down, even as Aurora had done, and he licked my face.

Ruby Mae stood on the porch, watching my approach. "Dog likes you," she said, opening the screen door so that I could enter the living room. She asked about my grandfather, served me sweet tea.

"Heard you got a good offer on the property," I said.

"Over two million. They move fast, want to close in a few weeks."

"Where will you go?"

"Staying here for the present. Ethan asked me to keep this house and the graveyard on the hill as his share. I'll live here until he returns from prison, then move to town. I figure to try some of that country club living, maybe join a book club."

I couldn't resist asking. "Did you bury Otis up on the hill?"

Her lips tightened. "That's a *family* plot. Cremated him. Sent the ashes to the folk back home, have him scattered there, not here."

We looked at each other, and the questions in my mind were blocked by her direct stare. I had no doubt that if she'd been at Tavasci Marsh she'd have pulled the trigger on Otis Stroud herself, to protect her family.

"Did you bring your camera like I asked you? Need you to take some pictures for me."

We talked over her plan, and it seemed sound. I took shots of her and the other family members as she specified.

Then I walked out to where the whiskey still had been. It appeared somebody had been busy. The distillery was burned to the ground once more, leaving scarred and blackened ruins. I shot pictures of that location as well.

When I came back to the house Ruby Mae gave me a check that I tucked in my pocket. "Go see Ethan, now, before you leave. He's out in the barn with the pups."

Reckless gamboled about me as I walked through the late fall sunshine to the barn. Ethan was sitting on the floor surrounded by a whirling vortex of red energy. He got to his feet and brushed off his pants. Reckless waded through the puppies, licking one, tumbling another out of the way.

"Peg, good to see you. Momma said you'd be out." He offered a hand and I shook it.

I took some more pictures of him and the redbone coonhounds. As I turned to leave, he clipped a leash on Reckless. He held the line out to me, his jaw set in a determined line. "You promised."

Reckless settled into the SUV like he owned it. He turned once on the back seat and then settled down, comfortable.

I left the SUV at the station, told Shepherd I was taking the rest of the day off. He didn't object, just nodded and went back to his paperwork. "Nice dog," was his only comment.

Reckless and I walked back to my apartment. I opened the front door and let him loose. He clattered up the stairs. By the time I reached the top he'd settled in the middle of my bed. "This is just temporary," I warned him. "Don't get too comfortable." His tail whapped the bedspread in response.

I changed into blue jeans and T-shirt and closed the door on Reckless. Then I walked over to HT's place to borrow his old pickup. It had a nasty habit of quitting on me, but maybe it would make the trip to Phoenix one more time.

I stopped at the office supply store on the edge of Cottonwood before I left the Verde Valley as Ruby Mae requested. Then I drove out Highway 260 to I-17 and headed south to Phoenix.

***

The traffic was heavy, and I didn't reach Big Al's place until late afternoon. His secretary was gone, but he waved me into his office. We looked at each other over his battered desk.

"I'm here in an unofficial capacity," I said.

"Heard about the land sale. Figured somebody would be down." He leaned forward. "You got something for me?"

259

I put the manila envelope on the desk and pulled out the pictures I'd had made at the copy center. One by one, I turned them his direction: The ruined whiskey still, inoperable now that both Cal and Otis were dead. A picture of Lucas that Ruby Mae had given me, the first of the Nettle clan to die at the still. Janny with Aurora in her lap. Darbie still in hospital garb with baby Ruby Janell. Ethan with the redbone coonhound pups.

Aldo inhaled on his cigar, then placed it in the crystal ashtray. He picked up one picture after another, studying them. "Family," he declared. Then, "Don't see Howard Nettle in here."

"Howard needs to fend for himself. Maybe he and Pietra will make it."

"Maybe so. He's a terrible car salesman, though."

I set down one last photograph, turned it so he could see. Ruby Mae on the porch, shotgun in hand, chin raised and a glint in her green eyes.

Aldo chuckled. "Wouldn't be wise to cross that momma bear."

I agreed. Then I pulled the check out of my pocket and pushed it toward him. "Ruby Mae says this is your share."

He picked it up, frowned. Flicked the paper with his finger. "Doesn't include enough interest."

"Rough times on that family because of the whiskey still," I countered. "Lucas dead. Darbie's child missing a father. Ethan going to jail."

He still looked doubtful.

"And Aurora needs surgery on that burned hand..."

He studied on it a moment. "Doesn't mean I won't come up to the Verde Valley. To take in the sights, say."

"But not with the Nettle family."

He paused for a long moment, thinking. "Fair enough."

We shook on it, a matter settled. He walked me out to the street and looked at my granddad's old truck.

"Give you a great deal on a new car. Drive it off the lot today."

His dark eyes sparked as he opened the pickup door for me, not expecting an answer.

He didn't get one.***

My official statement was never questioned. Why would it be? There'd been a murder suspect convicted. Justice had been served.

But Otis Stroud's actions marked all the Nettles, even though he was no longer on this earth. And it branded me as well. I knew that both Howard and Ethan watched Otis die and did nothing, even as he had watched their father suffocate on Ruby Mae's porch.

That omission in my statement became another hill-country secret added to the others I carried deep within my soul.

Someday I'd go see the lady doc again, talk about it. Until then I was working through it, day by day, the best I could.

AUTHOR NOTE TO READERS

I hope that you have had as much enjoyment reading this novel as I have had sharing it with you.

Although I've set this story in the fictitious town of Mingus, the mining region of central Arizona is still alive and thriving, and the historical setting that I've provided is accurate. The Tuzigoot Indian ruins do still stand guard over Tavasci Marsh.

There are other novels in the Pegasus Quincy Mystery Series available through the Amazon marketplace. Please visit my website at www.LakotaGrace.com to get news of upcoming novels, to read my blog, or to give me feedback on my work.

Because an Indie novelist survives through word-of-mouth recommendations, if you enjoyed *Blood in Tavasci Marsh,* let others know about it. Tell your friends and neighbors! And please, if you will, consider posting an online review at Amazon.

Visit me online at my Amazon author page, my website: www.LakotaGrace.com, or on Facebook at Lakota Grace, Author.

I'd love to hear from you.

ABOUT THE AUTHOR

Lakota Grace has called the American Southwest home for most of her life. She has a doctorate in counseling psychology and has written stories since age five.

Lakota has an abiding love for the high desert plateau and the abundance of life it supports. Quail and red-tail hawks visit her feeders; bobcats and coyotes wander by. She maintains a cautious co-existence with the scorpions and javelinas who visit her backyard.

Most of all, she enjoys getting up before dawn, watching the sun hit the red rocks, and sharpening her pencil for yet another writing session.

Made in the USA
Lexington, KY
15 October 2018